SEER SERIES

SEER

Ken —
Thanks for
your advice and
thanks for a wonderful
cover! People find it
intriguing! All the best ~
Larry

Larry Austin

outskirtspress
DENVER, COLORADO

SEER
Seer Series: Book One
All Rights Reserved.
Copyright © 2016 Larry Austin
v3.0

Cover Design by Berris Pictures Original Illustration by Rosalio Terrazas
Author Photo: vsoutherlandphoto.com © 2016.All rights reserved - used with permission.
Editing Guidance: Rosemary Riordan Williams and Margie Austin

Outskirts Press, Inc.
http://www.outskirtspress.com

ISBN: 978-1-4787-7190-6

Outskirts Press and the "OP" logo are trademarks belonging to Outskirts Press, Inc.

PRINTED IN THE UNITED STATES OF AMERICA

Dedicated to Grandma, for passing the torch, and to Ricky, for helping to keep the spark lit in the dark times.

Thanks to Phillip C. for asking me to leave class when I was a freshman, then welcoming me back as a senior; to Jeff J. for his non-judgmental guidance before I learned to be reasonable; to the robinmob for their support and friendship; to Bobby A., tour-guide supreme at Monument Valley, for his kindness and openness in teaching us when we were there; to Portia P., because we will always remember; to Ken for his generous help and guidance; to Jerry and John for their contributions; to Marc and my colleagues; to Alex and Milo; and to The Dragonfly for floating into our lives when the Coyote had to leave.

A very special thanks to Ro for her friendship, honesty and encouragement.

But most especially, my thanks to Margie, the love of my life, for being there when I needed her most.

What's being said about SEER –

"This exciting, dystopian view of the near future combines the suspense of *Outbreak* with the intrigue of *Blade Runner*. Mr. Austin has come up with a completely unique vision and lays out the story in an amazing fashion. A must read!" Ken Berris, author, *Wild Cards*

"As a youngster I read George Orwell's *1984* with fascination, but disbelief. Many years later I live in a vastly different world and *Seer* has recaptured my imagination with its realistic view of the not-so-distant future. This could be a survival guide. I can't wait for the next book in the series." Jerry Cordasco, Security Consultant

"When we read speculative fiction about the survival of humankind we see where the hard choices necessary for survival can make us question our humanity. *Seer* will have you asking those questions." John Foley, author, *Guitar Music For the Mid-Life Crisis*

THE NEWSCASTER ON the monitor, a thirty-something man with perfectly coifed blonde hair, bared his over-whitened teeth to the camera in what was supposed to pass for a smile. He was dressed in a collarless cream-colored shirt over dark brown slacks. The tips of his shoes were pointy enough to qualify as weapons. The set behind him was standard comline issue: a large bank of monitors all bouncing back and forth between images and text of one of the news stories to be covered during the show.

Sitting on a tall, four-legged chair, one leg casually draped over the other, he furrowed his brow slightly in an attempt to look serious as he announced that Triton Research and Development was about to reveal information the company said would revolutionize the life of virtually everyone on the planet.

"Like everyone else in the comline news field, *we*," he said with a self-important pause, "were skeptical that the company was simply trying to get free air time to reveal a new product, but Triton has guaranteed this is not about a product, adding that they do not want to give anyone an exclusive. They're simply providing the feed that any news show can tap into."

"Like all the other news programs, we know little else, because beyond that information Triton has kept us all totally in the dark." He cocked his head slightly to one side, narrowed his eyes a bit, trying to imply suspicion, then continued filling air time with background facts. "Triton has been a major player in defense contracting. Subsidiaries of Triton also manufacture and distribute computer hardware, software and security systems." He paused for a moment, his eyes darting back and forth at a prompter. "And I'm told the press conference is about to begin. We go now to the corporate headquarters of Triton Research and Development where the CEO is waiting to make his announcement."

The new camera shot showed a white room, empty save an unadorned podium, the post of which was a silvery metal less than six inches thick. Behind that, large black lettering boldly broadcast the name *Triton Research and Development,* under which a smaller set of red letters followed up with: *We are the future....*

A middle-aged man dressed in an impossibly crisp white shirt and medium-dark blue pants walked into view of the camera. His black hair, combed straight back, had a slight sheen to it. He stepped in front of the podium and immediately looked directly into the lens, trying to exude confidence. The resulting look bordered on arrogance.

"To all of you watching this, I want to welcome you to this press conference. My name is Edward Mortland, and I am the founder and CEO of Triton Research and Development.

"I will be very succinct in what I have to say. In the coming days I will have more announcements to make, but I feel that what I will reveal today must be fully taken in before the release of any other information."

He drew in a breath and let out in a slow, controlled manner. "Over the past century and a half, we have moved more and more toward being a disposable society. Things are made to break down so as to artificially create enough business to keep factories and companies viable. We buy an item that has a short life-expectancy, after which we have to buy another of the same product. While many have come to accept this as the way things are, Triton views this as incredibly wasteful." He paused for a moment.

"Triton Research and Development has developed a process to effectively meld plastic and steel. Triton's new material is called plasteel. Our research has shown this material to be durable beyond any known today. Products manufactured with plasteel will be virtually indestructible. You will only need to buy staple items once in your lifetime, instead of again and again."

He reached into the shelf under the lectern surface and pulled out an object and a single piece of paper. The camera zoomed in on this, showing the object to be hatchet-shaped and the color of gray-green vomit. He slid the hatchet blade lightly down the paper. It easily and cleanly sliced the paper in two.

"This hatchet is razor-sharp and will hold its edge without any sharpening for many decades and perhaps centuries, to come. Lighter than steel, it is also stronger and more durable than steel, yet it is virtually indestructible and will not decompose or lose its properties in any way, shape or form. Imagine the applications and uses of this material." He almost smiled as he held the hatchet up to the camera, then lowered it by his side. The blade lightly brushed his right leg at the lower, outer thigh, cutting a small, but noticeable slit in the cloth. A small whitish patch of skin showed for an instant, but a moment later, the pants material started to darken. His attention went briefly to the back of the room. As he returned to looking at the camera, he stepped slightly to his left, effectively hiding his bleeding leg from the world.

"Please take this information in. I will hold the next press conference in two days' time and will then reveal more. Thank you."

The new camera shot showed the newscaster again. "Pretty fascinating stuff," he said, his eyebrows raised high, "but what's with that color?"

Within twenty-four hours the company's stock had quadrupled in value.

—————•《◊》•—————

Triton incorporated the new material into many household items, as well as vehicles and heavy equipment. The announcement of the development of plastiseal was made within six months of that initial press conference. Plastiseal could be manufactured in sheets of various thicknesses and had the same properties as plasteel. New goods made of plasteel and plastiseal seemed to appear weekly. Little retooling of the factories Triton leased or bought was needed, as both plasteel and plastiseal could be poured like steel or injected like plastics when in their liquid forms.

The handful of original venture capitalists who had invested in the R & D phase of the new technology were paid back a thousand of times over, putting them on all the usual lists of the world's richest people. An additional stock offering of five hundred million shares made to the public was sold and bid up in record time. The money obtained funded an exponential expansion of the company, one that, according to the conventional rules of business, should have failed for being too big, too bold, and too aggressive. Triton simply plowed along like a steamroller over a field of wildflowers.

Two years after that initial announcement, in April of 2030, Forbes Online declared Triton to be the largest, richest and most powerful company in the history of the world. Six months later, Edward Mortland and the board voted to take the company private. He gave each member of the board an extremely generous bonus upon buy back.

<hr />

In December 2031, a new illness, a type of cold, started showing up in children and the elderly, a few at first, then larger and larger groups. Researchers worked to isolate the cause. The predominant theory was that it was some sort of mutated rhinovirus. Most of the symptoms were similar to the regular cold, with one addition: a temporary numbness that occurred first in the arms, then in the legs starting on the third day of the illness. This odd symptom lasted only a few hours total and puzzled doctors greatly. It quickly became known as the numbing cold. Scans of all types showed nothing out of the ordinary in the brain and spine. Conventional blood tests also revealed nothing unusual.

As the weeks passed, the cold-like illness showed no signs of letting up in the population and did not seem to tone down or disappear as the regular cold did when spring gave way to summer. In fact, it was no longer being found only in the very young and old, but in anyone of any age. The disease did not seem to do any permanent harm, with symptoms abating in a little less than two weeks' time. It was somewhat unpleasant, as any cold could be, but was otherwise innocuous as far as doctors could tell.

Researchers eventually isolated the virus, one a thousand times smaller than any they had previously seen. In labs, it replicated rapidly but then seemed to consume itself completely in less than two weeks' time, coinciding with the duration of the illness in humans. What was left in the growing medium was a single, misshapen virus that was either totally dormant or out and out dead. Further experiments could not bring this lone bug back to life.

The search for the origin of the virus began. Computer programs were used to trace the virus back to its starting point. Ground zero turned out to be Triton Research and Development's original manufacturing plant for the first plasteel products. Further studies showed that each of the Triton manufacturing plants was the center of an outbreak that started one year and nine months almost to the day after the plant started working with the new materials.

Triton had opened thousands of manufacturing plants around the world. Similar outbreaks occurred around each of these plants. A pandemic was declared. No one was sure whether it would turn deadly. Some people had died, but there were always mitigating circumstances: compromised immune systems, old age, and other illnesses that had weakened a person physically. Scientists were unable to determine the point or method of infection. Though it was believed to be airborne, this was never proven. Information and research from around the world was quickly shared in an attempt to deal with the illness. Misinformation spread even faster.

Triton, pressed hard by world governments, finally acknowledged that it had created a new virus to achieve its miraculous plastic-steel melding. The virus, considered a new life form, had not been registered and approved as such, but simply hidden within the molecular structure of the melding agent, as Triton called it. Government officials imposed what they thought of as a hefty fine. The company considered it budget dust.

It took less than six months to get Triton to agree to shut down manufacturing at all its plants. In the end, it was not through any legal process, but a financial one. As scientists revealed what had been found, most of the public stopped buying plasteel products. The material was then viewed very suspiciously. Many of the people who had purchased plasteel products, thinking the products themselves were dangerous, took them to collection sites that had been hastily set up.

Triton very quickly announced that it had located the source of the contamination and just as quickly announced that it had plugged the leaks in the process at each of the plants worldwide. The CEO agreed to keep the plants closed unless it was deemed safe to reopen by the regulatory agencies. The company, after all, had made profits of hundreds of billions of dollars and could survive for many years without any cash inflow. Triton even invested five billion dollars into the research to find a way to deal with the illness.

The cure was found late in 2033 and fast-tracked to release by the FDA. The new medication, rynchiphyllidine, proved to be very effective. It worked by speeding up the process in which the virus consumed itself. In addition, it stopped or severely limited the peripheral numbness usually experienced. The duration of the illness was reduced to three days or less. Though researchers worked to develop a vaccine, none was ever found. Scientists also observed that some members of the population did not seem susceptible to the illness, and while this was studied, no reason for their immunity was found. Computer models, using myriad data gathered from around the world, projected that eighteen percent to twenty percent of the world population would be immune to this new disease.

The U.S. and world governments declared the pandemic under control and allowed Triton to reopen its manufacturing plants, albeit under closer regulatory scrutiny. Triton had not been inactive during the shutdown. New applications and products were pushed into production quickly. The public's short attention span and blind faith in the government allowed the company to quickly resume its hyperbolic rise.

<hr />

In January 2036 a new illness appeared. It was quickly determined that all those who developed this new illness had had the numbing cold. The initial presentation of this new disease included confusion and bouts of what appeared to be dementia. Memory deteriorated at an alarming rate, as did the ability to function at even the most basic levels. These patients had to be fed liquid diets through feeding tubes, as their ability to chew food simply disappeared. They were confined to bed as they very quickly lost the ability to even sit up by themselves. It was as if they had forgotten how.

More long term care facilities were hastily built as it became clear the existing ones would soon be overwhelmed. Empty warehouse buildings were quickly converted. Over the next two years, twenty percent of the population of the U.S. became residents in these facilities. Statistics from around the world showed similar findings.

Unemployment was reduced to near zero for the first time in the history of the country. There were not enough workers to fill all the vacancies created by the illness.

Scientists rushed to find some way of dealing with this new illness. They were able to isolate the virus quickly enough. It was the misshapen one that had been left as dead, and it was replicating itself. As it did, it very, very slowly started melding all of a person's brains cells together into a pile of greenish gray mush.

Triton simply closed its doors and waited. Lawsuits were filed by the government and by class action; all sides started filing endless motions and briefs. The protracted battle was never resolved. There was not enough time, and eventually, there were not enough people left to pursue the matter or to even care.

—•《◊》•—

Dr. Michael Macalister pushed his desk chair back from his thirty-two inch monitor. The government had given him a large, fifteenth-floor, corner office at Massachusetts General Hospital as a sign of the prestige and responsibility they were heaping on him, but he kept the blackout curtains closed to minimize distractions, opening them only for a few minutes each day as he ate lunch. His office was pinpoint neat, the only sign of mess being on the simple, antique, twenty-inch square whiteboard he kept next to his screen. There were words and partial sentences scrawled on it, some erased only to the point of leaving little black marks on the white surface.

He was a bit over six feet tall, of medium build, with close-cropped light brown hair. He rubbed his hazel eyes lightly, drew in a long breath and sighed out his frustration.

He had always been the prodigy, entered Harvard on a full scholarship when he was sixteen, graduated with a dual major in biochemistry and synthetic biology with top honors at nineteen, then entered Harvard Medical School, graduating at the top of his class and receiving his M.D. at twenty-three. He went on to specialize in infectious diseases, was considered one of the top in the field internationally, and had been juggling his time between research and the large group practice he had put together, until just before his thirty-second birthday. At that time, two years ago, he had been persuaded by the government to give up his practice so that he might concentrate fully on this terrible new disease. Their persuasion came in the form of offering him ten times what he had been making, along with numerous other bonuses and benefits.

He was the one who had determined that the virus progressed from one phase to the next with an almost mechanical precision previously unseen in disease. Four years and thirty to thirty-one days after the initial onset of symptoms of the numbing cold, persons with this illness had to be committed to full time, long term care.

Michael loosened his tie even further and unbuttoned another button on his deep pink shirt. He gave a verbal command, putting the computer into sleep mode, stood up and stretched, and walked out of his office, heading next door to the room of his nearest colleague.

"I am getting nowhere at breakneck speed, John," he said to the man staring at a large screen filled with diagrams of molecular structures.

Dr. John Cummings, at thirty-five, was just under five-ten, his longish hair graying prematurely. He had built up a fair-sized gut that telegraphed too much food and too much time in front of a computer. He played nervously with one earlobe as he stared back at Michael through bloodshot eyes. Yin to Michael's yang, Cummings' office was in utter disarray. He was quick to point out to any who commented on this, that he knew exactly where everything was.

"Same here. I've never encountered anything even remotely like this little bugger. You'd think that with all this technology around us we'd at least find a hint of something useful," John said, shaking his head.

"All the technology in the world is only as good as the humans who do the programing and data entry," Michael said. "And then humans have to interpret the data spewed back out. Sometimes I think we depend too much on technology."

John gave a nervous laugh. "Sometimes I think we're just not going to make it happen on this one. Look, it's after seven, my friend, time for both of us to go home. Let's get a fresh start tomorrow morning. Come on, I'll walk with you to the parking lot." He turned his head and said, "Computer: sleep."

Home was a three thousand square foot Tudor in Brookline, small for the neighborhood, but more than large enough for him and his wife, Sherilyn. She was five-eight, drop dead gorgeous, madly in love with Michael, and waiting for the next and final phase of the illness to rear its nasty head inside of hers.

He ran his hands through her short blonde hair, kissed her on the mouth and pulled her in for a long hug. It had been over a year since either had asked *how was your day?*

"Anything?" she asked. He shook his head.

She had gotten the numbing cold just after Thanksgiving in 2033 and had taken the new medication for it. If the typical pattern held, and it would, they both knew she would be unable to function on her own in less than a month, just after the holidays. This had sat between them like a thick stone wall.

"Well, I still feel fine," she said, rubbing his back with one hand.

He pulled her in closer and started to cry.

"You'll find it, Michael. I know you will."

He didn't.

<hr>

By Christmas Sherilyn spent more time out of lucidity than in it. A week after New Year's Eve Michael signed her into a long term care facility. That it was the best in the area would make no difference to her at all, and did little to assuage the guilt he felt for his failure, but in his less-dark moments he allowed himself to pretend that the bright décor and more attentive staff would be of some comfort to her.

At every visit he would sit and talk to her, tell her what was going on, how much he loved her and how sorry he was for failing her. She was half-sitting up in the hospital bed, propped up against a thick pillow, a soft strap keeping her from falling to one side or the other. She stared straight ahead. Her head didn't move, nor did her once vibrant eyes, which were now dull and bloodshot.

Michael spent longer and longer hours at his office in the hospital, avoiding going home to a house that felt cavernous and filled with mocking ghosts. Every room reminded him of the end result of what he had not been able to accomplish. He sometimes even slept on a gurney in a closet at the hospital, just as he had as an intern during long shifts, though these days there were few interns vying for closet space.

Harvard was the only medical school still open in the Boston area. The administrators of all the regional medical schools had decided to consolidate the programs into one because there were fewer professors still able to teach, and even fewer students entering the medical programs.

The inhabitants of the world were being consolidated as well. Michael knew this all too well. As a diversion from the intensity of his research, he had created a program to project what would happen to the world population...and when. He had finished inputting the latest data and was letting the computer run scenarios. It announced availability of the results with a single, repeating beep. He pressed a spot on the screen to display these, and stared at the computer screen, eyes wide and unblinking.

"Oh my God."

Within two months he sold his house to a colleague who had lusted after it for a few years, and because his mortgage had been paid off by the government as part of a signing bonus, he was able to bank a sizable amount of cash. He moved into a small one bedroom rental apartment close to the hospital so he could walk to work. He liquidated all his investments and sold anything he had that was of any value, knowing it would all grow closer to worthless with every day that passed.

A few months later he was the proud owner of ten medium and large tracts of farmland and woodland in northwestern Massachusetts, for which he had paid cash. None was within eighty miles of the other. He knew what was going to happen and he'd formulated a plan.

In January 2038 the deaths that Michael knew would start to happen, did. The original people who had had the numbing cold were dying in large numbers. The funeral parlors and crematoriums kept pace at first, but soon became inundated. Temporary refrigeration units were built to house the backup of bodies waiting to be dealt with. Ten percent of the world population was now dead. Thirty percent of what was left was now confined to long term care facilities, many of which consisted of little more than cots placed in row after row in any building available, and the available buildings became more and more plentiful as businesses shut down. There were also fewer and fewer people to care for the sick and dying, or to work in factories or companies or supermarkets or anywhere. While many of the country's farms were still producing enough food, there was less of it available because there were less people to manage its transportation.

The government stepped in, offering firm reassurances to the public that everything would be all right. They started offering very attractive salaries to bring in enough workers to move food and supplies to where they were needed. Michael knew the feds were simply printing reams and reams of money because they knew what he knew, that life as it had been was coming to an end, and the full faith and credit of the United States government would be little more than the punch line of a very sour joke in a few years' time.

There were rapidly becoming only a few businesses that were viable and growing, transportation of food being one, the business of caring for the sick and the business of dealing with the dead, the others. States were activating National Guard units to dig mass graves in an attempt to quell the stench of dead bodies that was starting to permeate large sections of most cities and suburban areas. Other diseases related to dead and festering corpses sprung up and took hold. There was a steady stream of people leaving the city and moving to the more suburban areas. All the deaths were resulting in more and more houses being placed on the market, and that resulted in the cost of buying a home plummeting to all time lows.

The cost of properties remote from the cities was, however, moving solidly in the other direction. Fueled by fear, people with any means were getting into bidding wars to buy land and houses in distant, secluded areas. The further from a city, the higher the price got bid up, and many were offering cash at closing. Groups were forming, pooling resources to buy land. Michael easily sold eight of his ten tracts for over twenty times what he had paid. His plan was working.

Because the virus had been designed and constructed to be tamperproof, neither Michael nor any of the many people in the country who worked in the research labs found a cure or even any promising leads. He did develop a simple blood test to determine who was or would be immune. He took it as far as testing himself and his colleagues, but never brought it beyond that. Like his work, it had become superfluous to what was happening. Those who were immune would not get the disease; those who were not would eventually line up in the exit queue or cut in line via their own hand or that of a kind relative or friend. A quiet desperation set in at the facility, but the government kept paying him his exorbitant salary knowing that the odds were against anything coming from his work. And he kept accepting their money.

<hr />

On his last visit to Sherilyn, he brought a transdermal syringe and a single vile of clear liquid. He smoothed her light blue hospital gown and spoke to her calmly as he had always done. He kissed her lightly on the lips, stroked her hair for a few moments and told her one last time that he loved her. In a total vegetative state, she was but a lump of flesh and hair clinging to life by the most tenuous of threads. He loaded the contents of the small bottle into the syringe, set it for a full dosage and pressed it against the crook of her right arm. He hesitated for a moment, then pushed a button on the side. He heard the pop of air that injected the liquid through her skin and into her vein. She was dead in less than fifteen seconds.

Tears dripping from his eyes, he sat looking at her. Putting his hand to her cheek, he said goodbye. No one would investigate her death or call for an autopsy. No one had the time or the energy or the willingness to care anymore. Death meant little else than that a bed opened up, only to be filled within the hour. He wouldn't be surprised if he didn't even get a call.

———— ((●)) ————

John sat in his office chair, his face crimson red, eyes desperate and angry.

"What do you mean, you're leaving?" he asked. "How can you leave at a time like this? We've got to find the cure! We need you!"

Michael looked back at him through tired eyes, deep sadness showing. "I gave notice a few weeks back. It's over, John. You know as well as I do that if we haven't found the cure yet, it's not going to be found. We haven't even gotten any substantial leads. We're not going to be able to save anyone except ourselves."

John's fingers curled into fists. "I can't believe you'd be that fucking selfish. Son of a bitch! I don't believe it! I thought I knew you!"

Michael lowered his head for a second, then raised it back up. "It's not selfishness. Its self-preservation, for me and a bunch of others who want to take a shot at surviving, at starting again. I showed you the projections a year ago. You know I've always looked ahead to what's coming down the pike, and all I see is a billion car pile-up happening in slow motion, and I can't do anything to stop it, but I can get out of its path. This way of life is coming to a close. The government project to upload information and knowledge to their not-so-secret satellites just backs up what I'm saying. They're preparing for the end."

"Like that's been some great success," John said.

Michael and many others knew the feds had created programs similar to his, and that their projection results had come up the same. They, too, were making preparations. At first there were only news reports of mysterious rocket launchings. The lack of quality control specialists and competent, qualified workers resulted in only two of the eight rockets launched actually delivering the satellites into fixed orbits above the country. Failure had become more imminent than success. Speculation and rumor ran rampant as to the purpose of the launchings, but then a person Michael knew in the Harvard University Medical system told him on the sly that the feds had had their people in to upload medical teaching databases into special, portable storage devices. He told Michael that an insider he knew told him what they were doing, that they were creating a database of survival and historical data.

The Harvard person told him later that an armored vehicle with no markings had dropped off a dozen boxes that were immediately moved to a secured storage area. Through his connections and a large bribe, the man had gained access to the area and opened one of the boxes. It contained forty-eight smaller boxes, each of those containing odd-looking devices made of plasteel, with each unit consisting of a device with a screen, two pairs of viewing glasses, and two small solar power chargers.

The man went on to explain that he had figured out the devices were for accessing the satellites which contained the survival database, and he was willing to sell Michael one of them. He named his price. Michael offered him a higher amount and bought twenty. The man agreed and added that there were no manuals in the boxes explaining the devices.

"You have to decide how to act, John," Michael said, "be it sitting here hoping beyond hope to find a cure that has eluded us for how many years, or by taking your knowledge and talents into the new life that is starting as we speak."

"I've never been one to quit. You know that."

"This is not...." Michael stopped as someone walked past the office. "This is not quitting," he said, lowering his voice. "Quite the opposite. This is getting right out there in the beginning and doing something useful. Eighty percent of the world's population contracted the numbing cold. That means eighty percent of the world's population is going to die, leaving twenty percent of us to start over. It's inevitable."

"And that is why we have to find a cure!" John said loudly.

"I felt the same way for a long time after Sherilyn went into care. I started putting in even longer hours to find the cure, to make up for failing her. I'm betting that losing Jenny brought that same feeling out in you.

"Look, John, I've got some last minute shopping to do tomorrow, but I'll be heading out Route 2 early on Sunday morning. It's still fairly civil out there, but you know as well as I do that that's going to change over the next year or two. We're talking out and out chaos, violence, killing, as people scramble to get away from the death they believe lives in these areas. I have my place in western Mass and I'll be there sometime after lunch on Sunday. I could use your help. We could make a difference doing this. We could really help people again," Michael said. "Listen: why don't you take a few days off and at least come up and see what it's all about. Think about it, and if you change your mind, call me or be at the apartment by six a.m. day after tomorrow. And if you miss that time, here's my vehicle locator code so you can find me. And please: keep it quiet." He handed John a small piece of paper.

John stared at him again, searching for words, searching for anything that would make their parting okay. He knew there was no convincing Michael to do anything else. He drew in a deep breath and let it out as he stood up and approached Michael, then put his arms out. Michael extended his and hugged his close friend.

"Good luck to both of us," John said.

The alarm went off at 4:30 Sunday morning. Darkness wouldn't yield to first light until close to 6:30. Michael opened a window and felt the harsh sting of the mid-February air hit his face. In the overly bright, bluish glow of an LED streetlamp he saw a light and steady snow falling, adding to the five inches leftover from the last storm two days earlier. He knew the roads would be a mess. There were few qualified people left to man the city or state plows. He took a shower, made coffee and breakfast, washed and packed up the last of the dishes and silverware. Habit brought him to absentmindedly check for the newspaper outside his door. He let out a quiet laugh as he remembered that he'd cancelled it a few days earlier. Like many things in his life, it had ceased to matter. He took out his phone and set up a text to his landlord that he was leaving, giving only the vaguest of reasons why, and told the woman that he had transferred six months extra rent to her bank account. He set the text to automatically send at noon.

He waited until 6:30, hoping to hear the knock on the door that never came. He put on his dark green, arctic parka and black wooly cap, brought the last of his few belongings - packed in plasteel containers - out to the truck and loaded them in. Leaving the apartment keys on the kitchen counter, he closed the door and twisted the handle on the door to make sure the place was locked.

Stepping up on the running board of his hybrid solar/fuel cell Honda Expanza, he glanced around the neighborhood one last time before sliding into the driver's seat. Stopping at the local supermarket, he bought the last nine bags of ice left in the freezer, packed them into the large plasteel coolers half-filled with perishable food stuffs.

He had been right. The roads were poorly plowed at best, slowing down his pace to an average of twenty-five miles per hour. As he drove over another washboard stretch, he realized he'd be lucky if he made it by three o'clock, and that was if it didn't get any worse.

Two hours onto the road he decided to pull off at a rest area to relieve himself, parking at the outer edges of the lot, away from the few vehicles present. The building that had once housed five fast food establishments now had only one open, and that was operating with only two people, one give-a-shit teen at the register and one harried adult scurrying around the cooking area like a crazed animal. The men's room stunk of urine and feces from lack of being cleaned. He grabbed a large coffee to go, then headed across the parking lot.

Though the truck was fairly fully packed, he caught a glimpse of a moving shadow through the rear side windows. Someone hanging around the other side of the vehicle. Moving quietly and cautiously to the front side of the truck, he braced himself for confrontation if it came to that. He knew that in these times, people were starting to get edgy about a lot of things, especially about the lack of goods available. There had been more theft in the past year or two than ever before.

Coming around the truck, he saw a man standing with his back to him, wearing a heavy, dark blue winter coat, the hood up. The man was peering into the truck. "May I help you?" he asked from a few feet away.

Startled, the man spun around quickly, then pushed his hood back. John smiled. "Where's *my* coffee?" he asked.

Michael broke out into a wide grin and extended his right hand. "I'm glad you changed your mind."

"I was awake the whole night after you left the office…thinking about what you'd said. I knew it was true. This whole thing - society - is going to blow wide open within a year or two, if it even lasts that long, and being anywhere near Boston is going to be really bad. But then, so will trying to get away from it. So here I am."

"So here you are. Where's your car?" Michael said, looking around. "Go get it and follow me."

John scrunched up his face a bit and looked away for a moment.

"What's that for?" Michael asked.

"If it's not all right, please feel free to tell me," John said.

"If what's not all right?"

"What I did. It doesn't have to happen…I mean, I made that clear."

"Made what clear and to whom?" Michael asked, starting to get a little annoyed.

John scrunched his face up again.

"Just say it, will you?"

"I know you said to keep it quiet, but I sort of invited a few others along. I told them it might not work out, that you might not let them go…so they're prepared for that."

Michael stared at him for a few moments before sighing deeply. "How many?"

"Three others."

"Three? Who?"

"You know Marcy."

"Sure, head of bio-chem."

"Yes. And she's very good with computers, too," John said, sounding like a comline sales person making yet another desperate pitch.

Marcy was in her mid-thirties, a lanky, well-toned five-nine, with brown eyes and dark brown hair that was always in a ponytail at the office. There was a grace about her movement that almost didn't match her physical appearance. She seemed more to glide, than walk from one spot to another.

Michael stroked his chin a bit and looked very serious. "I don't suppose she eats very much, being that thin and all."

"No, I don't suppose…" John stopped, looked at Michael and broke into a laugh.

"And the others?"

"Neighbors. My age, too. He's an engineer. She's an M.D. - OB/GYN. I thought a specialist or two might be of interest."

Michael thought for a minute, considering what this would mean. More mouths to feed meant the food he'd stored wouldn't go as far, but he could still stock up pretty easily. He wondered how they'd hold up doing physical labor. There would be more than enough of that to go around. The brainy life would be the smaller part of what was to come. *Still,* he thought, *an engineer, a biochemist and an OB/GYN would probably be very useful. But I'm getting ahead of myself.*

"Okay," Michael said.

"Yeah, I thought so...wait a minute. You said okay?" he asked, surprise in his voice. "Okay!" He turned and waved his arm.

The lights on a small, glacier blue hybrid SUV flicked to life and the vehicle moved silently toward the Expanza, Marcy at the wheel.

A man and woman got out of the back seat. He was of average height, wearing an arctic parka similar to Michael's, but even under its bulk it was clear he was solidly built. He pushed his hood back to reveal green eyes and a full head of blonde hair combed straight back.

"Bob Williams," he said, taking off a glove and extending a thick hand.

"Michael Macalister," Michael said, shaking it.

A thinner hand with long fingers was extended by the woman next to Bob. "Heather," she said, shaking his hand with a firm grip. She was petite, wearing a white, waist-length micro-down jacket that hugged her body. A wide pink headband held back medium length light brown hair. "I hope this isn't throwing your plans all to hell," she said. "John said you've always been a meticulous planner."

"He probably left out the part of me also adapting quickly to new situations. We'll make it work," Michael said. "Pleased to meet you both."

He turned slightly to Heather's right. Marcy stood there wearing jeans, work boots and a dark brown thigh-length micro-down jacket. "Marcy, nice to see you again."

"Michael," she said, smiling warmly.

The breeze stiffened a bit as the snowfall turned heavier.

"Welcome aboard," Michael said. "Get coffee if you want, then let's hit the road. We've probably got another four-and-a-half to five hour drive if the roads are this bad all the way out. John, you want to ride with me?"

<hr />

The narrow, winding road leading to Michael's new place was just over a mile long. Freshly plowed, five-foot high piles of snow formed a whitish wall on either side. Patches of hard-packed dirt showed in places. There were cutouts carved into the sides of the road here and there in the event that two vehicles were heading in opposite directions at the same time. The multitude of tall red pines standing guard on either side were tipped with snow and quickly blended into each other, forming a hodgepodge wall that limited sight into the woods. Between that and the curves in the road, they could never see more than twenty yards in any direction. This and the thickly clouded sky gave the sensation of driving through a dream.

As their two-vehicle caravan came to the end of the road, the trees suddenly opened up and they drove into a large, circular area where they were greeted by two tall, large young men holding plas-teel assault rifles. Both were dressed in white camouflage parkas with the hoods down, white wooly caps protecting their heads from the cold. One waved upon seeing Michael's truck, and dropped his rifle to his side. The other looked suspiciously at the second vehicle, his eyes focused intensely on it as it slowed to a stop. His gun stayed at the ready across his chest.

Before them stood a massive structure made of dark brown logs, the front wall two hundred feet long, the side, one hundred fifty. Off-center of the front wall, a normal sized metal door was fitted into the middle of a significantly larger one that was twelve feet high by ten feet wide. Ten by six windows adorned the front of the building's lower section, ten on the left side of the door, six on the right. Smaller ones were interspersed evenly across the second floor. The four-sided roof peaked at fifty feet, with four large gables on each of the two visible sides. The logs used for the construction of the first story walls were each about a foot thick in diameter. The second story logs were half that size.

"Ted, Bill," Michael said as he got out of the truck. He nodded to the second vehicle. "Its okay: they're with me." He made introductions. "Would you two mind unloading my truck. The coolers go into the kitchen; everything else can just be stacked in the living room for now. Thanks."

Bob, the engineer, whistled as he looked the place over, taking in its size and construction. "It's a fortress," he said to no one in particular. He turned to Michael. "Who designed it?"

Michael motioned them to follow him. "I did. The logs used for this building are uncut except for some shaving on the interior side, to allow for one-by-twelve inch pine boards to be nailed in flush. The exterior is treated with a fire suppressant. The windows are a poly-glass composite, flame and heat resistant, bulletproof, shatterproof. It would take a tank to break through the walls, and we cannot be burned out, should anyone feel the need to try. Come on in. I'll give you the cook's tour," he said, approaching the door. He took his right hand, curled his thumb and fourth finger to his palm and pressed the fingertips of his fore-, middle-, and pinky-fingers against the center of the smaller door. There was the sharp sound of metal sliding against metal before it opened. He stood back to let the others pass.

"Biometric security," Bob mused out loud.

"With each person's code a mix of fingers," Michael added. "If one places all five fingertips on the pad, the lock would remain set.

This probably sounds very gruesome, but if an intruder wanted to enter the building and he or she cut off the hand of one whose fingertips were coded in, the intruder would have to come up with the right sequence of fingertips in two tries. After two, the computer shuts out another attempt by the same fingertips until reset from inside the building. Of course, there's always the doorbell...and there are cameras to let us know who's out there."

John turned toward the others, raised his eyebrows and said, "Always thinking ahead."

They entered a room that was fifteen by fifteen, with walls made of plasteel panels. A single, high wattage LED bulb, sitting behind a thick poly-glass lens, threw stark light down on them from twelve feet above. As Michael shut the door, a heavy, metallic clicking-thudding sound followed.

"Eight inch titanium dead bolts, four of them, one in each direction of the door's edges," Michael said. "The walls of this room are two-inch thick plasteel and cannot be penetrated with anything less than large, armor piercing rounds, which, to my knowledge, are not to be found outside of military storehouses. The gun to fire such rounds weighs in at about two hundred pounds. Not something someone just carries around.

"The grates you see in the floor," he said, pointing down, "allow gas to enter and fill the room, if necessary, and be drawn back out as well. What gas, exactly, has yet to be determined."

He again pressed his fingertips on the center of a smaller door inside one big enough to drive a large vehicle through. Only the bottom half of the door opened, and that seemed to be made for someone half the size of an average person. It opened back into the room they were in. He stooped to walk in, waited for the others to follow. "If anyone not invited does somehow breach the room's defenses and opens this door, they have to come in stooped over, which will slow them down. Because the door opens back into the foyer, there are also clear shots from any direction inside," he said in a matter-of-fact tone.

"Expecting a siege?" Marcy asked.

"Expecting? No. Prepared for? Yes."

They entered and stood on the edge of a one hundred by eighty foot room. A second floor balcony, twenty feet up, hugged all the outer edges of the room, allowing viewers to look down into the area. The great room was filled with dozens of boxes. Couches and chairs were set up in such a way as to create three distinct sitting areas around a central one. A massive walk-in hearth dominated the center of the wall furthest from them. Two large, wood burning stoves stood off to either side of the fireplace, and two more were placed halfway down the interior front walls. In a corner, in the last open space in the room, was a concert grand piano, twelve feet in length, covered with thick, blue movers' blankets. Cases were stacked under and around it.

"Stringed, brass and wooden instruments and drums of various types, with enough spare strings, skins and hardware to keep us in a lifetime of music, and then some. It is unlikely that any of the instruments, strings or skins will be made again for some time to come, as things out there move into total collapse."

"You're cheery today," John said.

"Realistic," Michael answered with a smile. "You're welcome to leave your coats here, if you want. Just drape them over a couch or chair." He removed his parka, tossed it over the nearest piece of furniture.

He started walking, but hearing no footsteps, turned back slightly. The four of them were caught up in gazing at various sections of the great room. He caught their attention, then extended his arm and gestured gracefully for them to follow him through a tall set of French doors at the end of the room furthest from the fireplace. These led to a large dining room with a cathedral ceiling. One large table, forty feet in length, occupied the middle of the room, with smaller tables for two or four diners lining the outside walls. All the chairs save seven were stacked on top of the outer tables. A small wet bar was built diagonally across one corner. A wood stove, also set diagonally, lay across another corner near the front windows. The pale tone of the light green walls had a calming effect. A glow from overhead panels enveloped the room with soft light.

John pointed to one of the side tables. "I see you brought along your chess set." He turned to the others. "Michael is beyond a master at chess. Well, Marcy, you know that. You've seen some of the lunch-time games at the office. Never seen him beat. He's always at least five or six moves ahead any anyone else."

"We'll have to have a game," Heather said. "I was captain of the chess club in undergrad."

Michael smiled and nodded at her, then walked through a set of full-sized, swinging double doors, moving the group into a very large and spacious kitchen. "Commercial grade, with six six-burner stoves flanked with double, over-under hyper-convection ovens, six spectra-wave ovens, six high-efficiency refrigerators, six huge freez-ers, four commercial-sized dishwashers and enough prep space to keep twenty-five or so cooks out of each other's hair. All of it is solar powered with battery backup. And there is a very large pantry be-hind that door over there."

They looked around, fixated on the myriad cookware hanging from racks suspended from the ceiling over the prep space and the islands, or bolted to the walls, all the grayish-green color of plasteel.

Michael read their thoughts. "It will last our lifetime and prob-ably many more, as well. What has created the death of so many, may end up being an integral part of what keeps those of us who are left...." He paused. "...alive."

He continued leading them around. The spaces between the dining and kitchen areas and the exterior walls were divided into rooms of various sizes, all meant for storage, he explained.

"By the time I'm finished supplying the place, we will have pretty much all of the most important staple items we'll need to survive for quite some time," he said, showing them a room filled with boxes stacked neatly from floor to ceiling.

"What's in all those boxes?" John asked.

"Duct tape and WD-40."

They moved back into the great room area.

"There are two main staircases to the upstairs from the living area, with another smaller one accessible just off the kitchen, as well as a ladder that goes from the basement to the second floor. That one goes through a closet and can be used to access this first floor, also. There are fourteen bedrooms up there, all about twenty-five by twenty-five, all set up for double occupancy - couples or roommates. I also have a number of bunk beds and cots in storage in case we need a little more sleeping space. Each bedroom contains a bathroom complete with linen closet, sink, shower, composting toilet and bidet."

The two women looked at each other and gave a short laugh. Heather spoke. "Pretty fancy, putting in bidets."

"We'll all appreciate it much more when we run out of toilet paper in three or four years," Michael said with a slight smile.

"You keep saying *we*," John said. "You mean us?"

"I guess I'm using it in the sense that there will be more people than just Ted, Bill and me," he said. "Now, if you'll grab your things and go upstairs, I invite you to choose whatever rooms you'd like. All the doors are open save one; that is my room. I'll finish unpacking the supplies. So freshen up and settle in a bit, then join me for a snack in, say, thirty minutes."

The others put their coats on and walked outside, unloaded Marcy's SUV, and went back in. Michael helped Ted and Bill finish unloading his Expanza. He then stepped back, took out his remote and pressed a button once, then twice. The vehicle started to whir. The cargo area slid slowly and smoothly into the passenger section, effectively reducing the vehicle's size by half.

"I love this truck!" he said to himself.

———— ◦《◉》◦ ————

The meal Michael made that night was simple: two herbed, roast chickens with mashed potatoes, giblet gravy, and peas and Brussel sprouts from the freezer. He opened bottles of pinot noir and chardonnay.

Bill and Ted joined them for dinner. Both were slightly over six foot tall. Bill had black hair which he kept on the longer side and parted just off-center. His full beard was neatly trimmed, his broad shoulders covered by well-toned muscles. His skin color displayed his love of the outdoors, and the energy he gave off was open and friendly. His smile, wide and on the toothy side, came easily. His green eyes sparkled cheerfully, playing off his bright red and white checked flannel shirt. From his participation in the conversation, it was clear he was intelligent and well-read.

Ted shaved his head and face except for his eyebrows, which were brown and thin. His dark, steely eyes looked at the world from behind a barricade of suspicion, as if he were sure the next attack would come at any moment. He wore black jeans and a black tartan flannel, the sleeves rolled up enough to reveal a set of intensely toned forearms.

Though they hadn't known each other previously, both had lived their entire lives in the northern high country of Wyoming, and had answered an intriguing ad Michael had run a year and a half before. Both were used to the cold. Bill thought the New England winters were mild; Ted referred to them as pussy. Seasoned hunters and fishermen, both had done farm work and possessed a wide body of knowledge about construction, mechanics and living off the land. Neither had any family left. Bill participated in the mealtime conversation; Ted only listened and watched.

"John, you remember that long weekend I took some time back?" Michael asked. "That's when I flew out to Wyoming to meet with these two gentlemen. I explained everything I believed was going to happen. When they didn't flinch, I told them what the job entailed. When they didn't flinch again, I invited them to join me. Currently they are on salary, but if...no," Michael said, as if correcting himself, "*when* the shit hits the fan, they understand that money will mean little, if anything, but they know they'll have a place to call their own." Michael chuckled a little. "If, on the other hand, I turn out to be a total space shot, they will have fairly sizable bank accounts to fall back on."

"I think it's all gonna happen," Ted said, not bothering to look up from his plate. His voice was devoid of any emotion or concern. It was his only participation in the conversation.

"Gentlemen," Michael said to them as the meal finished up, "you are welcome to stay with us or to retire back to your cabins. We are simply going to hang out and chat about things."

Ted left immediately, with a single terse nod to the group. Bill stayed until he heard the door shut, looked at Michael and motioned with his eyes and a subtle nod of the head to follow him. Michael excused himself, followed Bill to the back door of the building.

"That guy is fucking nuts," Bill said. "I mean, it's been just the two of us for quite a few months and he rants and raves about all kinds of shit, how he can't wait until people start coming after the place so he can shoot them all dead."

"I'll be around now, and pretty soon we'll have more people, so there'll be more of a buffer."

"That'll be a little better, but he still scares the shit out of me. There've been a few times when I questioned - and not in a challenging or angry way - some of the negative shit he's spewing out, and he's given me this killer look, like I'm the enemy. I'm just telling you, he's a frigging stick of lit dynamite and I surely don't know how long the fuse is."

Michael took in a deep breath, let it our slowly. "I hear you. Keep an eye out; I'll do the same. If need be, I'll talk to him."

"Y'all'll want to be carrying when you do that."

Michael thought for a moment after Bill left before turning to go back into the dining room. He invited the group to move into the great room, telling them to leave the dishes. He remained behind for a few minutes, and then rejoined them, carrying a tray with five cordial glasses and three bottles of liqueurs. He offered cognac, pear brandy, and a homemade cranberry liqueur. Each went to the tray and poured his or her choice. He lit a readymade fire in the nearest wood stove, the flames dancing around behind the thick glass doors.

He talked about his computer projections and explained further what he had been putting together.

"So what you're saying is that with the projected twenty percent of the population left, people will simply walk away from their jobs?" Heather asked.

"Or the jobs will - so to speak - walk away from them. Let me ask you a question," Michael said. "If you weren't getting paid to do what you do, would you continue to do it?"

Heather thought about that for a moment. "I guess it would depend on the conditions."

"Such as?" he asked.

"I might volunteer my services. I've done that before, gone someplace in need and worked without pay for a few weeks."

"Now let's put some other conditions on the situation, then you tell me what you'd do. Start with this: there is no money. It has become worthless, useless."

"I would barter," she said without hesitation.

"For what?"

"I don't know. Food, I guess."

"And if food became scarce, maybe too scarce for people to want to give it up in barter, yet that was what you needed most in order to survive?"

She thought on that. "Interesting condition."

"And then let's add this: food, on a larger scale, is grown outside of the cities, in regions like this."

She remained silent.

"And the stench of death was permeating most places where humans had lived en masse?"

Marcy had folded herself onto a dark brown loveseat, legs tucked to one side, her back leaning half against an overstuffed armrest. She cut in. "But people survived way before money was used, so wouldn't people just revert back to that way of living?"

Michael smiled. "Marcy, you are now stepping onto the path I'm on. You are correct. However, before that reversion, what will happen?"

"Well," she said, pausing for a moment, "Survival will dictate that people go back to farming, hunting and gathering, making what they need with their hands."

"Agreed. But my question is what will happen before that? How many people know enough to do all that, know enough to survive, know how to hunt or farm or what to gather? Make clothes? People have become so incredibly dependent on technology. How many will know how to survive without it? Without supermarkets? Without someone else making things for them? A lot of that type of knowledge has disappeared from the lives of the average person. How many of you would know how to make steel, for instance?"

"Well," Marcy said, "I could tell you what goes into the making of steel, and I could probably figure out the process."

"But if push came to shove, could you actually make tools or weapons out of steel?"

She thought for a moment before answering no.

"And what about clothes? Would you know how to make clothes?" he asked.

"I could probably weave reeds together or something. If all else fails," she said with a smile, "there're always fig leaves."

Michael smiled back. "So much of the knowledge of how to do things has been lost to computers and machinery and automation."

"Whoa! Now I see where you've been going in that brain of yours. You've been projecting the critical path of reversion back to farming, hunting, gathering, et cetera," Heather said. "And now I know why you annihilated me in three games of chess this afternoon, the way you not only think ahead, but how you get there."

"So now you're seeing what I've been seeing. Add this in: if there are no replacement parts being made for technology for when it breaks down, it will start to disappear little by little. How many people do you think will be preparing for that possibility?" Michael asked.

"Oh, my god," Bob said. "Most people will be caught off guard, then scramble to find what they need…except, everyone else will be trying to do the same thing."

"The farmers and the hunters become those who will have," John said.

"And hunger is a powerful motivator," Bob said, "so…chaos, violence, anarchy."

Michael let this information sink in. "I know there are many who would say I'm paranoid, maybe even psychotic in my thinking," he said, "but this is what I believe to be coming."

"So you see this all happening within the next year or two?" Bob asked.

"Not much longer than two years, if even that," Michael said, "but it will seep into life as we've known it, little by little."

Marcy complimented him on the cranberry cordial he'd made. "Michael, I know your work and your uncanny ability to be forward-looking and -thinking. Speaking for myself, I believe in what you're saying and doing. I've been watching all of us at the office make no progress at all. I've worked on some tough bugs in my time, but I'll tell you: I don't think we're going to beat this thing. I like what I see here, how you've thought things through and set things up. For myself, if you're open to it, I'm in. It may take me a while to get it all together to move out here, but if you're okay with it, that is my intention."

John, slumped back comfortably in a chair, spoke up. "You've always been the godfather of foresight at the office, and, quite frankly, I followed your career and work for a bunch of years before we actually met. Your thinking always seemed so radical at first, but then the payoff came, and all of a sudden your thinking made perfect sense. I know what I was saying to you last week, but the more I hear about this, the more I think you're on the money. Like Marcy, I don't know how fast I can make it here, but I'm in."

"Bob and I have obviously not talked this over, but I'm inclined to think being here is the best shot we'll have."

Bob looked at her and smiled. "Makes two of us."

John smirked. "You knew we'd do this. That's why you kept saying we. Always thinking ahead of everyone else."

Michael smiled. "Then I guess this is sort of our first town meeting, though I would consider it an unofficial one. I also believe it will be a brief one. I'm quite tired from the ride and what's been going on lately, and I assume you all are as well. We need to have clear heads to properly discuss what we'll be doing. So, the only order of business I have for this evening's get together is to welcome each of you on board as we prepare to sail into uncharted waters. I'm sure we will try to retain some things from our past lives, but much of what is before us will force us to create new ways. I would like to propose a toast: To making it up as we go along!" he said, raising his glass.

"To making it up as we go along," they said, almost in unison. They clinked glasses, then drank.

"May we survive and thrive!" Heather added, raising her glass. Again the group joined in.

"Before this wonderful pear brandy kicks in and my brain turns completely to mush, and, apropos of our conversation," Michael said, "I would like to formally invite you all to the first official town meeting tomorrow. It will commence after a hearty breakfast. I will leave you with this: first and foremost, we need a name for our new town or whatever it's called. Secondly, we must start coming up with a plan."

The others went completely silent and turned to John, who turned to Michael. "I told them you had this all planned out. Don't you?"

"I know what needs to be done," he said, smiling at them. "The plan we need is *how* to do it."

The others still showed apprehension. It was Bob who stood up and faced the group. "I know what he's talking about. It's like figuring out the structure of a building to be constructed. We may know how we want it to look, but we have to figure out how to make it strong and lasting."

"That's what I'm talking about," Michael said, standing up. "I'm going to clean up and then go to bed."

"I'll help," Marcy said, putting the glasses on the tray.

The two of them gathered up the dishes from the dining room and headed into the kitchen.

"Michael," Marcy said as she loaded the dishwasher, "I know you're very methodical in your approach to things, so I certainly don't mean to step on your toes, but I have to tell you that that guy Ted scares me a little...well, maybe more than a little."

"I got a similar feeling when I first met him," Michael said, "but he knows his stuff and he's a hard worker. He's a survivalist, so there's that mentality at play. Think about what we're trying to do here: survive. So who better to help out than someone like him? His bit of paranoia offsets my tending to be too trusting. I know he's a bit intense, but I think he's okay. I hope I'm not proved wrong."

"It's just that he tended to stare at us. Maybe *glare* is a better word. Seems angry."

"Let me know if he does any…well, just let me know."

⸺◦⟨◍⟩◦⸺

As was his habit, Michael got up quite early. After showering, shaving and dressing in jeans and a dark blue, long-sleeved tee shirt, he turned off the bathroom light and moved back into the bedroom. A three-quarter moon hung low to the tree line, its waning radiance still bright enough for him to move into the hall without turning on a light. Heading down the stairs to the living area, he saw a flickering glow off in one corner, outlining a person on the floor. Marcy was sitting cross-legged between two candles, dressed in jet black tights with white leggings pulled up a few inches above her knees, her ever-present ponytail trailing a foot down her back. An un-tucked, bright blue and white checked flannel draped down over her waist. She had a hand resting on each knee, palms open.

"Good morning, Michael," she said quietly, without turning around.

He moved around in front of her. Her eyes were closed.

"Good morning. How'd you know it was me?" he asked softly.

"You have a certain way of walking, a very distinctive sound to your footsteps. You drop your right foot just slightly harder than the left," she said, without opening her eyes.

"Your powers of observation are quite honed. That's a detail few would be aware of," he said. "myself included. I'll leave you be."

She opened her eyes, gave a warm smile. "It's okay. I'm done. I brought my own," she said, standing up and handing him one of the two-inch square candles. She took the other one. "I didn't know what you had or didn't have."

"I've got a few tucked away in the kitchen and my bedroom. We're off the grid with battery backup, so I'm not so concerned about losing power. However, moving out of practical mode, candles do have other, more esoteric uses," he said. "So, yoga?

"Meditation. Ever try it?"

He shook his head.

"Mrs. Dabrakow, a very kind teacher at Franklin High, who had taken me under her wing when I was in my angry, chaotic teenager phase - she suggested it. I found it very calming. Been doing it ever since. Nothing fancy; just sitting quietly for a half-hour or so, focusing on my breath. Hardly a day goes by when I don't start this way. Helps to keep me centered. I'm into mindfulness: being where I am, doing what I'm doing…like that."

He motioned her to walk with him. "I guess I'm more into letting my mind wander when I relax."

"A type of meditation in and of itself. That's probably how you get your creativity flowing…maybe how you came up with the ideas for this place," she said, smiling. "Would you like some help getting things set up for breakfast?"

"Sure," he said. "I'm going to get started on making some cornbread. You want to put coffee on?

"I love cornbread. What mix do you use?"

"No mix - from scratch."

"I'm impressed,' she said. "Where do you keep the coffee pellets?"

"Fridge."

"Uh, which one?" she asked.

He laughed. "Sorry, I forgot. For a moment I was back in my

little apartment. I guess I could use some of that mindfulness you're talking about. The one to your right, in the door's top shelf. And I don't use pellets. I prefer making mine the old fashioned way, using ground beans, so fill the pots to the twelve-mark and use twelve scoops in each coffee maker. The yellow canister is caff, the green, decaff. Maybe make a pot of each, and put on a kettle of hot water. I know John likes tea. Are you a tea or coffee person? Or neither?"

"Coffee. I can't remember the last time I had coffee brewed liked this. I think it was at a museum or something. I'm not sure how to do this."

"It's easy," he said, verbally walking her through the steps.

She watched as he moved through the kitchen gathering ingredients, noting that he wasn't reading from a recipe. His manner of preparation was quite fluid when he was measuring cornmeal, cracking eggs and mixing batter. They chatted a little or worked in silence, getting cookware together, lining up eggs, slicing bacon from a large hunk of pork belly that Michael told her he had bought from a local farmer.

He cracked ten eggs into a large bowl, picked a medium whisk off the wall rack in front of him. After putting in a dollop of sour cream, he mixed the eggs with the whisk.

"That's kind of quaint," Marcy said, nodding at the whisk. "Don't you have an electric scrambler?"

"Nope. It's one of those things I decided to do without right from the get-go."

"Yet you put in dishwashers," she said, a puzzled look on her face.

"So what was I thinking?" he asked her, smiling. "The dishwashers will certainly break down after a while and become useless. But in the beginnings of this place they will save a fair amount of time, time that can be spent doing other, more useful things. And," he added, "I have cabinets already made up that will fit in the spaces when the dishwashers break down for the last time and we remove them."

"Good lord, you do think ahead," she said.

He went into the pantry and came out with a box in which button mushrooms were growing, picked two handfuls. She helped him rinse these off, then watched as he selected a long, large-bladed knife. He snapped off the stems, started cutting the mushrooms into slices, then into small pieces using a fast, precise rocking motion of the blade.

"How do you do that so quickly without slicing the tips of your fingers off?" she asked. "I'd be chopping one piece at a time."

"It's all in how you hold your fingers and how you angle the knife blade. Watch." He demonstrated his technique, going slowly so she could see easily. "Now you try," he said, handing her the knife. "You'll want to go slowly at first…that's right, just like that. After a while you'll get used to the motion and you'll be able to pick up the speed little by little. In angling the blade like that, it's almost impossible to cut yourself."

He selected a large plasteel sauté pan and put a chunk of butter in it. When it had melted and was starting to sizzle a bit, he scooped up the mushroom pieces and put them into the pan, swirling it around to spread them out evenly, then reduced the burner to a low-medium heat.

She stood to one side of him. "Now you'll probably do the pan-flip thing, which anytime I've tried to do, I've ended up doing a major cleanup on the stove and floor," she said.

He looked at her and gave a slight smile, then turned back to the stove, stepping slightly to the side so she could watch. He grasped the pan handle and tilted the pan slightly away from him. As the pieces moved toward the side, he quickly moved the pan up, tilted it slightly back, and flipped the contents. He did this a few times, then swirled it again.

"Okay, now I'm totally impressed. Where did you learn all this?" she asked.

"Watching my mother. She was an amazing cook and I just soaked up whatever I could in her kitchen," he said. "Want to try the pan-flip?"

"Maybe with a smaller pan sometime. I'll just spill a lot and make a mess," she answered.

"Wouldn't be anything I haven't done a thousand times," he said. "That's how we learn."

This feels good, she thought. *I could get used to this.*

<hr />

They decided to hold their first meeting in the dining area. All were dressed casually in jeans or cords, flannels and turtlenecks. Michael purposefully did not sit at the head of the table, but instead chose a corner chair. The others joined him at that end. Each person was given a Softapple Konectable tablet for notes. He called the meeting to order and announced that he was the facilitator only for this meeting. Each, he proposed, would take his or her turn in order.

"Before we get started," John said, unrolling a ten by fourteen inch piece of paper, "I'd like to present the group with a drawing I did of the after-dinner get together last night. I was kind of wound up and couldn't sleep when we went to our rooms, so I started drawing. It sort of commemorates our first gathering." He held it out for them to see. "On archive quality paper. *Guaranteed to last a lifetime and then some* is the company's advertising slogan."

"I know how much you enjoy sketching and drawing, John, so maybe we should make you our pictorial historian," Michael said, raising his eyebrows, half-joking.

"I'll pick up a large portfolio case when I get back to Boston," Marcy said, jumping right into the exchange. "Maybe somewhere, sometime in the future our descendants will get a kick out of seeing how we started."

"There's a thought," Heather said. "What we're doing here could have implications that go on for generations."

"Right now our main focus needs to be on the here and now, with an eye to the future, but if we are successful, that scenario might actually come to pass," Michael said, sitting back in his chair.

The others pondered that for a moment before John broke the silence. "Yes, well, it's just a drawing," he said. "So, Michael, since this is your baby, what do you think we need to discuss today?"

Michael pinched his lower lip together and pulled on it slightly. "I guess it would be good for me say this up front. While I started the process of putting this place together, I really don't want to continue thinking of it as mine. I mean, who owns a...what do we even call this place... *town* doesn't seem to be the right word? Uh, *village*, maybe?"

"*Colony* might be a better word," Bob said.

"Colony? I like that," Michael responded. "So who owns a colony? I want everyone who lives here to consider it theirs...or no one's. You all have as much stake in this as I do."

"But you put this all together," John said.

"I started putting it together, but all of us will take it from here. Besides, the money I put into it will be useless in a few years, if even that long, so it's not like I could sell it, and I certainly have no designs on being the king of anything. I guess the point is that I want you each to consider this your baby, too."

They looked at him, not quite sure how to take what he was saying.

"Ours," Michael said, stretching out his hands, palms up, and looking at each of them. "Agreed?"

Each, in turn, agreed.

"Great! Now, as to what we need to do today...submissions of names for our colony...." He paused and smiled, feeling comfortable with the word rolling off his tongue. "...would be a good starting place. Beyond that, we need general ideas of how to do this, maybe some general plans for the coming year or maybe just the next month or two - set up a sort of calendar -, then an agenda for today and maybe tomorrow."

"Eden," Bob said.

"What?" John asked.

"Eden. A name. I'm submitting a name."

"Sort of putting ourselves a little high up, don't you think?" John said.

"All submissions will be voted on. We now have our first entry. I would invite you to submit as many names as you want," Michael said. "So let's take a few minutes now and put a few names into our 'tabs. You'll find a folder marked *names*. Use that, please."

They each activated their Konectables. A virtual screen appeared in front of each unit. Touching a spot on the virtual screen produced a virtual keyboard. Michael watched as they tapped the virtual keys, giving them fifteen minutes to submit names. He put in entries he'd previously thought of, then came up with a few more.

"Okay, we've got twenty-two submissions. The *names* folders are all synced together. Please hit share and we'll each have all the names to peruse. Closeout for entries will be just before the start of dinner tonight. We'll take the evening to consider the names, then each of us will cast five votes for our favorites by noon tomorrow. The program I've set up will tabulate the top five names. We'll all cast two more votes, get that down to two choices by four o'clock, and then have our final vote right after dinner tomorrow evening. Does that sound fair?"

They agreed.

"Next order of business: the general calendar. Who wants to be the secretary for today? John…good. So let's proceed," Michael said.

The discussion started with a slew of questions: how long the stored food would last? Where was the nearest supermarket? Should they conserve right from the get-go? Where would new food come from? What would happen when things started to break down in the outside world? Bob raised the issue of growing their own food, wanting to know how the five of them could possibly do that with little to no experience.

"I would remind you that the two members of this colony who are not attending this meeting have quite a bit of experience in farming. I have ten climate-controlled greenhouses already set up in a field not too far from here, so growing many things in the winter will not be a problem. We also have computers and the 'net, at least for now, so we'll have access to a great deal of information. There's also a general store in Warren, the nearest town, that has a feed and grain department. I've chatted with the owner - Bert. Nice guy. He'll guide us a bit. The hard work part…well, we're going to have to get used to that," Michael said. "And who said it's just us?"

"You invited more people?" John asked.

"Not yet. So let's discuss our needs in the people department, then figure out how to meet them."

"But we can't just keep hiring people," Marcy said. "Where will we get the money?"

"Who said anything about hiring people? But speaking of money, who owns properties in the Boston area or elsewhere?" Michael asked. All raised their hands. "Then rather than just abandoning them at some point, how about you put them on the market and get some cash flow going. At this point, money can still buy us a lot of things we'll need, so the more of it we have, the better. It will mean going back to the city on a few occasions to deal with things, but in the end we'll all be here. And what about cash value in life insurance policies? Borrow it. You most likely will never have to pay it back."

After lunch, as the group was dressing for the outside tour, Michael passed around a box full of sunglasses and let those who hadn't brought any choose a pair, then took them out into the sunny, but frigid day to show them around.

Right off the back of the building was a large patio area and an outdoor kitchen complete with two large plasteel barbeques, one powered by a solar-charged battery, one wood fired. Plasteel picnic tables and chairs were leaned on their sides against each other, all in a row, half covered with snow. Food prep space was covered by an overhang. An island containing multiple sinks was covered with *plastiseal* sheets.

"I can't get past that color," John said. "Yuck!"

Michael laughed. "You'll get used to it after a while. Besides, I had regularly colored covers made up for the tables and chairs, anticipating reactions like yours."

"Smart ass," John said, whacking him on the shoulder.

"You've got a whole set up for kids over there," Heather said. "Slides, jungle gyms, swings, treehouse."

"I do expect there will be children, and I do have plans to construct a school building as things get going," Michael said. "Now those buildings over there are the six cabins we've built so far. That's where Bill and Ted live. Each negotiated for his own place. Both intend to take a wife when the opportunity presents itself somewhere down the road."

Bob asked about heating sources.

"Each building has three potential heating sources, the first being photovoltaics from direct sunlight, second being battery backup, which is kept fully charged by the photovoltaics, to run the heat grids, stoves, small refrigerators and lights when there's no sunshine for a few days. If all else fails, each has a high-efficiency wood stove, which will do a pretty good job of keeping the places warm as well as being suitable for cooking. I considered wind turbines but there were a couple of issues. The first was the cost, initially, and then with repairs. The second was the height, which I felt would add an element of danger, like advertising where we are. Besides, I got a lot more bang for the buck going the way I did. The backup batteries are cutting edge - lithium sulfur - and will charge quickly and store large amounts of power - enough to fully run each building for about two weeks. That also includes the main building. They will recharge many thousands of times before breaking down…and I intend to get more spares if at all possible, though I will say that I have my doubts. They've gotten incredibly expensive because manufacturing, as you know, has dropped precipitously. I've got sixty in storage and I've contracted for another twenty, but right now the backorder on them is over a year, so it may or may not occur."

Bob asked where the panels were for generating the power. "I mean, it's got to be a fairly large array just to power what you've already put together…and then, there's what's going to be set up."

"I was able to purchase the most efficient panels made, so the panels are much smaller than what is currently the standard for your average commercial use. New, high-end commercial buildings and military bases are the only ones using them. The generating capacities are huge relative to size, and life expectancy is around fifty years. As to where they are, let's just say they're within reach, but well-hidden. My thoughts were around protecting the array from sabotage in case of attack. When the weather improves, I'll take you on a tour."

He turned back to the cabins. "They are basic and identical except for personal finishing touches - two bedrooms, one bathroom, and a kitchen/living/dining room open floor plan, each around a thousand square feet. We already have the timber cut and prepped for six more, and my thinking is that newcomers will have to help ready the materials for one new house, then help build it after they move into one already constructed. Seems only fair. Our storehouse has enough plumbing, heating, cooking and electrical equipment to set up another fifty cabins. After that, they'll get a little more…uh… rustic, if we can't order more supplies. Sanitary facilities will have to be set up outside for the later-built models."

Michael stopped and let them take in the information. He knew they were starting to grasp the enormity of what they were about to engage in. These first days they spent here would seem more like a vacation, and maybe a fantasy one, at that. They would exist in this winter wonderland free from want and need, everything provided for them from his various stockpiles. In the beginning, they would talk more than do, live in a think tank that was only part of what was to come when the weather broke.

He had already spent countless hours and sleepless nights thinking and planning and wondering and buying and getting started, only to realize that for every problem he solved there would be two more presenting themselves, and many more that were, as of yet, totally unrevealed. And when people started joining the colony, there would be more issues, unexpected ones, to be dealt with. In addition to building a place, they would also be building a community. But more than that, they would be building a new way of life.

The meeting that followed lunch lasted most of the afternoon. They talked over what a colony would need. A dentist was one such need. Heather mentioned that she had an oral surgeon in her social circle. She agreed to speak with him in private, see if he might be interested. Teachers would also be good, another said.

"And security," Michael said, "will be a big issue. We would indeed be naïve to believe that the chaos that results as society collapses would not lead to violence in some…or maybe many. People will want, and we will have, and that is the recipe for conflict."

"Cops!" John said.

"Soldiers would be better," Bob added.

"Let's take a walk," Michael said. "I want to show you something."

He led them to one of the two staircases that led down into the basement area. The space was mostly open. A few rooms had been fully constructed; others were framed out. Piles of lumber and composite wallboard were stacked in the middle. Boxes were lined up in an orderly fashion in many areas, some draped with plastiseal tarps, others left bare. He pointed out one finished room he had built that had been rough-plumbed with the thought that it would be their lab.

"Time and money are the current issues in setting that up, buying the equipment and all. I've spent a fair amount on more basic needs and want to make sure I get what is absolutely necessary for survival. In a few years' time, we could probably ride into Boston and take what we want in lab equipment and supplies, assuming the facilities don't get ransacked. But what I want to show you is here in this room."

He pressed his fore, middle and fifth fingertips against the biometric screen on the wall. There was a metallic snap. A light flickered on automatically as he opened the door. One by one they stepped inside.

"My friends: the arsenal."

The room, about thirty feet square, had a sterile feel to it. A number of black metal racks cut the room into rows, with various types of rifles leaning against the frames, two levels high. Many of the guns were made of plasteel. A separate set of shelves ran the length of one wall, fully lined with handguns. Marcy walked down one of the aisles like a kid in a candy store, looking back and forth at the various weapons, letting her fingers brush against some of them.

"We have about two hundred rifles of various types: assault; twelve and sixteen gauge shotguns; small, medium and large caliber lever and bolt action for hunting, and a handful of very powerful pump-action air guns. And John? Did you notice that I actually got some of the rifles and handguns in something other than plasteel? Just for you, my friend," Michael said, smiling and raising and dropping his eyebrows quickly. "Some ammunition is stored in the far end of the basement in another room, sunken and lined with four foot reinforced concrete walls and ceiling, with an exhaust port in case of explosion. I call it the powder room, like they did back in the old days. There is also another outbuilding containing more ammunition, as well as a box of grenades. It's simply amazing what one can purchase on the Internet. The room adjacent to this one is full of compound bows, crossbows, arrows, camouflage gear, fishing rods and reels and tackle, many miles of extra line, fly-tying supplies and tools, et cetera, et cetera, et cetera."

"Where did you get the money to do all this?" Heather asked.

"Sherilyn had a rather large insurance policy provided by her job. I borrowed against my own policy…and my house brought in a pretty penny. And that ridiculous salary the feds paid me…well, let's just say that I've lived like a state college student in my little apartment for the last few years. I also did a bunch of land deals a while back that paid off big time."

Bob scratched his head. "My question is how did you get all this stuff? Any individual buying up this amount of guns would be flagged by the feds pretty quickly."

Again, Michael smiled. "There are ways around most anything. As I started buying up a few rifles and handguns and went through the background checks, I realized there was an easier way. I already had a close-to-the-top security clearance through work, so I went through the necessary scrutiny and paperwork and permitting process, called in a few favors, and I bought into a partnership with a man who owns a sporting goods store just outside Boston. In addition, I registered this place as a warehouse for stock. I not only got most of these weapons wholesale, I was also able to buy up some large amounts of ammunition without garnering any unwanted attention."

"This is some serious shit," Marcy said, almost muttering to herself. Picking up one of the plasteel semi-automatic handguns, she checked that there was no clip inserted, pulled back the slide to check that it wasn't loaded, them pretended to aim and pulled the trigger. "Ten millimeter with recoil dampers; fifteen- and thirty-shell clips. Close up shot would pretty much tear a person's shoulder to pieces. And wheel guns...and speed loaders. Smart."

"Revolvers? Aren't they sort of old fashioned?" Bob asked.

"The chance of a jam is infinitesimal," Marcy said. She put down the handgun, picked up one of the hunting rifles and pulled open the bolt. "Thirty-thirty. Well-placed shot'd take down a deer. You have scopes?"

The others looked at her oddly.

"What?" she asked. "My dad was really into guns. I used to hunt with him when I was younger." They continued to stare. She waved her hands in front of them. "Hello, people: we're not going to be able to grow all our food. Some of it will have to be caught or shot and killed."

Michael laughed a bit. "I am so glad you're here, Marcy. Now let's go back upstairs and start figuring out our assignments."

After dinner, the night before the others were leaving to go back to Boston, Michael announced the winning name for the colony.

"Berk Shire," he said. "Has a nice ring to it."

"Sounds quaint and comfortable," John said, looking up from his sketch pad.

"Berk Shire. Like a village in England from medieval times," Heather said. "I like it."

"And to whom do we owe thanks for this name?" Bob asked.

"Actually, both Marcy and I submitted the name," Michael said. He raised his glass to her; she did the same back. The others follow suit.

"So," Michael said, "we have the Colony of Berk Shire, and then the village proper."

Heather and Bob decided to return to their respective jobs while they worked on selling their house. John and Marcy returned to Boston only to give a few weeks' notice and clean out their houses enough to get set up with a real estate agent and lawyer who would handle all the details of selling their places for them.

Their first few days back at Berk Shire were spent organizing themselves for the sequence of events coming up. They tended to the young plants in the greenhouses, brought in supplies from the general store's feed and grain department, and kept unloading the stacks of boxes in the great room. They also assisted Bill and Ted in the construction of rooms in the basement.

On the fourth day, Michael walked down the stairs from his bedroom with a small flashlight and presented himself to Marcy for his first session of mindfulness training. She talked to him about being in the here and now, and taught him to close his eyes and focus only on his breath, instructing him to give himself permission to relax and do only that for the next ten minutes.

"Your breath occurs in the moment, so if you're focused on it you have to be in the moment, also."

When she sensed he was getting fidgety, she spoke calmly to him, reminding him to refocus on his breath.

"That's a lot harder to do than I thought it would be," he said to her. "I found my thoughts drifting away from my breath again and again."

"Mindfulness is a practiced art," she said. "The more you do it, the better you get at staying focused. But for the first time, you did pretty well. Most people I've taught this to have a hard time even lasting that long. We'll take it up again tomorrow morning…that is, if you want to continue."

"Absolutely," he responded.

She got up, stretched her back and took her candle. "Now, for my cooking lesson."

————)((O))(————

The weather broke the third week in March. Bill and Ted went to work plowing twenty acres of the farmland closest to the compound, using two of the five, full-sized, six-wheel drive Honda tractors stored in the machine shed. Michael provided them with lettuce and spinach plants he had started from seed. While they were doing that, he, John and Marcy planted a few long rows of peas and sugar snaps inside an area that had previously been fenced off to protect these crops from rabbits, deer and other animals. In April, plots of corn, wheat, and oats were put in next, using seeds hybridized for quick germination and growth in the cooler sections of the northeast. Seed potatoes were also put in the ground. All would be staples for their food needs. The property also contained remnants of small apple, pear and peach orchards that needed to be reclaimed from the ubiquitous weeds and nursed back from the neglect they had suffered.

As May rolled in, cucumbers, peppers, tomatoes, squash and pumpkin plants, all started in Michael's greenhouses, were carted out to the fields and put in by hand, one by one, all five of them working long days to get this done. There was enough rain and sun for everything to grow well. As diseases and pests appeared, they sprayed and spread accordingly, using commercial products. Marcy started researching more natural ways to do this, analyzing and formulating fixes from natural sources using the lab equipment she had brought in from Boston. They knew that the first season was not only about growing food to be eaten, canned and stored, it was also for experimenting for the future. The more quickly they became self-sufficient, the better. After all, there would be a time soon enough when driving to the supermarket or the feed and grain store would be an exercise in futility. There would be little or no products to buy if the stores even stayed in business.

June brought a minor heat wave with temps pushing into the upper eighties. Michael decided to take one of the tractors out to try his skills in turning over a new five acre plot of land for a second planting of corn and wheat. Dressed in jeans and a deep pink dress shirt with the sleeves cut off, straw cowboy hat on his head, he climbed into the two-seater enclosed cab, looked at the automatic plowing option touchpad connected to a GPS unit and flicked the switch to manual. He moved along the field the way Bill had taught him. It felt good to be out doing this kind of work after having sat in front of a computer in an office for so many years. There was something about growing things, getting his hands into the soil that felt so much more real.

He'd bought the air conditioned tractors in green, red and gray, had chosen a red one for himself because it felt more farm-like to him, like old pictures he'd seen as a boy. It was quite large and fairly boxy, standing over twelve feet tall and fifteen feet wide. The dual electric motors provided high amounts of torque, giving the machine massive amounts of pulling power. The combination tool dragging behind the tractor not only broke up the soil, but also set up raised beds as well. It was adjustable for bed size, was made of plasteel, and had been way more expensive than he'd figured, but he knew that in the long run it would pay for itself many times over.

Recognizing the childlike excitement of playing farmer for the day, driving the tractor and plowing the land just like he'd pretended as a four year old, he laughed out loud. He acknowledged he wasn't *playing* a farmer; he *was* the farmer.

He saw Marcy's small SUV zip out of the woods and onto the edge of the field, turning onto the access path next to him. She smiled and waved as she drove in tandem with him down the plow line to the end of his run. He shut the tractor off, climbed down the six steps from the cab and headed toward where she'd parked.

She got out of her vehicle wearing cut off jeans and a sleeveless shirt tied up off a well-toned midriff. As she walked to the back of the truck, little swirls of dust kicked up behind her work boots. She dropped the tailgate and started reaching into the back. Her ponytail was threaded through the strap hole in the back of the baseball cap she had taken to wearing in the sun, keeping her hair off her neck.

"Hey, Marcy. What brings you out to the far reaches of Berk Shire?" he asked.

"Come here," she said, motioning him to the back of her truck. "I thought you might be hungry. You didn't take any lunch this morning so I brought you some food."

He said he'd forgotten, thanked her and looked at what she had brought: buttermilk biscuits, fried chicken, coleslaw, Granny Smith apples and manchego cheese. She handed him a beer and patted the tailgate. He sat down.

"Quite the spread," he said. "What possessed you to fry up chicken and put this all together?"

"Tired of sitting in front of a computer downloading shit. I needed to get out and I thought this would be the quintessential country picnic spread. I also wanted to practice my burgeoning cooking skills. I like that deep fryer you installed."

She handed him a cloth napkin and a plate, then held out the basket of drumsticks and thighs. He chose a piece, accepted some slaw and a biscuit.

"Fresh-churned butter, too? You really thought of everything."

"I tried to," she said, fixing a plate for herself. They chatted about how things were going and what kinds of information she'd been downloading. She told him about her progress coming up with *plant potions* as she called them, naturally based concoctions that would fertilize the crops or rid them of unwanted pests and diseases and quell the growth of weeds. Her idea was that next year they would use them on half the crops to see how well they worked.

"And," she said, grinning, "I figured out how to synthesize that knockout gas we talked about. I can get it into a very concentrated form. I called Bob. He's going to pick up what I need in Boston. Pumping it into the foyer is no problem, but I thought we might want to be able to bottle it in some way, just in case we have to use it to subdue people outside of the building. So, Bob said he already has some ideas about how it might be delivered, some sort of spring loaded canister."

"You are quite the wonder woman," Michael said, "and you're developing a healthy sense of paranoia."

"We all know it's not a question of *if* we'll be attacked, but *when*," she said, cutting up slices of apple and cheese and presenting them to him. He smiled and ate, sipped his beer, pointed to her chin; she wiped.

"Well, I've got to get back to work. I'm hoping to finish this up by dinner time," he said. "Thank you so much for doing this. It was just what I needed."

"I'm enjoying this day way too much to go back to my computer. Why don't you show me how the tractor works," she said.

He helped her climb up, motioned her into the driver's seat, sat in the passenger side and started giving her instructions on how to operate it and site a straight line. He had her go slowly at first, carefully completing a new set of rows. She stopped at the end of the field, stood up and let fly a very loud *yeehaw*.

"I did it! My first rows! I want to do more!"

"Well, if you're going to do more, you're going to need proper attire," he said.

She tilted her head at him and squinted, questioning him with her eyes.

He removed her baseball cap, threading out the ponytail, and put his hat on her. "Now you're official. Go. Plow."

She gave him a smile that said *thanks*. He felt the connection, enjoyed it for a few seconds before a vague and ghostly image of his last visit with Sherilyn drifted along the far edges of his mind. He nodded forward and made a circular motion with his hand. She turned the machine around and started the next set of beds.

Here; now, he thought.

By the early fall, Heather and Bob had sold their house, albeit at a lower price than the place had been worth at their first visit in February. Real estate prices were continuing to plummet. Still, after paying off the mortgage, they were able to put a decent sum into the bank. Borrowing against life insurance policies yielded more, as did taking cash advances from their credit cards. Bob had figured out that by putting a set amount aside, he could pay the minimum on each card each month for three years and they could still raise a fair amount of cash for Berk Shire. Their actions were all predicated on Michael's projections being fairly accurate. If he was off....

Sitting in the great room with Michael, Bob said, "I've worked since I was fourteen years old, so I'm not sure how being unemployed is going to sit with me. This feels really weird. Of course, I sort of feel I'm on vacation."

"Well, enjoy it while you can, because that feeling will likely end early tomorrow morning," Michael said. "You get this afternoon and tonight to settle in, then it's off to work you go. I'd say we're averaging about twelve, thirteen hour days. We're smack in the middle of heavy harvesting, and we've got a lot of squash to pick and put up. Next week we'll be cleaning off the tomato and pepper plants, cooking and freezing them. You'll be working harder than you've ever worked."

John and Marcy had entered the room to greet the new arrivals. He was wearing a baseball cap, white sleeveless shirt, and jeans with work boots. His gut was gone and his arms were well-toned and larger than when they had last seen him.

"Amen to working harder," John added. "But it's strangely satisfying work to do."

Marcy, dressed the same, had dirt smudges up both arms. "Yes, strangely satisfying," she echoed. "Kind of like shooting your first squirrel, huh, John?"

John broke into a wide grin. "Kind of icky, skinning and gutting it. But I'll tell you, I didn't know it could be that good! Tastes like chicken."

Heather made a face. "Yecchh!"

"Marcy has taught us quite a bit about hunting and shooting," Michael said, laughing a bit. "But don't worry. Tonight's menu is a bit more conventional. We'll start with a Berk Shire style caprese salad: freshly sliced tomatoes, fresh farmer's cheese - which, I might add, we've learned to make, olive oil, fresh basil, with sea salt and ground pepper. That will be followed with rib eyes off the wood grill, roasted corn we picked this morning, and potato salad with our own freshly picked 'taters and fresh egg mayonnaise.

"The predominant word seems to be fresh. You did well growing things?" Bob asked.

"We lost as much as we grew - pests, diseases. But this year's experimenting has taught us a lot about how to do it and how not to do it. Marcy has been coming up with some viable natural alternatives to the chemicals we'll soon no longer be able to get.

"We could go on talking, but why don't you settle in and we'll give you the updates at dinner. We'll be eating out back," Michael said. "Oh...I forgot to mention, we also learned how to distill our own vodka, thanks to Bill, and can now make our own version of apple-, pear- or peach-tinis, with, yes, vodka infused with *fresh* apples, pears and peaches. So, cocktails at five."

The late afternoon weather had turned slightly cooler over the past few days. The dwindling sunlight slowly stole the vividness from the birch leaves' early foray into reds and yellows. The outdoor lights automatically snapped to life as dusk took hold. The group, all wearing sweaters or sweatshirts, brought chairs closer to the wood-fired grill to take in its radiating warmth.

"This is excellent," Bob said, holding up a corn chip with peach salsa on it.

Michael smiled. "Glad you like it. Marcy and I concocted that over the summer with fresh tomatoes, medium hot peppers and peaches."

"Just the right amount of heat. You made the chips, too?"

"We did."

Sipping apple-infused vodka, Heather explained that the oral surgeon she knew had said he was in if things kept going down the tubes. She and Bob had also spoken with some friends and family members who were interested in escaping the city sooner rather than later if things didn't start to pick up.

"Why is it people can't see the writing on the wall? Are they still waiting for the government to swoop in and save the day?" John asked, picking his head up from his sketch pad.

"People hope against hope," Marcy said. "They don't want to believe it's coming to an end. Did you?"

"Point taken," he said, returning to his drawing.

Michael said they needed to meet soon to figure out how fast they could expand. Bob offered to set up a program to project how many newcomers the food stores would reasonably handle.

"Also, I think we should get started on a few more cabins," Michael said. We've got another four erected, but we haven't had time to cut and prep timber for more, at least as of yet. I suppose we can work on that over the winter. What I had originally thought was that we could put people up temporarily in the main building, but now we've only got ten bedrooms open."

"If it came to it, couldn't we set up dormitory living in the basement?" Marcy asked.

"That's an idea," Michael said quickly. "Bob, how fast can you get that program together?"

"Depends. You have ProCode loaded?"

"I do."

"Then maybe four to six hours if someone can put together a good list of what we have, input the data onto another 'tab so it can be synched in later."

"I can do that," Marcy said.

"ASAP, please, both of you. I hate to put pressure on you during the harvest, but we need to be prepared. According to my projections and what you and Heather are reporting from Boston, the whole thing's going to collapse big time within eighteen months, twenty-four on the outside."

Heather started to cry.

"What's going on, babe?" Bob asked, putting his arm around her shoulders.

She wiped her eyes, sniffled. "I guess I'm really starting to take this all in - what's happening out there and what we're doing here. It's really sinking in: this is real. Life as we've known it is swirling towards the drain." She dabbed at her eyes, then cocked her head to one side, a slight smile crossing her lips. She moved from crying to laughing.

"Okay, big change. So, what's funny?" John asked.

"I just heard a voice in my head saying, *Ladies and gentlemen, this is your pilot speaking. Please put your snack trays up, return your seats to an upright position and fasten your safety belts. We're in for a rough ride.*"

"It is going to be a wild ride, isn't it?" John said. "Well, I think that calls for another round. This one's on me." He waved his hand in the air. "Oh, waiter?"

Heather had a lever action rifle in her hands, its brown stock braced against her shoulder. Marcy, standing right next to her, adjusted the hand holding up the barrel. Heather had already gotten comfortable and proficient with a .22 caliber rifle, repeatedly hitting the six-inch square wooden target Marcy had hung from a branch fifty feet away.

"Line up the sights, then squeeze the trigger," she instructed.

The gun recoiled as it fired, pushing Heather's shoulder back abruptly. The target didn't move.

Marcy tapped her left ear protector once, activating the headset mike and spoke to Heather. "Yeah, it's a bigger bullet with a little more kick. Now open and close the lever to load another round. Tuck it in a little harder and try again."

Heather raised the rifle back up, pulled it tighter to her shoulder, sighted the target and gently squeezed the trigger. The target jumped, bounced around for a few moments, then returned to its original position. A clear hole could be seen slightly off center.

"Girl, you're on your way to becoming a dead eye," Marcy said, patting her on the back. She had not activated the mike and realized Heather had not heard her. She twirled her right hand and mouthed, "Go again."

Fifty feet away, Bob was getting instructions from Bill. He was firing a bolt action thirty-thirty and had missed the target as much as he had hit it, but seemed determined to learn to use the weapon well.

Fifty feet further down, Michael and John were practicing with handguns. Both had started with a semi-automatic 10mm and had moved on to the .45 caliber wheel guns. The first shot John had fired resulted in him hitting himself in the forehead with the barrel as it recoiled.

"The same thing happened to me the first time, too," Michael said. "We're using a pretty hot load in the round. Try again."

The second shot went a little better.

"Good!" Michael said. He tapped the left ear of his headset twice to key him in to the entire group. "All righty, safeties on, headphones off! Let's call it a day."

On the walk back to the lodge, John pointed out a rabbit to the others. They all stopped to watch. The animal was frozen in place, pretending to be invisible to the group. Bob remarked how nicely its light-colored fur blended in with the bush twigs. There was the crack of a rifle and the rabbit dropped, blood seeping from its skull.

Heather lowered the .22 she had fired. Her eyes filled with tears. Marcy slid the rifle from her grip, engaged the safety.

"Why, babe?" Bob asked.

Heather stared at the lifeless body. "If this is the way we have to live...well...I think I needed to get that first one out of the way. Someone show me how to clean it...dress it...whatever the hell you call it, so I can get it ready to cook. I need to eat rabbit tonight." She took the rifle back from Marcy and slung it over her shoulder.

"Here," said Bill, pulling his knife out of its sheath and handing it to her. "I'll walk you through it."

<hr>

Two weeks before Halloween, the group, dressed in jeans and sweats with kitchen aprons tied on, staked out sections of counter space in the kitchen. Each one had selected a pumpkin and was cutting away. The seeds would be squished out of the pulp later and set aside for roasting or for drying for next year's plantings. They laughed and chatted and carved, drinking homemade vodka and reminiscing about their favorite Halloween costumes and candy.

"Those were the days," Heather said. "Can't say I don't miss those simpler times."

"I'll tell you what I'll miss moving forward. I'll miss limes, lemons, and oranges. Didn't have much at Bert's store today. Supplies are getting a little scarcer every time we visit there, especially the stuff he has to ship in," John said.

Michael explained that he had plugged in whatever new data he could get for his projection program. "From here it's going to go down very quickly, maybe by Christmas next year, definitely by the summer following that. I think we're going to find more and more scarcity in everything."

"Then we should buy all the coffee pellets we can," Bob said. "I'm going to miss coffee when it's all gone. I'm really going to miss coffee."

"I ordered ten more of the large greenhouses. Poly glass, just about impossible to break. Lets in sunlight and heat, but an outgoing R-factor of sixty holds it in well. That'll give us twenty," Michael said. "They should be in soon. Put an additional heating and grow-light source in each and we can probably grow coffee and tea, hothouse tomatoes…maybe we can even get some lemon and lime trees over the 'net. That would be good."

As each finished his or her carving, the pumpkins were placed in a row on the center island. They stood there wiping orange goo off their hands, admiring each other's handiwork.

"You said you had some candles around. Are they handy?" Marcy asked.

"Sure," Michael answered, heading for the pantry.

"Yeah, there's another thing we need…bees for wax," she said to the group. "Oh, my God. There is so much we haven't thought of…so much to do. I'll start researching beekeeping tomorrow. We'll need those suits, I guess."

"And then we'll have honey, too," Heather chirped in.

"Let's hope we can still get queens," John said. "You either need to buy a queen and drones or set up a hive and hope a swarm comes by and finds it attractive enough to inhabit."

"So you know about beekeeping?" Michael asked.

"Not really, but I remember that from a nature program I watched once."

"I like yours," Marcy said, pointing to Michael's pumpkin as he lit the candle. "It's scary, but not too scary."

<hr />

The first of November brought with it an early winter storm that left six inches of light, fluffy snow on the ground. The birch branches were neatly dusted with white powder, the pines frosted from top to bottom. Michael and Marcy walked silently through the woods, invigorated by the crispness of the air and the hunt they were on. Both had lever-action Winchesters slung over their shoulders.

"There," Marcy said quietly, pointing to turkey tracks and droppings. "Probably eight or ten of them. Leave the biggest one - that'll be the tom. We need him to keep making hens for us. Let's get three or four. They freeze well. All right, let's see...I believe they're going... this way."

They followed the tracks for over a quarter mile before spotting the flock. Crouching behind some low growing bushes, they pulled off their gloves, then each sited a bird. Marcy whispered a very quiet *now* and they fired simultaneously. Two birds went down. The others started to scatter, some on the ground, some flying up toward the lower branches of trees. She immediately fired a second round at one in its awkward flight, bringing it down. Michael fired two more rounds at one running on the ground but missed both shots.

"Got to work on moving targets next," he said.

"When they're moving, by the time you site one and go to pull the trigger it's moved. Lead just slightly. It's like the animal will run into your line of sight. Anyway, we got three."

They worked to quickly remove the feathers before the birds got cold, then cut off the heads and strung them up by the feet to bleed them out. Michael put down a sheet of *plastiseal* for dressing the birds. They saved the hearts, livers and gizzards, put everything in bags and headed back.

"You're quite the outdoors person," he said to her. "I never would have known from seeing you locked up in the chem lab all those years."

"Well, it's been a while, but it's all come back pretty quickly," she said. "I never would have thought you'd put something like this together. Guess we surprised each other."

They walked quietly for some time. Marcy broke the silence.

"I'm not quite sure how to say this, so I'm just going to blurt it out. Michael, I've been thinking about getting pregnant."

"Well…okay," he said, raising his eyebrows and smiling. "Where'd that come from?"

She explained her line of thought, that the world would need to be re-populated, that she was thirty-six and had always thought about having children, and that now seemed as good a time as any.

"You know: *tick tock* and all that," she said.

"In more ways than one," he answered.

"Since Bob is married, that leaves you and John. I didn't really consider Bill, and Ted…well, it goes without saying that I'm not going there. So I did the most random thing I could think of to make that choice - I flipped a coin. It came up John, so I spoke to him a week ago." She fell silent.

Michael stopped and looked at her. He waited, but she didn't speak. "But…."

She bit her lip, looked uncomfortable. "I feel like I'm sharing something I shouldn't share, but I need to. John told me he's sterile."

"But Jenny had two miscarriages. Oh: in vitro."

"No, the regular way. After she'd gotten the numbing cold and things were declared under control, before knowing it was fatal, they kept trying, but no pregnancy. They wondered if she'd lost fertility with the illness, so she got checked out. She was fine. Turns out he wasn't."

Michael looked puzzled. He and John had been close almost from the day they'd met at the research lab. They had shared a lot of deeply personal information over the years, but this seemed to be at a whole other level.

Marcy went on to explain that no reason could be found for his sterility. John had told her he suspected it was from the illness, even though he hadn't actually gotten sick.

"He was immune, like me and you. I checked all of us at work to help validate the immunity test I developed. So...so, that means I might also be sterile." He stopped talking and thought for a few moments. "I guess I don't know how I feel about that possibility."

"Could you check?" she asked. "Because if you're okay, I'm asking you to get me pregnant. Would you do that for me? I'm not asking you to marry me or pay child support or anything...I mean, I like you, but...but I just want to get pregnant."

His eyes opened wide, his eyebrows rising up. He took in a breath, held it for a moment, his cheeks puffed out, then let it go through pursed lips. "I...I...I'd be honored."

"Check yourself, then we'll talk about when we let the group know. But I want to be clear, I am definitely not putting this to a group vote."

<hr />

Michael spent some time on his own in the makeshift lab that night. He placed a slide on the video-microscope, flipped the switch on and looked at the screen. A few seconds later he shut it off, washed the slide and went to his room.

A morning sunbeam streaked across the dining room floor. The group sat in bathrobes or sweats, sipping coffee and finishing breakfast.

"Good eggs, Marcy," Heather said, pushing her plate away.

Marcy glanced at Michael, who smiled and gave a subtle nod. "I hope so," she said.

"Who's on cleanup?" John asked.

Michael raised his hand as he wiped up egg yolk with his last piece of cornbread.

"And who's going on the deer hunt today?" Bill asked.

John and Heather raised their hands. Bob remarked what a huntress she was turning into. He announced that he was going to stay in the warmth all day and work on trying to figure out how to activate the little computers Michael had bought from the mystery man at Harvard.

"Michael?" Bill asked.

"Not today. Ted and I are going to keep working on assembling one of the greenhouses that came in. Maybe next time."

He gathered up the dishes from the table, put them on a tray and brought them into the kitchen. He returned with a damp cloth to wipe down the table. Marcy downed the last of her coffee and followed him back through the double swinging doors.

"That's good news," she said. "I'm happy for you...well, for both of us."

He asked her when she would be ovulating next. She told him her basal temperature had been rising. Heather had told her that the best time would probably be the next three days.

"She said it was okay if we...if we...got a little drunk, that it wouldn't affect conception."

"And why did she tell you that?"

"Because I asked. I don't know about you, but I'm pretty nervous about this. It's not like we've been dating or anything. So, to be clear, it doesn't have to just be…I don't know…well…clinical sex."

"I've never had clinical sex before, have you? Could be more exciting than it sounds," he said, a little smile on his face.

"My room is the furthest away from everyone, so just show up and be ready to party, say, around 9:30? They're all sound asleep by 9:00. I'll leave the door unlocked. Just come in. I'll take care of everything."

"Probably a good thing I made the rooms fairly sound proof."

She looked at him, smirked a little, walked over and kissed him on the cheek. He smiled, looked into her eyes and kissed her lightly on the mouth.

"Trial run?" she asked, then kissed him back, just a little longer and a little deeper.

———— ((•)) ————

"Now what the hell do we do?" John asked, looking at the dead deer in front of them.

Bill unraveled the rope he'd been carrying, swung one end over a sturdy branch, tied the other end around the rear hooves, and called John over. They hoisted the animal up until it was a few feet off the ground. Heather tied the end of the rope to the trunk of the tree. The deer swung back and forth a bit before Bill steadied it.

"First we either cut the throat or cut off the head. While we're waiting for it to bleed out, we'll cut some of these small birches and lash them together to make a little sled. Then we'll gut it and drag it back home. We can skin and butcher it back there. How's that sound?" Bill asked.

"Peachy," John said, smiling weakly.

Heather asked the best way to decapitate the animal. Bill

pointed out what he would do. She repeated back what he said using clinical terminology, mentioning each muscle, tendon and bone by its Latin name.

Bill stared at her for a moment. "It's always so nice to be clearly understood," he said, deadpan. "And before you begin, you definitely want to put on one of those plastiseal moon-suits we brought. It's going to get messy." He handed her one suit, slipped into the other one himself.

She suited up, took out her knife and did the work while Bill steadied the carcass. As blood started to drain, John turned away and looked off into the distance. A few minutes later, he startled when Heather put her hand on his shoulder. As he turned towards her again, she handed him a plasteel bow saw. After making the sled, Bill showed them how to slit the belly from the groin down. The guts spilled out. John promptly walked away and threw up.

"I'm used to bloody babies and afterbirth coming my way. From what I understand, John was always more of a researcher," Heather said, explaining his reaction. "Of course, in my book, this is research - just a different sort."

Bill laughed. "Let me show you how to scrape out the inside of the carcass."

She watched him work. "Kind of like a D & C," she joked, "but a little more in your face."

The fire in the living room was down to a glowing pile of embers. A faint, smoky scent hung pleasantly in the air. All were present except Ted.

"That was a good hunt today, guys. Heather that was a great take down - one shot did it. Nice six-point buck," Bill said. "More than a hundred or so pounds of meat, I'd say. We got chops, ribs, steaks, roasts. Keep us going for a while."

He talked to the group about varying their hunting grounds so they didn't thin out any one herd too much. That way, he said, they could keep a steadier supply of meat in store. He recommended they get to know the different herds, be able to tell the deer apart. He explained what things to look for.

After a loud yawn, Bill excused himself to go to sleep. The others followed suit shortly afterwards, moving upstairs to the respective rooms.

Michael took a quick shower, put on a fresh shirt and pair of jeans. Walking barefoot down the hall to the far side of the building, he raised his hand to knock on her door, remembered what Marcy had said, and walked in. The room was empty. Soft music was playing. A dozen lit candles were set about the room. Two small cordial glasses and a bottle of vodka sat on a tray. The door to the bathroom was closed, but the shower was not running.

The door opened slightly. She stuck her head out. "I'll be right with you. I've just got to finish drying my hair. I've had one already. Why don't you catch up?" she said, closing the door without waiting for an answer.

He walked to the nightstand, picked up a glass, filled it three-quarters full and took a big sip. It was the apple-infused variety, the one he preferred. She liked both the apple and peach versions, but preferred the latter. He'd been in the doorway of her room before, but had never been inside since she'd moved in. He looked around the room, saw some of the things she'd brought with her from Boston. There were fifty or so antique books on a shelf, most in good to excellent condition. He glanced at a few of the titles: *The Complete Works of Shakespeare, To Kill a Mockingbird, Swiss Family Robinson, Brave New World, Lord of the Flies,* three books with *The Hunger Games* in the titles, and multiple books with *Harry Potter* in the titles. Underneath them was a small doll that had the worn look of having been a child's favorite years before. A picture of a tall, gangly, teenaged girl in a ponytail was propped up near the doll. He saw three very old photographs on her work desk and went to look.

"Parents, grandparents, great grandparents and my favorite aunt," Marcy said, entering the room. "I like keeping some sense of connection to my family and my childhood, even though they're all gone. Kind of like the life we're starting: we'll hang onto some things and let others go."

Michael turned to face her. She was wearing only a silky thigh-length blouse, the outline of her nipples showing through the material. Her hair, usually in a ponytail, was flowing down her shoulders and back.

"Hi," he said, almost in a whisper.

"Hi," she said back quietly.

After a quiet pause that lasted a bit too long, they both chuckled nervously.

"So, how about those Red Sox?" he said.

She laughed.

"Kind of awkward, huh?"

"We'll get into it," she said, picking up the bottle and walking over to him. "If that's your first, knock it back. I'm ready for another, and just for the record, I do not like to drink alone."

She refilled both glasses. "To getting to know each other a little better."

He tapped his glass to hers. "Probably qualifies more like a *lot* better." They laughed again and emptied their glasses.

"We can take our time. I've always enjoyed your company."

There was another pause, though shorter in length.

"God, I feel like I did the first time," he said.

"Me, too. But it's kind of exciting, too; kind of *Oh, yeah!* mixed with *Oh, shit! Now what do I do?*"

She motioned to the couch on the wall opposite the foot of the bed. He sat down. She brought the tray over, set it down on the coffee table. She sat down at the other end of the couch from him, realized what she'd done and laughed again. "Look at me, all the way over here. That's not going to work too well, is it?"

She got back up. Standing in front of him, she bent over and slowly poured two more glasses. The front of her blouse, already undone three buttons from the top, opened a bit more, revealing cleavage. She handed him a glass, clinked hers to his and drained it. He followed suit.

Without saying a word, she moved up onto the couch next to him, her legs folded under her. She put a finger across his lips, leaned in and kissed him. They went slowly at first, lightly touching each others' faces and necks and shoulders. She took his hand and moved it onto one of her breasts. He hesitated, staying motionless for a moment, before caressing her gently. A few moments later he undid another button and slid his fingers onto soft, bare flesh. She breathed out a quiet moan of approval and put both of her hands on his face, kissing him more deeply. He pulled his tee shirt off and tossed it aside. She pushed the coffee table back, moved onto the floor in front of him and undid his jeans, sliding them and his underwear off in a single motion. She pulled him into her mouth, gently teasing him.

He lay back, enjoying this attention, soaking in the pleasure. Slowly he leaned forward and pulled her face up to his, kissing her mouth and neck. She pulled back slowly and stood up, undid the last two buttons of her shirt, dropped it to the ground and stood naked before him for a brief moment before taking him by the hand and leading him to the bed.

⸎

She invited him to come to her room two nights later, saying she felt that fully taking advantage of her ovulation cycle might increase her chances of getting pregnant. He smiled, gently touched her arm and said he'd be there.

——»«◦»«——

"I'm going over to Wayne Roberts' place today to meet with him," Michael said. "I want to see if I can either buy or barter for some horses in the spring. We need to get a small herd started for field work and transportation when the vehicles start breaking down."

John looked a little puzzled. "But that's going to be many years…." His voice trailed off. "And I'm telling that to the guy who *never, ever* thinks ahead. My apologies, Michael."

"No apology needed, John. Anyone want to join me?"

Each said they had something they were working on. Marcy was the last to respond, saying she'd be happy to tag along.

Roberts' farm was a little over three miles away. He was the man who had sold Michael the tract of land that was now Berk Shire. He was still rugged and strong well into his sixties. His wife, Gladys, had *got the cold way back*, as he put it, and had died a few years ago. He said she got it because she'd gone to the city to visit her sister when all that was happening. Michael had tested Roberts, found him to be immune.

As they turned into Wayne's driveway, they received vacuous stares from some of the milking cows standing near the feeding troughs in the snow- and mud-field that bordered the main road. The smell of cow dung quickly filled the truck's interior. Michael had come to actually like the smell; Marcy didn't seem fazed by it at all.

Two border collies greeted them with a few loud woofs as they pulled up to the farmhouse. A few sniffs later, they became indifferent as Roberts walked out from the side of the house, barn coat and cowboy hat on, and greeted them with little fanfare. Michael introduced Marcy, then got two large containers out of the back of the Expanza. Wayne invited them in for coffee. He led them through the front door and down a hallway into his kitchen. He motioned to a table in one corner as he hung his coat and hat on a wooden peg next to the back door. A ring of short gray hair circled around the sides of his otherwise balding head. He'd been a solid six-one in his younger years, but a slight stoop cut an inch or two off that.

Marcy and Michael put their coats over two of the chairs.

"I brought you some venison, Wayne," Michael said, placing the containers on the countertop. "I figured chops and steaks would be easiest to cook."

"And I brought you a loaf of bread I baked fresh this morning," Marcy added.

Roberts turned to them and smirked. "Trying to butter me up so you'll get a better deal?" he said in a thick New England accent.

Michael laughed. "Just sharing the bounty. I don't know how much you get out hunting these days. And since Marcy has never met you before and doesn't know about your incredible baking skills, she brought bread."

Roberts stared at her for a moment, pushed his tongue into his cheek, then smiled. "I can barely turn the damn oven on," he said with a chortle. "'Scuse my lack of manners, miss. I do appreciate your bringing that. I'll slice up a little and get out some raspberry jam I traded in last month."

The coffee was strong and slightly bitter, but a little sugar and some sweet, heavy cream from Wayne's cows made it tolerable. He told them about getting the jam from Tom Robbins' wife.

"Aggie always puts up the best. Makes damn fine pie, too," he said. "Tom was one of the first hereabouts to die from that damned disease. Shame. Helluva good man."

He started to take a piece of bread, withdrew his hand and offered the cutting board to Marcy.

"You a doctor, too?" he asked.

"Yes, but not medical. I have a doctorate in bio-chemical engineering."

"Fancy woman you got there, Doc," he said.

Michael told him about Marcy's hunting skills and how she had been teaching them all how to shoot. He told him about the turkeys they'd gotten, and the buck that was taken a few days back.

"Well, Miss Marcy the other kind of doctor, you're my kind of people." He took a bite of the bread. "And you bake pretty damned good, too. My Gladys wasn't much for hunting, but she sure could cook up a storm when I brought something back. She was pretty good at skinning, too." He looked away for a moment. "Damn, I miss her."

Marcy looked at him, saw his eyes starting to water up. "I'm sorry I didn't get to meet her."

"I'm betting she'd a liked you a lot."

"You're invited to Thanksgiving dinner, Wayne. It'll be quite the spread. You can meet the others, see how things have progressed since your last visit."

"Last time I was there you were just getting started, just hired them two boys from out west. The one guy's okay, but I don't much like the other one," Roberts said, sipping coffee. "Seemed like a hare-brained idea when you first told me what you thought was going to happen, but I'm watching the comline now - and I'll tell you, there ain't much left in the way of shows to watch anymore - and I'm starting to think you're on to something. Seems like things are starting to fall apart just like you said they would."

He put his head down for a moment and sighed. "So how about we get to horse trading," he said. "Way I see it, money's not going to be worth a damn in a year or two. Probably not worth a damn now, the way the government keeps printing up so much of it. Guess they know it's all coming to shit, just like you do."

He paused again, stood up and walked over to his back door, stared out at the three outbuildings close by. He continued facing the outside as he spoke again. "It's like this: I got nobody in this world since my Gladys died, just me and my two dogs, and the bitch is probably only good for one more litter in the spring before she gets too old for that sort of thing.

"So here's what you need that I got: five mares and a hot shot of a stallion; sixty head of milkers that are a royal pain in the ass twice a day; one ornery bull; forty or so hens and chicks and two roosters that don't much like each other, but still manage to get the job done. I also got ten hogs, but they're a pain in the ass and smelly as shit, so I'd suggest turning them into ribs, chops and bacon right quick. In addition to all that, I've got fifty sheep I can just about sheer when it's time, and the restaurants hereabouts ain't buying much lamb these days on account of there ain't much business anymore. The sheep pretty much just keep the dogs entertained." Roberts turned around, ran his hand over his bald spot and looked directly at Michael. "So here's the dollar figure for all of that: zero."

Michael talked about what they had to trade: meat, corn, potato and wheat flour, and root vegetables. Roberts just shook his head at all of it.

"Here's what you have to trade that I'm most interested in: when it all goes to hell in a hand basket, take me in. I'm getting too old for what I'm doing now. I mean, I do it, but I'm real tired all the time. I want to be able to sit and do some reading, take naps when I want, maybe tend a small vegetable garden…like that. You promise me that and you can have all my livestock. Hell, I'll throw in all twenty-five hundred acres of farm, the tractors and the accessories, for whatever they're worth, they're so damn old. That way, you're all set up with a working operation.

"We both know that when the shit hits the fan, some of those left will take to violence to get what they want. Never fails when things fall apart. It's just gonna get taken from me anyhow. I'd rather what I got goes to good people and good use.

"So," he said, turning back to look at Michael, "the price too high or do we have ourselves a deal?"

<hr />

On the ride home they talked about how to deal with what was being given them. Marcy brought up that they'd also just added their first new member to the group. She called Wayne crotchety and cute, said he'd make a good advisor on growing crops and tending the livestock.

"It's also kind of fitting," Marcy said.

"How so?"

"Be nice to have a grandfather around."

"Tell me you know you're pregnant already?"

"Don't know. I've been getting this slightly metallic taste in my mouth. Heather said that could be an early sign. One way or the other, it'll happen eventually. And speaking of it happening, I really got into it with you. It'd been about three years or so since I'd done the deed. Didn't realize how much I missed it. I don't know if you'd be interested or not, but I'd be open to a friends-with-benefits situation."

He thought about it for a moment. "Probably been twice that long for me. I'd be lying if I said I didn't enjoy being with you. But I don't know. It could be…well, it could be sort of dangerous," he said, a serious tone in his voice.

"How? It's not like I'm worried about getting pregnant, you know."

"Feelings. One might start getting feelings, the other might not."

"Aren't women the ones who are supposed to be concerned with that kind of thing?"

Michael explained that he didn't want things to get complicated between them. He brought up that as they expanded the group, she might meet someone else, want to move on. She brought up that he might meet someone as well.

"Well, I'm not planning on it."

"Michael, I'll always be your friend, whatever happens," she said. "I can deal with it," she said.

He thought about it for a few minutes. "I guess I'll deal with it, too. Hope those aren't famous last words for either of us. Okay, I'm in."

"Interesting choice of words," she said, smirking a bit. "Got anything on your calendar for tonight?"

Breakfast three days before Thanksgiving was going as usual, with the group having a conversation about what they would be focusing on that day. Halfway through the meal, Marcy got up and, without a word, moved quickly into the kitchen. A moment later they heard her vomiting. They all got to their feet instantly.

Heather motioned for them to sit back down. She walked toward the swinging doors, stopped, looked back and smiled. "I believe its official," she said.

All told, they had twenty-three for the Thanksgiving meal. Wayne had contacted Michael to come over and meet the local veterinarian when the doctor made a house call to tend one of the horses. The vet, Mark Carlson, had raised the issue of what was happening near Boston. Wayne had simply nodded to Michael, who proceeded to tell him about what he and the others were setting up. Carlson was interested in seeing the compound. Michael invited him and his wife for Thanksgiving.

The oral surgeon Heather had spoken about in February came up Wednesday afternoon to see what it was all about. Dr. Theo Parks, a tall black man, brought his husband, George, and three others, one an organizational psychologist, the other two a just-retired Red Sox pitcher and his girlfriend.

"Theo Parks," the dentist said, introducing himself to Michael, "and this is my husband George. Thanks for having us."

"It's our pleasure," Michael said, shaking their hands.

He turned to the woman next to Theo. She was pushing forty, shy of Marcy's height by two inches, with long whitish-blonde hair, teased up and out. She had steely blue eyes and wore a white, waist-length, faux fur jacket, stretched tight by a large bust. Black pants clung to her like skin, with black boots cresting each knee. Even in her winter clothing she managed to show a sizable amount of cleavage.

"Dr. Macalister, I'm Dr. Elizabeth Angel," the woman said, extending her hand palm down, almost as if she expected it to be kissed.

Michael took her hand into his, turned it slightly and shook it gently.

"But don't let the last name fool you," she said. Her lips curled up just slightly as she said it. Getting no reaction from Michael she said, "I've heard a lot about you and have been looking forward to meeting you."

"Welcome, Elizabeth," Michael said, withdrawing his hand from hers. "I hope you enjoy your stay."

"Friends call me Lizbeth." Michael simply nodded.

A man, who was taller than Michael by at least four inches, stepped forward. His brown hair was on the longer side, parted on one side and aimed slightly back. He extended a long arm, took Michael's hand and shook it vigorously. "I'm Will Loren, and this here is my girlfriend Chrissy."

A petite brunette stepped forward just a bit, put her hand out. "Chrissy Martin."

"You both sound like you're from southeastern Kansas," Michael said. "I have cousins there."

"Yeah, Kansas," Will said with a big smile. "Small town named Cherryvale."

"We were high school sweethearts," she added, talking in a drawn out mid-western accent.

"Well, we'll have to find some time to chat about that town of yours," Michael said.

The rest of the visiting group consisted of neighbors from the surrounding farms, some of whom had known about Michael's plans, others who were just being introduced to his ideas. All brought things to add to the meal, including wine, side dishes and desserts.

Michael and his group enjoyed the company. They had been to the stores in the nearest town, had met and talked with others, but this type of socialization outside of just the group had not occurred in earnest for any of them in quite some time.

For dinner, Michael had thawed out two of the turkeys he and Marcy had shot, each one around eighteen pounds, and brined them overnight in salted water with fresh herbs from the hothouses. Those who had had wild turkey before all remarked how tough it could be, but how tender and juicy these were. He promised to share his recipe.

Aggie Robbins brought six of her *ho-made pies*, as Wayne put it - three pumpkin and three apple.

As they finished the meal, Michael invited them all to join him in the living room, where the furniture had been reconfigured to accommodate the entire bunch in one large sitting area. More coffee and after dinner drinks were served. The conversation jumped around at first, with the farm people talking about the past season.

Will, the celebrity ball player, quickly became the focus of the group as he launched into a story about a particular game.

"What you may not know about pro-ball players is many of them love to caff up before and during a game, get an extra boost of energy. So both locker rooms have a large pot running at all times, real brew, quality stuff. You remember Billy Ramirez? First baseman, played from '25 until '31, when he died in that plane crash. Anyway, I had just been traded to the Sox when he did this. The visiting club house manager, a guy named Benny, was setting us up with the big party perk, making the coffee extra strong for more juice, just the way we liked it. So Billy tells Benny that he's going to take care of the visitors' coffee that day, slips Benny a thousand bucks. Benny takes the money and says, *Knock yourself out.* Billy goes and loads their party perk up with decaff. Needless to say, they were dragging butt the whole game. Now we all knew, but we never told anyone, not even our manager."

Eventually the conversation came around to what was happening in Boston and around the nation. Some wondered if the federal government was going to be able to pull the country out of the tailspin it was in. Others believed it was already too late, that the feds were just prolonging the inevitable as long as was possible.

"Theo, what are you seeing out there?" John asked.

Theo sipped from his drink and thought for a moment. "What I'm noting is an interesting mix of reactions from the people who are referred to me. Some have been putting off work for a while because they were wondering what was going to happen…sort of a *why bother* attitude. Others seem almost overly eager to get the work done because they're not sure if things will keep going along, business as usual."

"So…uncertainty?" Michael asked.

"The energy most people are giving off is of an anxious nature. I mean, there are certainly people I've spoken with who seem blasé about what's happening. Maybe it's denial. They seem to believe that everything will work out fine because it always has in the past. Again, denial."

"What do you believe?" Marcy asked.

Theo paused again, took another sip from his glass. "I would like to believe things will work out all right, but I'd be lying if I said I actually believed that. I guess I'm still on the fence, but I'm leaning more and more to one side. Financially, I've been preparing for the worst…just in case."

He asked Michael what he thought would happen if the decline occurred as he was predicting.

Michael thought for a moment. "My belief is that things will move into collapse, and in the beginning people will remain - for the most part - civilized. They'll share what they have with relatives or neighbors. But as supplies start to dwindle, those who have will move to not wanting to part with what they have. They'll be rationing what's left, even to themselves. Hunger is extremely motivational, so people are going to start fighting tooth and nail just to survive. Some will do better than others.

"I think people who form into groups - like this one - will also try hard to hang onto as much of life as it had been, as is possible: rules, regulations, social mores. And some things will keep working for a while, like our vehicles, but will eventually start breaking down. Most people will not have the resources or the knowledge to fix them, or to fix any of the machines or technology. I mean, how many of us would know how to trouble shoot a broken down car? And even if we could answer that in the positive, where would we get parts? Who is going to be manufacturing parts? Some with the knowledge and skills will cannibalize the broken down vehicles to fix others, but that can only go on for so long.

"I think things will stay partially the same for a while. People will have to learn to hunt, fish, grow food, forage. But then - and again, this is my opinion - I believe civilization will start going backwards for a while."

George spoke up. "What exactly do you mean by backwards?"

"As the vehicles break down and become useless, transportation will mean walking or riding some sort of animal. Our farm equipment will eventually break down and we'll run out of spare parts. How will we plow the fields? Horses, probably. And eventually there will be no more ammunition for those who have guns. Hunting will be by bow and arrow, spears, snares, throwing rocks, whatever."

"So you see civilization headed into a deconstructive phase, a sort of Dark Ages, part two," Theo said.

Michael simply said, "Not as dark, but yes."

The silence in the room was deafening.

"Scary," Will said. The others *hhmmed* in agreement.

"Most people are sheep," Lizbeth, the organizational psychologist, said. "Most people will follow someone who says they know the way. It doesn't matter whether that person actually knows the way or not, most people will simply follow without question."

"So what are you saying, Lizbeth?" Michael asked.

"Leaders will emerge. Some will be natural leaders with good intentions. You, for instance, seem to have thought things through fairly well from what I'm observing, and you seem to genuinely care about people doing well. People will start following you...already have. Others will see an opportunity to take power and will seize it, and the more people who follow those leaders, the more engorged their feeling of power will become. That has been a part of human behavior since time began. Those leaders will most likely look to take from others who have, as a way of shoring up their power base, proving their superiority to their followers."

"Are you saying that you see a classic battle of good versus evil burgeoning as things go into decline?" Michael asked.

"Essentially: yes."

"Interesting point," John said.

There was a brief silence before George turned to Michael and asked, "So, when do you see this collapse taking place."

Michael talked about his computer projections showing that it would all fall apart in twelve to eighteen months. "Give or take a few months."

"I'd love to see the data you have and how you configured your study," Lizbeth said.

"If you're going to be here for a day or two, I'd be happy to show you," Michael responded. "I tried to program in as many variables as I could when I first set it up. I've also re-entered data as it comes in, both from this country and others around the world, updating and recalculating every three or four weeks. I keep getting the same results, but I'm always open for a fresh set of eyes on my program."

Her eyes sparkled as she looked at him and smiled. "I'll be around. I drove up with Theo and George, and they're not leaving until Monday morning."

"Okay," Michael said. He saw Marcy stand up and glanced in her direction. He watched her turn away from him very quickly and head for the kitchen.

"Do you play chess?" Lizbeth asked, pointing to the board that was sitting off to one side.

"I do," Michael said. "Can I interest you in a game?"

John brought the board over to the coffee table and placed it near Lizbeth. "This should be interesting," he said.

The first game lasted a little over twenty minutes, with Michael winning.

"Well-played, Michael," she said. "Now that I see how you think, I'd like a rematch."

Michael started setting up his pieces. Thirty minutes later, Lizbeth had him in checkmate.

"Well-played, Lizbeth," he said.

"I don't believe it," John said, shaking his head.

"Time for one more?" Lizbeth asked.

Twenty minutes later, she said, "Checkmate."

John scratched the side of his face. "Sonofabitch," he muttered under his breath.

<hr />

Shortly after breakfast the next day, as they were walking out of the dining room, Will and Chrissy pulled Michael aside and asked to speak with him privately. Michael led them to his office in the basement. Both said they believed Michael's predictions would come true. Will's financial advisor had talked about the events taking place in the country and discussed possibilities. The man had advised him over a year ago to start turning his investments into cash and to buy gold.

"Not gold stocks or futures, but buying bullion and storing it someplace safe. I did buy a bit of it, but I'm also sitting on a ton of cash."

"Probably a good move," Michael said, knowing exactly where the man was going.

"I don't know if you're letting more people in, but what we're thinking, me and Chrissy, here, is that we'd like to be a part of this."

"You'd have to work very hard. This is all about very tough work, farming and tending animals, cutting and splitting wood, building things. Some people don't care for that kind of life, but that's what's going on here."

"Hell, I grew up on a farm! And besides, it'd be a good way to keep in shape," Will said. "So how about it."

"Fine by me, but I have to put it to the group."

"Tell them I can add over two hundred million to their bank

account."

⸻•⸻

Michael met with Lizbeth in his office on Sunday morning after breakfast. She showed up jeans that had been painted on, heels and a blue checked flannel shirt over a white tee. From the pendulous sway of her breasts, it was clear she was braless.

Michael set up a chair next to his and explained how he had set up his program, what data and variables he had inputted, and went through the initial set of results as well as subsequent sets showing the new data on his computer.

"I knew the government had hired you," she said, "saw you talking on the comline a few times. I checked you out on the 'net and kept running into terms like *forward-thinking, visionary*. Hell, my first thought when I saw a picture was, *Damn, he's cute*." She paused for a moment. Getting no reaction from Michael, she went back to talking about his projections.

She continued flirting, some of it toned down, some not so subtle, and made a point of walking around the room every now and again to swing her breasts in front of him. He smiled politely, but didn't buy in.

"So you and this Marcy," she said, "an item?"

"We're very good friends. Marcy has been here almost from the beginning, and we worked together before that for over five years. She's an integral part of Berk Shire. In fact, she came up with the name."

"Her claim to fame," Lizbeth said with just the smallest inflection of sarcasm in her voice. "Well, if you're not an item...."

"I do have other guests I have to attend to, Lizbeth," Michael said, cutting her off, "so how about I walk you back up to the living area?"

She hooked her arm into his. As they reached the staircase,

Michael stepped aside, freeing his arm.

"You go ahead. I left something in my office," he said.

"I think I'll go get a cup of tea," she said.

"Sure. Help yourself."

Marcy was in the kitchen opening a box of loose, black tea, when Lizbeth walked in. They looked at each other for a second before Marcy said she was fixing tea and offered her some.

"That's just what I came in for, so thanks. Anything I can do to help?" Lizbeth asked.

"I'm all set," Marcy said. "So what'd you think of Michael's projections?"

Lizbeth leaned back against the middle island, crossed one foot over the other. "Pretty interesting stuff. I've done enough research in my time to know that his program is set up well, so I believe the results are pretty much spot on."

Marcy hung the tea ball on the lip of the pot, poured the kettle water into it. "I looked it over, too, when I first got here. It's never been published and duplicated, but it also struck me as well constructed."

Lizbeth giggled a little. "Like him. He's quite the prize you've got there."

"Prize?" Marcy said, grabbing two mugs out of a cabinet.

"You two are together, aren't you?"

Marcy looked at Lizbeth, thought for a moment before answering. "Michael and I are very good friends."

"So, *very good friends*…that's it, then?"

"That's it, then," Marcy said.

"Well, that's a relief. I'm not into those kinds of games."

Marcy gave her a tight, closed-mouth smile and moved the teapot to the middle counter by Lizbeth, then told her she had guests to attend to and walked out.

By the time the last guests left mid-morning on Monday, seven of them had spoken to Michael about their desire to be a part of Berk Shire. He conveyed this to the group, without talking about the money Will had offered or the come-on by Lizbeth. They discussed the benefits each of the seven offered. Marcy challenged the value of bringing in an organizational psychologist, saying she saw no need for such skills. John thought it would work well, arguing that as the population grew, group dynamics would become an issue. Lizbeth, he said, might be able to help them get in front of problems before they started.

"Well, I think we're perfectly capable of managing the group as it grows. We've done just fine so far," Marcy said, a slight edge in her voice.

When the meeting had ended, Michael followed Marcy into her basement office.

"What was that all about?" he asked.

"What was what all about?"

"The thing with Lizbeth."

Marcy looked him straight in the eye and said, "Other than a set of big boobs and a willingness to bounce them around for everyone to see - especially you -, what does she really have to offer?"

Michael looked at her, stayed quiet.

"Oh, shit. It's happening, isn't it?" she said. "Shit! I'm sorry, I didn't mean that. I'm so sorry!"

He went over to her and pulled her into his arms. She rested her head on his shoulders. He held her, rubbing his hands over her back.

"I've never had a jealous bone in my body. I must be getting hormonal." She looked up at him. "I'm really so, so sorry."

"It's okay," he said.

"No, it's not. She really could be a big help. We should bring her in. Besides, you're a free man; you can go where you want."

"Other than concern for the health and growth of Berk Shire and how she might aid in that, I have no interest in her. Besides," he said, nodding his head and faking seriousness, "yours are better."

Marcy's eyes brightened and she smiled a bit. "You really think so? You're not just saying that? Oh, God, listen to me. Like I care whose are better."

"Feel like a visitor tonight? I don't mean for that. Just to hang out."

"Sure." She laughed, undid two buttons on her shirt, grabbed her breasts and pushed them together creating cleavage. "How about I hang out and we'll see what pops up?"

Michael looked at her and smiled.

<hr>

Two weeks later the entire group, minus Ted, donned snowshoes and went out into the woods after breakfast, toting a chainsaw, bow saw and clippers. A fresh foot of light, powdery snow had blanketed the area, causing the sunlight to sparkle and dance off the frosted boughs of the pines and birches. The conversation wove its way through their tales of experiences during the holidays when they were kids, favorite presents or foods at family gatherings.

They moved from tree to tree debating the pros and cons of each. As they considered one tree, Michael broke off the tiny tip of one branch and rubbed it between the fingers of his glove, then held his hand out for the others to sniff.

"Smells sort of like tangerines," Heather said.

"Frasier fir," he said. "The entire great room will start to smell like that."

"I'm sold," she said.

The others nodded their approval and the twelve-footer was

cut down. They also cut branches from cedars and junipers for wreaths for the windows and swags for decorating the mantle of the main hearth.

Heather and Bob had brought their ornaments from their home, a good-sized collection that had been acquired over their ten-year marriage. They had also picked up over two hundred boxes of LED lights both for the tree and the outside of the building. They explained they loved decorating so much at Christmas that they wanted to make sure there were enough lights for years to come.

The group spent the afternoon decorating the tree. Michael opened up two bottles of champagne he had stored away. Salmon that had been caught and smoked by a neighbor who had been there for Thanksgiving, was sliced thin and put on little squares of store-bought pumpernickel bread smeared with fresh sweet-butter. A toast was made to their first Christmas all together. All drank. Marcy sipped only a bit and put her glass down for Michael to finish.

"We have got to learn how to make champagne!" John said.

"And pumpernickel bread!"

"And how to catch salmon and smoke it!"

Michael called for the group's attention. The group looked at him. He looked at Marcy and bowed his head to her. She asked the others to sit down and, when they had, she stood up.

"The pregnancy appears to be going very well, according to my own personal OB/GYN. My due date is somewhere at the end of July or the beginning of August. Though Michael was kind enough to do the honors, each of you will be expected to share in the duties of raising this child. Each of you will be mother, father, aunt and uncle to him or her. And try as you may, *none* of you will escape diaper duty!"

"Then here's to changing lots and lots of diapers!" John called out, raising his glass.

The Christmas gathering grew to over fifty people. The neighbors who had attended Thanksgiving dinner were encouraged to invite their neighbors and friends. Theo and George returned, bringing with them two of their neighbors. Will invited another former Red Sox player, an outfielder he'd known for many years, who brought his wife and teenaged daughter and son. Lizbeth returned as well.

The dining room tables were reconfigured to accommodate the crowd. In setting up for the meal and chatting about how large the gathering would be, the core group talked about having to move it into the great room for the next holiday if things kept growing as they were.

Ten of the fourteen bedrooms were to be occupied by guests who were staying for various lengths of time ranging from overnight to a full week. The first houseguests arrived on the twenty-third. Will introduced his former teammate, Clint, to the group.

Clint was a tall, almost gangly man with black hair, laughing eyes and exceptionally long arms. His claim to fame as a ball player was having made a throw from deep centerfield all the way to home to make the final out that won the World Series for the Sox a few years back. His wife, Jan, had medium length auburn hair. She was five-eight, light in complexion, and had a few extra pounds on her that she carried well. She was quick to see the humor in things and had a hefty laugh that backed that up.

Their son, Billy, who was sixteen, had his father's height and build, his mother's hair, and his own way of smiling. Their daughter, Susan, rail-thin, was almost as tall as her mother, with long, dark brown hair with just a bit of curl to it. She was thirteen, just starting to mature physically, and was a little shy at first, opening up more as she got to know some of the others.

"Pleased to meet you all," Michael said. "Why don't you grab your things and I'll show you to your rooms. I don't have connecting rooms for you and Jan and the kids, but I can line you all up in three rooms that are right next to each other. When you're done, come on down. We're going to do a little tour of the area in about an hour."

By the early-afternoon of Christmas Eve day, all the guests who would be staying over had arrived. They were invited into the kitchen and divided into five groups. Michael and Marcy had printed out recipes for each group. Large bowls filled with fresh hothouse tomatoes were set out for sauce and slicing. Hunks of cheddar and asiago cheese sat on cutting boards. Newly made mozzarella, sitting in water, awaited slicing for caprese salad. Greenhouse garlic, picked a few days earlier, was to be chopped for the sauce as well as for garlic bread. Wheat flour would be kneaded into dough, then ground through a pasta maker for spaghetti. Potatoes were there to be cooked and shredded and formed into gnocchi. For dessert, a bushel basket of apples sat waiting to be peeled and cored.

Michael put out four pitchers, explaining what was in each one.

"First, we have eggnog, no alcohol. You may add from the bottle of rum as desired. The next two are peach- and apple-infused vodka. The last one contains a concoction called a French Ninety."

"What's in that?" Chrissy asked.

"I'm glad you asked," he said, holding up the pitcher, "because it comes with a warning, of sorts. It is a combination of brandy, simple syrup, lemon juice and triple sec. When you've poured from the container, top it off with a little of the champagne sitting next to it. Drink one too quickly and its Air France, so if you head in this direction, please buckle up and imbibe responsibly. And Billy and Susan, if 'nog is not your choice, we also have apple and peach juice in the fridge. Sorry, no soda, but we have learned to make seltzer so you can add some of that for fizz."

"What about beer?" Clint asked.

"Also in the fridge. Here's the deal: we are making what we're going to eat for dinner, so proceed carefully. Marcy and I will wander about the kitchen to check on progress, advise on timing, and answer any questions. This will probably take about four hours to make and cook, so we should be eating by 6:30. We also have snacks by the drinks. That's it. Now, let the preparations begin."

The group poured drinks. Billy asked for some paper towels to wipe up a spill. Michael explained that they did not use paper towels anymore and handed him a cloth one instead.

"Jeez," Billy said, "if I did that at home I'd get it!"

"Won't happen here," Michael said. "It's how we live."

Each group read their recipes and divided up the tasks. Inquiries were made about where certain cookware or spices were. Michael and Marcy answered questions, watched, waited, and guided the group members. At one point when one group had a flare up at a stove, Michael jokingly took to walking around with a small fire extinguisher at the ready. People talked and laughed and sang along with the Christmas music playing on wireless speakers that had been brought into the kitchen.

An hour later the kitchen smelled of sauce, olive oil, sautéing garlic, asiago cheese and apple pie.

"Hey, Michael," Lizbeth called out, a slight slur in her words. "How about another French nightie over here?" She held up her glass.

He moved over to her, leaving the pitcher where it was. "You nailed that second one kind of quickly, Lizbeth, so I'm going to suggest it might be good to slow down a bit."

"Honey, I'm just getting warmed up," she said loudly, hacking out a laugh and brushing the backs of her fingers across his cheek. "Why would I want to stop now?"

He leaned in close to her ear. "Because you're starting to slur."

"I'm just having fun," she said back loudly.

"I know," Michael said, keeping his voice low, "but slow it down for a bit. Please."

She shot him a nasty look, went to the pitcher, poured herself another drink and walked out of the kitchen. He went to follow, caught himself and went back to helping supervise the cooking.

Marcy walked by him slowly. "She going to be trouble?" she asked quietly.

Lizbeth rejoined the group for dinner, offering no apology for her behavior. She participated in conversation at times, but never said anything to or looked at Michael or Marcy.

The food turned out pretty well, with no disasters. The pasta was a little overcooked and the pie crust wasn't as flaky as some would have liked, but everything tasted good. A few people volunteered for cleanup duty. The rest moved into the living room where more Christmas carols were sung, with Michael playing the piano, accompanied by John on guitar. Bob produced a Konectable and pulled up *The Night Before Christmas.*

Michael turned down the lights in the room, leaving on the tree lights to create more of a Christmas atmosphere. Bob sat next to an end table with two large candles burning. He started reading. As he was finishing the poem, Michael, who had been standing by a window, walked over to the light panel and flicked on the outside security lights.

Slowly, each one in the room turned to the main windows and looked out. Snow was falling, steady and straight. They all watched quietly for a few moments. Someone started singing *Silent Night.*

<hr>

They awoke Christmas morning to the aroma of brewing coffee, freshly baked cornbread and applewood-smoked bacon. Marcy had gotten up early and started preparing for breakfast, chopping mushrooms the way Michael had taught her. There were presents under the tree, either brought in by the guests who had come in from the Boston area or from the core group members who had gone out en masse in the weeks before to scour the few shops still open in the surrounding area.

Marcy received the lion's share of the gifts, mostly maternity clothes of various styles and sizes for the coming months. Michael presented her with a replica of an antique rocking crib he'd made with Bill's help and guidance. She gave each of the core group a package containing a dozen cloth diapers and instructions, complete with hand drawn illustrations of how to change a baby. There were also plenty of gifts of wine and favorite liquors which would soon be difficult to buy and even more difficult to make. Tequilas were the predominant alcohol gift, along with triple sec and bottled lime juice. Half of them had agreed that they would miss a good margarita on a hot, summer evening.

Those coming in just for dinner started arriving shortly after two o'clock, with the meal being set for five. As before, each set of guests brought in some contribution to the meal, which ended up being a true feast and had to be set up in the great room. Two legs of venison were slow-cooked on a rotisserie on the wood-fired grill outside, as well as a few chickens for those who didn't enjoy game. Two large pots of potatoes were mashed. Thick, rich mushroom gravy was made with drippings from the venison. Vegetables that had been frozen just after picking were cooked and served piping hot in large bowls. Baby onions were steamed and creamed. Butternut and acorn squash were cubed and roasted with sage and a generous splash of apple cider. Twelve pies went into a warmer oven for later. Fresh cream from Wayne's cows was whipped with just a little sugar added to sweeten it up.

When the meal was finished and people had taken some time to digest a little, Wayne broke out a jug of his homemade apple jack, which he simply referred to as *jack*. This was passed around, along with brandy and other cordials. Wayne banged his empty coffee cup on the table to get the group's attention. As they quieted down, he stood, holding up his glass. His face turned slightly red.

"Those of you who know me know I'm a man of few words. I'm not one for making speeches or even talking to so many people in one place, but I feel quite compelled to make not one, but two toasts this evening. The first is to say thank you to John, Marcy, Heather, Bob, Bill, Ted and Michael for providing the place for such a wonderful feast, the likes of which I have never seen in my entire life."

He raised his glass higher, then drank. There were some *here-heres* and *thank yous* offered up.

Wayne cleared his throat loudly to bring the group back to silence. "I need to start the second toast with a bit of a story. When Michael first approached me to buy some land I had put up for sale, we got to talking about what was going on in the country. My Gladys had died a few months earlier from that new disease, and the TV was reporting that there were a lot of deaths because of it. So Michael, for whatever reason he had at the time, shared with me what he was thinking of doing. At first, I thought this was some flatlander's harebrained idea, but the more I watched the news, the more I got to thinking he might be on to something. Some weeks back he came to me to buy some horses. First time I got to meet Marcy. So I decided to give him the horses, and the cows, and the chickens and the sheep, and even those damn hogs I've been threatening to butcher for the last few years. Threw in the farm, too." His eyes watered up a bit and he coughed and cleared his throat a couple of times. "Well, enough *speeching*. Time to get to it. I would like to propose a toast to Michael for having the foresight to see down the pike and get this together before it all goes to hell! To Michael!"

All glasses were raised. Someone yelled out speech and others joined in. Michael looked embarrassed and raised his hands to say no, but they persisted. He sipped from his water glass, stood up and looked around at those in the room.

"There were plenty of times I also wondered if it was a hare-brained idea, and maybe it will still end up being so. Maybe someone will save the day at the last moment...but I don't think so. I also don't want to be taking too much credit for what's happening here. Each of you is, in some way or another, helping to make this dream a reality. Each of you is helping turn this into a fine community of good people.

"I want to give special credit to the founding members of Berk Shire: Bill, Ted, John, Bob, Heather," he said, then looked warmly to his right, "and Marcy. And also a special credit and thanks to Wayne, without whom we would not have had the land to get started with. Thank you, my friends." His eyes watered up a bit. He smiled and sat down. Marcy gently put her hand on his arm.

⸻ ⸜(●)⸝ ⸻

Clint had asked about the hunting in the area. He was an Iowan, raised hunting elk and deer. He, Michael and Will took rifles and handguns and headed out into the hills in search of game. Each had a backpack with snowshoes attached, should the snow get too deep. The air, crisp and dry, made the freezing temperature bearable.

On the hike in, Clint said he and his wife had talked it over and were interested in joining Berk Shire. "If that's even possible," he said. "I mean, I don't know if I have to pass a test or be interviewed or if I have to have special skills or something. I'll work hard and so will Jan and the kids."

"You're most welcome to become residents of Berk Shire. There's no test or anything," Michael said. "Living conditions will not be what you're used to. The cabins are small, though we've been work-ing on designs for bigger models for families."

"I've got money. Lots of it. Will and I have the same advisor, so

I've been turning everything into cash and buying up some gold, as well. How long do you think money's going to be good?"

"As long as people think it's worth something. But realistically, there are less and less goods being made, so there's less and less for sale. I'd say that by June it's going to be a lot tougher to buy much because supplies are already starting to dwindle, and money's going to be worthless when the government starts to go down, probably around late fall, maybe a little into the next year."

"But it's still good now, right?"

"Yes."

Clint hesitated for a moment, looked at Will, then back at Michael. "I can make about a hundred and fifty million available to you right after January first, like Will's done. That'll leave me enough to live on. We would want to let the kids finish out the school year, probably move up here the end of June, maybe July. Would that be okay?"

"If that's what you choose to do, that would be fine. You probably won't be able to sell your house then. No one will be offering much for anything even remotely near the city. You might consider selling now and then renting a place until you move," Michael said. "Look: tracks."

An hour later they had brought down a doe and were stringing it up to bleed out. Clint was right at home working on the animal. The three of them built a makeshift sled and dragged the carcass back to the main building.

"I'm liking this already," Clint said.

<hr />

New Year's Eve was a more intimate affair than Christmas. Clint and his family, Will, Chrissy, Theo, George, and Lizbeth stayed. They were able to pull in a comline feed from New York

City showing the Times Square celebration that had been going on since the mid-nineteen hundreds. The Square itself was less crowded than it had ever been. Not only were there fewer people alive, but fewer living there, or in any city. Many of those attending wore surgical masks.

They watched in silence for a while. There was no ball to drop, so video of a past year was used, with the old year digitally removed and 2040 pasted in. Everyone yelled *Happy New Year* and started hugs and kisses. Marcy got to Michael, put her arms around him, looked into his eyes for a moment before giving him a long kiss. He held onto her for a few moments, then kissed her again.

Lizbeth, dressed in a tight, clingy black outfit that left little to the imagination, gave Michael a cursory peck on the cheek and passed Marcy by altogether. She'd spent much of the evening hanging around Ted, trying to get him to dance, and generally letting him know she was quite open to his attention. Shortly after midnight, they disappeared.

Michael and Marcy said goodnight to the others and walked upstairs together.

"My place or yours?" she asked.

"How about mine tonight," he said. "Why don't you stay over?"

"That's a first."

"It's a new year. How about it?"

"Let me get a few things and I'll meet you there."

<hr />

On the second, the group met to discuss the state of affairs at Berk Shire. They talked about how the main house had been duly tested out over the holidays, and how fast they seemed to be acquiring new members. Michael pointed out that he had figured it would be slow at first, but would rapidly pick up when the government shut down and chaos set in. They agreed that they needed to prepare for a much larger influx of people over the summer and fall.

"I made a deal with a logging company that still has a few crews available. Hardly anyone is buying trees from them, so they're wide open to doing business with us. I've got a deal that will bring in ten trailers a month of large, prime pines cut, trimmed and debarked, starting by the end of January, weather permitting. Each trailer provides enough wood to build two houses of our current design. Of course, we have to work out the footage needed for a bigger design for family cabins."

"I'll have the design finished in a day or two," Bob said.

"So here's the issue for this meeting. Marcy, you want to play secretary? Thanks. We are going to very quickly find ourselves not being able to buy things more and more in the coming months, but for now, we can start scooping stuff up from various places. The question is this: what will we miss the most and need the most to sustain us?"

"Tequila," John said.

"Hey," Heather said, "this is serious."

"I am serious. We can't make it unless we find a source of agave, which is unlikely. Also, triple sec and lime juice. I mean, look at how many bottles of both were given at Christmas."

"Point taken," she said.

Michael told Marcy to log it into the tablet.

"Seeds for new plants, not the ones we've been growing - we saved enough seeds from last year - but also for new kinds of veggies, and flowers, too. Bulbs. Tulips and daffs, etc., etc."

"And speaking of seeds, shouldn't we be planting something for grain and hay for the cows and horses at Wayne's?"

"I'll ask him about that, "Michael said.

"Garden tools."

"With seeds, we should bring in different kinds of beans,

including soy. We should have an alternative plant protein source. Don't know if we can grow rice here. Probably not."

"Parts for our vehicles and the tractors. Hell, another couple of tractors, bigger ones than we've got, if they exist, and two or three more backhoe attachments."

"Bolts of all kinds of cloths, miles of thread, thousands of needles, buttons…and scissors, zippers."

"Razors."

"Surgical equipment and supplies."

"Medicines."

The suggestions kept coming for four hours straight. Marcy keyed it all in, saying she'd put it through a sorting program later. In the end they had come up with over a thousand items.

"Between Clint and Will we will have access to over three hundred and fifty million in addition to what we have left, so let's get ready to go shopping," Michael said. "A lot of things we can get over the 'net, but other stuff we're going to have to locate, then go and pick up in person. Let's get the list sorted and divvy it up into sublists. Everyone will take a list and start doing the research, making the calls, etc."

"Before we go," Marcy said, "I want to raise an issue. What are we going to do with those who cause trouble here?"

The group looked at each other in silence. No one, not even Michael, had considered this.

"I guess we're going to have come up with some rules and consequences," Heather said. "Whoa! Starting a new government, we are."

<hr />

January and February were spent locating the products and supplies they needed and wanted, and setting up either delivery or pickup schedules. The winter turned out to be filled with snowstorms, and it seemed like they were constantly plowing and clearing new snow. Two more tractors were acquired to aid in that work. Two of the larger trucks were rigged for and fitted with removable plows. A four acre plot was cleared as best as could be to store the mass of logs that started coming in, two trailers at a time. All available indoor storage space was quickly being filled.

Will and Chrissy arrived the second week of February. Their house was on the market, but the agent had told him it would likely sell for much less than what it had been worth the year before, which was already low. Will told the agent to make the best deal he could, then call him. Mortgage free for years, it would add at least some money to the till. They moved into one of the cabins that had been set up last summer, but joined the group for meals.

Chrissy, it turned out, was great at organizing and cataloging. She set up a computer program to keep track of where everything was stored. Previously, Michael, Bill, Bob and Marcy had used their memories to know where things were kept, but since stuff started pouring in faster than it could be remembered, that was no longer viable. Michael helped Chrissy survey the property and buildings to take inventory.

The group continued its shopping spree, splitting up by twos to go out and pick items up. Will, who turned out to have an affinity with heavy equipment, worked with Bill and Ted to keep moving big items around in the name of keeping as much space open as possible for the next load of whatever was coming in.

Two more couples showed up a few days apart, about a week after Will and Chrissy had arrived. One couple the group had met at Christmas. Theo and George had texted about the other couple that would be arriving, ones they had mentioned at the Christmas gathering. Both had the furniture from their houses trucked in, and what was in excess of what their cabins could hold was put into storage for the use of others.

March brought the first break in the weather. Two more couples arrived. Seventy new acres were plowed under in addition to the original twenty-five. Containers of seedlings were stacked almost to the ceiling on wire racks in the twelve greenhouses that had been assembled. Eight more unassembled greenhouses, the very last ones the company had left in their warehouse, were stored on a wall of pallets outside the machine shop where the tractors and other heavy equipment were kept. The owner of the company had started closing down his business for lack of customers as well as the skilled help to produce the units.

By the end of the month, all the cabins that had been built were full. Two more of the bedrooms in the main house were occupied, leaving only a few open. A makeshift dormitory was set up in the largest room in the basement. All new arrivals were placed there, separated from each other only by cloth sheets, while they awaited the next open cabin.

Michael contacted the construction company that he'd hired to build the original structures. The owner, Chuck, had told him he'd let his crews go back in the fall for lack of work. No one was building anything new, and the only jobs that came in were pitifully small ones he could handle himself or with one helper. He felt bad about the layoffs, but figured they'd find work elsewhere with the labor shortage intensifying.

As Michael desperately needed skilled help to erect enough buildings to keep ahead of demand, he made Chuck a lucrative offer to reassemble as much of his crew as he could.

"I probably have enough work to keep a crew or two going for the next year or so," Michael explained.

"I'll see what I can do. I know three of the guys are still available, and I am as well. And hell, I've got enough heavy equipment just hanging around if you've got room for me to leave it there."

In the end, Chuck was able to assemble one full crew of six

men. Split into two and augmented with new residents as laborers, they could get a lot done quickly. Michael saw this as a godsend. He knew the influx of people was going to increase exponentially in the coming months. He needed cabins, barns, storage buildings and water towers.

He ordered twenty more trailers of logs.

Lizbeth showed up mid-March, stayed in the main house for a few nights before moving in with Ted. She was brought into the group meetings for her input in setting up the colony. Her skills were readily apparent. She created neighborhoods consisting of eight cabins set on cul-de-sacs, and suggested a common area for barbequing and socializing, giving each area an identity of its own while still being part of the larger picture. In each neighborhood, one family would be chosen to orient the newcomers. All this, she said, would help blend people into more cohesive groups.

New residents were only given two days in which to familiarize themselves with the area and set up their cabins. After that, they were assigned duties either within the village proper or in the fields. Since there were not enough bus drivers to pick up all the students in the rural area, school had become something of an option. For those kids who did not attend schools, all over the age of fourteen were expected to contribute to the health and well-being of the community. Those younger than that often helped their parents with small jobs and chores.

Michael gave up his duty as chief greeter to those coming in. John was given the task and did it with relish. Heather and Michael set up a medical clinic and manned it for two hours most days. When two other physicians joined, both specializing in primary care, Michael backed off. There was too much else to do. But he also knew that his medical knowledge would be needed in the days to come, so he continued at the clinic one day a week, taking the opportunity to sharpen rusty skills and learn from the others.

—◦—

There had been small pockets of unrest around the country, mostly in the form of protests that had been occurring for many months, but the first full-blown riot occurred in Washington, D.C. on April first. Five thousand people marched on the White House to protest the lack of progress the administration was making in addressing the problems created by the disease. The protest group, organized and peaceful at first, quickly degraded into an angry mob. National Guardsmen were brought in to back up the riot police, but the crowd would not back down. Over a hundred people on both sides were killed when the police and soldiers, slim in numbers and scared out of their minds, opened fire. Many of the protesters also had guns and fired back. Hundreds more were wounded.

The core group, which now included Lizbeth, Will and Chrissy, watched the news report on a computer comline feed.

"And so the next phase starts," Michael said, rubbing his hands over his face.

Marcy rubbed her swelling belly. "It's going to get really bad, isn't it?"

"We'll be pretty safe here, but we need to be prepared in case of attack," Michael told the group. "We need a plan and we need to do drills so everyone knows what to do."

"No one knows shit about defense like that," Bob said. "Making it up as we go," he added, his voice trailing off a bit.

"Chrissy, what is the count now?" Michael asked.

"Thirty-nine," she said, "and no one with police experience. A few were in the service for a couple of years, so maybe they could help."

"Could you arrange a meeting with them for tomorrow? Late afternoon would be best. Thanks," Michael said.

"If we get attacked, it'll most likely be mob behavior," Lizbeth told them. "Pretty unorganized, but they'll have guns, I'll bet."

"Any suggestions?" Michael asked her.

"Being prepared will surprise a mob. Organization, for the most part, wins out over disorganization unless the numbers are wildly out of whack. A mob is already in a chaotic state, so it feels more powerful to its members than it actually is, but there's little leadership and little planning. It's more about brute force. True power in a group comes from working together, having a plan," she said. "Is it possible to wire speakers in the trees around the house? Loud screeching sounds would hurt their ears, distract them from their attack."

"But that would also hurt our ears," Will said.

"We'd have to use earplugs and hand signals, and that would get complicated," Michael said. "Maybe we could wire headsets into the earplugs."

"That might be doable," Bob said.

The group threw out more ideas. What was decided was that creating a small armored vehicle that had weaponry and could split a mob up would be very useful. Camouflaged pits, deep enough to make climbing out very difficult, would be dug in the area leading up to the front of the main building.

"We'll also assemble a group of ten or twelve of the best shots and have them available to send out, if necessary," Michael said. "I guess we should use volunteers for that."

"I'm in," Will said.

"Me, too," Bob added.

"Me, too," John said.

Knowing John was the worst shot amongst them, Michael thought for a moment to find a diplomatic way to keep him off that team. "I'll be out there, too. But John, we're going to need someone inside to keep things steady, and I think you're the best one for the job."

"Really?" he said, a look of pride on his face.

"Really."

Marcy brought up the idea of sniper stations on the roof. Bob said he would get to work on how best to do that without affecting the integrity of the current construction.

—————◦《◦》◦—————

Marcy and Michael were lying in bed, spooning, his hand on her belly.

"There," she said.

"I felt it. Little soccer player he...or she is."

They lay there, not speaking or moving, very comfortable with each other's touch.

"This defense stuff scares me," she said, "but it's also kind of exciting. Must be the momma-bear instinct kicking in, protecting my turf and children."

Michael thought for a moment. "I sort of feel the same way, but there's this other feeling of intense responsibility. Sooner or later, if we get attacked, people are going to be killed. That's weighing pretty heavy."

She rolled over and faced him, caressed his face with her hand. "You've always been the leader here, so maybe you get that worse than any of us, but I've had those same thoughts, too. There's the whole thing of killing another human being. I've shot deer, squirrels, pheasants, chopped the heads off chickens and turkeys, but killing another person...well, that is a whole other thing."

Michael said nothing. He looked up at the ceiling, then closed his eyes. His lower lip started to quiver a bit.

"What's wrong?"

He didn't speak for a few moments, then sighed and told her about his last visit to Sherilyn, how he'd shifted back and forth on the decision to euthanize her, then walked in, allowed himself a few last minutes with her before giving her the shot.

"I just stuffed away my emotions for the second it took to do it, like going into clinical mode the way we were taught in medical school. Don't feel what the patient feels; don't feel the patient's pain or distress. They never discussed what to do when the patient was a friend or relative. They never discussed what to do with our own feelings. It was always about staying objective and focused on what had to be done."

"Objective? What you did, you did out of love for her. Didn't you ever talk about it with her when she got sick?" Marcy asked.

He said they'd talked about it again and again because they'd known what was coming. "But talking about it, that's way different than doing it. I don't regret what I did - it was the humane thing to do - but it just feels so heavy in me. Not a day goes by when I don't see that blank, lifeless look in her eyes from the disease, yet there was even a change in that look when she died, like there was still a tiny bit of something there."

She looked at him. "It was the kindest, most loving act."

His eyes filled with tears as he looked at her, seeking some sort of absolution that could never come from another human being. She pulled him to her and let him cry.

<hr/>

Will, who eventually moved all four of his vehicles to Berk Shire, donated a large SUV for the armored car. Bob worked on the design, printed out plans and passed them to Ted and Bill, who were both experienced welders. The suspension was greatly reinforced to handle the extra weight that would be added. Eighth-inch plate steel was cannibalized from two derelict pieces of ancient farm machinery Wayne had literally put out to pasture. Two radically sawed-off twelve gauge shotguns were mounted on each of the four sides of the vehicle, with only a few inches of what was left of the barrels showing. The wide dispersion rate would do the most damage. The double barreled rifles would be the easiest to reload from inside.

Slits were put in the metal, covering three sides of the vehicle. Each was about two feet long by four inches tall, and was covered by a poly-glass composite that was bulletproof for most weapons that a mob might carry. A minimal space was opened up for the rifles, limiting breach points by attackers, should any try to shove a gun barrel in. The front was set up in a similar way, with a slightly larger composite windshield. A set of servo motors were connected to the triggers on the rifles in front, able to be activated by the driver using micro buttons mounted on the steering wheel. The inside of the vehicle was also lined with six inch thick padding that would prevent any bullet fired into it from ricocheting.

One of the residents who had been in the military had been trained as a driver of armored personnel carriers. He was chosen to be the primary controller of the car, and taught what he knew to another former soldier. A third and fourth person were also trained, both for driving as well as for use of the weapons. Cross training was deemed the most prudent course, as they would all be in the vehicle, should it have to be sent out. In the event of any of those inside being wounded or killed, redundancy guaranteed the best chance for continued operation.

Sniper blinds were gradually installed on the edge of the roof line of the main building, with steep stairs inside providing access. Weapons were stored at the tops of the stairs. Boxes of ammunition for each were kept in a single room in the basement. Each box contained enough to keep the sniper firing, yet was light enough for any resident to lift, older children included. Specific people were assigned to the duty of delivering these boxes.

A single, weatherproof speaker which broadcast three hundred and sixty degrees was set on top of the tallest pine in the area and shielded from underneath. Since it was wireless, attackers trying to disable it would have to climb the tree, a formidable task since the branches had been cut off the lower twenty feet of it. This communication would be used to warn all within Berk Shire, including those in the fields and woods, as well as the nearest neighbors. A test showed it could be heard ten miles away on a windless day, more if the wind was with the sound, less if against it.

Assignments were given; drills were run repeatedly.

"For what it's worth, we are about as prepared as we can be," Michael said.

"Let's hope we don't ever have to use what we've put together," Heather said.

"And if we do, that it's good enough to protect us," Bob added.

⸻

The drive to the general store in town took Michael and Marcy past many of the biggest farms in the area, many of which had been abandoned. Seven and a half months pregnant, she had come along for the change of scenery. She had found herself getting more and more listless as her due date approached. Heather had put her on a restricted physical workload. Some of her time was spent in the kitchen, helping prepare fruits and vegetables to be put up. Some of it was spent in her basement office, doing research on natural pesticides and herbicides, but she grew tired of this easily. More and more of each day was being spent sitting in a chair on the patio area behind the main house or walking off the restlessness.

The owner of the general store, Bert, was fifty-five, with a full head of brown hair liberally peppered with gray. About two inches shorter than Michael, he had unloaded enough trucks and shifted around enough feed and seed bags to keep him in pretty good shape. From his chair on the front porch of the store, he saw Michael's truck coming, greeted them with a hearty wave, and motioned them to pull into the side alley to make the transfer of supplies easier.

Standing at the side entrance was the store owner's sole employee, Jimmy, a lightly freckled eighteen year old with wavy brown hair. He was as tall as Bert, but was still a little on the gangly side. Bert had taken him in when Jimmy's parents, Bert's younger sister and brother-in-law, had died in an auto accident when Jimmy was eight. Michael had met the boy well over two years ago when he first had dealings with Bert, and found him to be respectful and responsible and willing to engage with customers. He'd played football in the fall for the regional high school, and though he was never a star player, write ups in the local paper mentioned him frequently as assisting in many of the big plays. He was the quintessential team player. He had graduated in early June, but had decided to put college off because of the way things were shaping up.

Jimmy shook Michael's hand, then went to help Marcy get out of the truck. After a little pleasant chitchat, Bert asked the boy to escort Marcy to the porch rocker and get her something cold to drink. When he returned to the alley, the three of them loaded the many boxes of supplies into the truck. Michael had started to feel sorry for Jimmy, coming of age as the world was moving into decline. He remembered his own dreams upon graduation - college, medical school, residency, practice, marriage, children....

"I've also got a few more boxes inside," Bert said, "more of that tequila you've been ordering. The rep said production is way down due to lack of help in the fields and the distillery, so the supply is going to get scarcer from here on out."

"Thanks, Bert. Give the rep a call and offer him a bonus...a big bonus…for any more he can…uh…redirect."

Bert inquired as to how much of a bonus. When he heard Michael's numbers he said, "Boy, you must really love that stuff out there."

"Let's just say we're preparing for the future. Now, what do I owe you?"

After settling up the bill, he gave Bert a thousand more. "For all your help. You've been great, going the extra mile. And if I can ever do anything for you, you let me know."

On the way out, he pulled Jimmy aside and handed him a sizable tip. "Remember what we've talked about," he said to the boy.

"I know: spend it sooner rather than later. I got my eye on a brand new truck. Figure I'll need one anyway."

"I think a new truck would be a good investment."

"I got plans, Dr. Macalister."

"Jimmy, I think it's all right if you call me Michael."

"Well, then…Michael…I got plans, big plans. I figure I might have to make some adjustments if things keep going the way they're going, but I want to find my place in the world, whatever happens. I want to get married and have a bunch of kids. Yeah, I got plans," he said, nodding his head up and down.

"If there's ever anything I can do to help you out, please feel free to look me up. You're a hard worker, Jimmy, and that's exactly what's going to count no matter which way the world heads. I believe in you," Michael said.

Jimmy smiled and looked down for a few seconds. "That means a lot to me, Doc…Michael." The boy walked over to the passenger side of the truck, helped Marcy back in. "Bye, Ms. Gruner," he said with a big smile on his face.

"Call me Marcy."

"Okay…Marcy." The boy turned red.

Michael took Marcy to lunch at the lone local cafe, a place called

Lonny's. They both had cod that had been farm-raised in the waters just off Cape Cod. It was the special of the day, coated with a Ritz cracker, butter and onion mix, baked crispy. Both knew that this kind of seafood was becoming a rarity and might not be available too much longer.

"I think the kid's got a bit of a crush," Michael said. "See the way he blushed?"

Marcy shrugged it off.

"Can't say I blame him. Shows he's got good taste."

"You think a lot of him, don't you?" Marcy asked.

"He's a big part of the future, just like our baby will be."

On the ride home, they came upon a small, dark green car pulled off to the side of the road with its hood up. A woman stood behind it waving them down. There was no one else in sight. She was short, had on jeans and a light blue tee shirt, a baseball cap partially hiding brown hair.

Michael came to a stop about fifty feet away from the car, put his hazard flashers on and told Marcy to wait in the truck.

"I need to stretch a little," she answered, stepping out.

"Then please stay by the truck. I'll see what this is about."

He walked toward the woman, who stopped waving her arms, but didn't seem to relax much.

"I need help," she called to him. "My car broke down."

As Michael reached her, a man stepped out from in front of the car. He was a few inches taller than the woman, with a receding hairline, wore dirty tan pants and a brown tee. His skin was sunburn red. The pistol in his hand was shaking.

Michael recognized the wild, adrenaline-fueled look in the man's eyes: fear mixed with desperation. Michael raised his hands out from his sides.

"I don't want any trouble," he said to the man, stepping away from the woman.

"Me neither, mister. I…I…I just want your truck. I've never done anything like this and I'm really nervous, so just move away from your truck. Right now!" he said, his hand shaking harder.

A shot was fired. "Put your gun down, pal, or I'll drop your woman where she stands!" Marcy called out. She had a semi-automatic pistol held out in front of her, both hands locked around it. "I mean it!"

The man tried to steady his aim at Michael as he looked back and forth between him and Marcy, but his hand shook even more. After a few moments, he put one hand up and crouched down, put the gun on the ground and stepped back. Marcy moved forward, now training her gun on the man.

"Please don't hurt her. Please, I'm sorry. I'm really sorry. I didn't mean any harm. We're just trying to get away from Boston. They had a riot there this morning. People got all crazy and we just headed out. I'm really sorry," the man said, starting to cry.

Michael picked up the man's gun and checked it, found the safety still engaged. He popped the clip out of it, checked the chamber for a round, found none. He nodded once at Marcy, who lowered her gun.

"Where are you headed?" he asked the man.

The woman moved next to the man, wiped tears from her eyes. "We were just going, just wanted to be away from there. It's like we went crazy inside, seeing that riot happening," she said. "It was only about ten blocks from where we lived. He didn't…we didn't want to do this, hold somebody up. That's not us, but we had a bunch of cars just pass us by."

Michael introduced himself and extended his hand. The man hesitated for a moment before shaking it.

"Jim Talbot," he said in a tremulous voice. "My wife Barbara."

"We watched the riot in Washington a few months ago. Scary stuff and it's going to get worse," Michael said. "If you've got nowhere to go, we've got a place about ten miles up the road. You can spend the night. There's a bunch of us, so I'll be happy to send some of my friends back to tow your car in. Couple of them are pretty good mechanics, probably be able to fix you up."

The man looked at Michael in disbelief, then looked at his wife, who raised her eyebrows and hesitantly nodded yes.

"We're pretty loaded down," Marcy said, "but we can make some room."

"By the way, if you ever have to fire this, make sure you pull this top part back to load a round, then take the safety off," Michael said, handing Jim back his gun and clip.

Marcy apologized to both for pulling her gun on Barbara, said she was just bluffing to scare them.

On the ride back to Berk Shire, the conversation flowed. Jim turned out to be an investment advisor, his wife a grade school teacher. He talked about knowing the shell game the government was playing, using money to try to keep people calmer for longer. He had been seeing the market drop precipitously, then watched mystery money, as he called it, move in to prop the market back up, making it appear more stable than it was.

"The feds call it quantitative easing, but the bottom line is they just keep printing more and more money with nothing to back it up. Some of my colleagues kept going, making all kinds of money, ignoring the fact that it's become more worthless with every day that passes. The writing's on the wall."

"In capitol letters and bold print," Michael said.

"So this place of yours…you have a small farm or something like that?" Jim asked.

Michael looked at Marcy, who smiled back. He turned left onto the dirt road to the compound. "Something like that."

They were put up in the one of the few bedrooms left in the main house. Bill took a few guys and a tow strap out to bring the disabled car in. It took about ten minutes to determine that it was a popped breaker, which they reset on the spot.

The Talbots took less than a minute to accept the invitation to stay.

—«O»—

Michael walked into Chrissy's basement office for their weekly meeting, bringing with him two cups of tea. He placed one on her desk and sat down across from her. She had taken on the job of keeping track of all manner of things. She and Jim, who had been assigned as her assistant, monitored what was being used, built, born or grown not only in Berk Shire, but also on the neighboring farms that had unofficially joined with them.

"So, Berk Shire only," Chrissy said, reading from her computer screen. "Thirty-two laying hens, twelve breeders, three roosters - only one in the breeding pen at a time, and we rotate them to keep them happy - fifty-four chicks of various ages. Jim has done projections and says that if we maintain breeding at this level, we'll have enough eggs and meat to feed about one hundred and fifty people with no problem. Controlling the breeders is not an issue: just remove the rooster."

"Great. And milkers and beef cattle?"

"Slow there. We cut Wayne's milking herd back to twenty. That level produces around fifteen to twenty gallons of milk per day, giving us more milk, cream and butter than we know what to do with. It's being consumed by adults as well as children, so that's good, but it's still more than we need. The excess is mixed in with the pig swill."

She sipped her tea, put it back down. "As to the other forty from the herd, we cut out twenty-five, left the bull fifteen. Bill says that bull has a big 'ol smile on his face. We've got five calves, three more on the way in about three weeks, and a couple more births slated for November."

She kept going down the list, enumerating the sheep and hog population, then moved on to cabins built and timber left.

They both looked up as they heard someone moving quickly down the hallway, heading towards them. Bob burst through the doorway and looked at Michael.

Panting, he said two words only: "It's time."

Michael jogged through the halls to a room on the far side of the basement. He pushed open the outer set of doors. The inner doors were closed, with a large note taped on it: *Scrub in!* An arrow on the paper pointed toward the scrub sink they had installed in the sterilization area. He picked up the bottle of surgical scrub and a fingernail brush, poured a liberal amount on his hands and arms. He scrubbed thoroughly, then used his elbow to turn on the hot water and rinse off. He thought about the UV scrubbers he'd used back in the lab and wondered if he would still be able to buy one or two.

"There's a gown over there," Heather said as he entered the room. "Contractions are close, so it looks like its game time. Ever do a birth when you were in rotation?"

"No, but I helped Wayne with a breech birth on one of his cows a few weeks ago."

"Close enough."

"Hey, Marcy."

Marcy, drenched in sweat, was lying back on an OB birthing table Heather had trucked in shortly after she'd moved in for good. She grimaced with a contraction.

"SON OF A BITCH THAT WAS A BIG ONE!" she yelled. A split second later, she smiled at Michael and said softly, "Thanks for being here."

"No where else I'd rather be." He bent down and kissed her. "I borrowed a catcher's mitt from Will just in case."

"SO! FUCKING! FUNNY!" Marcy yelled. She relaxed as the contraction abated. "Sorry. Heather said I might blurt some things out SONOFABITCH! Not you," she said, looking at him. She reached out for his hand.

The labor went on for a little over two hours. Somewhere around the end of the second hour, Marcy started screaming things out, many of which were unintelligible. Michael looked at Heather.

"We in the field refer to it as speaking in tongues," she said. "You're doing great, Marcy. No, don't push. Wait until I say push. Right now, just breathe in a regular fashion."

A few minutes went by. "Okay, now push. Harder! Harder!"

Marcy let fly a run-on sentence of expletives aimed directly at Heather.

"I can't tell you how much I've longed to hear you say those words," Heather said coyly, batting her eyelids. She went back to her all-business tone. "Now relax. Couple more and I think we'll be there."

"WHATDOYOUMEANWEOHGODTHATHURTS."

"Michael, would you be kind enough to get my sippy cup over there?" Heather asked.

He picked up the glass and straw, held it to her lips while she drank.

"WHATABOUTMEMOTHERFUCKER?"

"Give our sweet talker a sip, Michael...but just a sip."

"Marcy? Are you ready? This is going to be a really big push. Push!"

Marcy pushed.

"Harder! The baby's crowning. Harder!"

A moment later Heather held up the baby. She handed the boy to Michael, clamped the cord and cut it. As the baby started to cry, she gave instructions for Michael to gently wipe off the blood. He brought the baby over to Marcy and placed it on her chest. Tears streamed down both their eyes.

"Okay, you might want to go wrap the baby up. We've still got a placenta to deliver," Heather said. "Yep, the contractions are starting. Okay, Marcy, we've got a little more pushing to do, but this will be a piece of cake. Push! Harder!"

Ten minutes later they were done.

"I'll go make out the birth certificate," Heather said. "What is it? August 7th? Okay. You two hang out for a while."

Mica Martin Macalister was introduced to the core group when they came to visit Marcy in her bedroom. She sat in a rocking chair wearing a light green silky robe. The baby, cradled in her arms, was wrapped in a small, soft blanket.

"He is so adorable," Bob said. He lightly touched the baby's fingers, which wrapped part ways around his.

"Oh, so beautiful," Heather chimed in.

"I love the name," John said. His voice trailed off a little.

Marcy picked up on his curiosity. "But you're wondering why we used Michael's last name."

"Well, that's your business," John replied.

"No, it's okay, really. Think about it: Mica Martin Gruner. Doesn't have the same ring to it. It's as simple as that," she said.

Michael stayed behind when they left. Mica Martin started to cry. Marcy pulled her tee shirt up and offered the baby her breast.

"You sure you want to move in here?" she asked Michael. "It's going to be a bit noisy and you're probably not going to get a full night's sleep for a while, if what Heather said holds true. I can handle it on my own."

Michael tilted his head a little and gave her a smile. He reached out and stroked her hair. "I know you can, but if you don't mind, I want to be a part of what's happening, day and night, sleep or no."

"Well, I reserve the right for you to change your mind if it gets to be too much," she responded, "or to throw you out if I see fit!"

"Well...," Michael said, not finishing his sentence.

"Well, what?"

He hesitated before speaking. "I'm wondering what you'd think about me moving in, like, you know...like...permanently."

The look on her face told him she had not expected that in a million years. "We agreed: no obligations. You get me pregnant, I get a child. You shouldn't feel like you have to do this."

"I know I don't have to, but I want to. In fact...." He dropped to one knee and produced a small dark blue, felt-covered box.

"Oh, don't you dare," she said, a look of shock coming across her face.

"Marcy, I'm going to make this short and sweet. I love you. Will you marry me?"

"Oh, shit! Shit! SHIT!" she yelled, then quickly lowered her voice. "You sneaky son of a bitch!"

"Speaking in tongues again? I love you."

Tears started streaming down her face. "Of course, I'll marry you! I love you, too," she said, glowing. "Wow! First baby, now first wedding. You do want a *wedding* wedding, don't you?"

"We'll invite the whole of Berk Shire and anyone else in the area!"

"I need to lose my baby belly first, though."

"You tell me when," he said.

She thought for a moment. "How about New Year's Eve?" The baby pulled away from her breast and started to cry again. "Don't worry, you're invited, too."

Mid-August delivered a sweltering heat wave. The residents were told to take it easy in whatever outside work they were doing, to stay well-hydrated. On the third day, Michael announced that outside work was only to be done in the earlier morning hours, that everyone should do half-days and stay inside the rest of the time where there was air conditioning. Some drove off to the nearest lake, about fifteen miles away, while others just hung out inside the main building in the great room or basement areas.

Michael came up from the basement from an early afternoon meeting with Chrissy and Jim, to find a small crowd gathered by the windows looking out onto the rear patio. He pushed his way through to see what was going on.

Lizbeth was lying topless on a chaise lounge.

Marcy and Heather slid up next to Michael and looked out.

"Is she kidding me?" Marcy yelled. "I'm going to go talk to her right now. Jeez, there are kids around."

Michael put his hand on her arm. "Maybe Heather would be better suited for this. Heather? You up for this?"

"I'll do it," she said, moving toward the door.

"All right, break it up," Michael said, realizing the crowd was mostly men. "Break it up."

Heather approached Lizbeth. Lizbeth looked out from behind her sunglasses but didn't acknowledge her.

"I can appreciate working on your tan lines, Lizbeth, but it might be better to do it in a less public place."

Lizbeth didn't move a muscle. "Like I care who looks."

"That go for children and teens? That sound smart to you?" Heather said.

Lizbeth pushed her sunglasses up on her head, shot a pissy look at Heather, then got up and walked away, not bothering to put her top back on.

Marcy turned to Michael, punched him in the arm and said,

"Told you she was going to be trouble."

———————

Clint told the group that he had been talking with someone from his old neighborhood, who told him that the start of school had been postponed. The robocall that went out cancelling school in the town ended simply: *For now.* He had made some other calls and found that other towns were doing the same thing. There were not enough teachers to maintain regular classrooms, and the skeleton maintenance crews made it dangerous for students to be in the buildings. Consolidation was an option being explored.

John talked about what he was reading in online reports. A lot of town governments did not have enough people to cover all the usual departments, so those who were able were now doing double or triple duty in an attempt to keep things working.

"It's all starting to collapse," Clint said, "just like you said it would."

Michael felt no satisfaction in knowing his projections were coming true. In fact, he felt a profound sadness attach itself to him, felt it dragging him down like a great weight. He went to his basement office, closed the door and looked at a picture of Marcy and the baby. Tears started dropping from his eyes as he thought about having just brought a child into this mess.

———————

The end of September brought with it a streak of warm days punctuated by cool nights, what Michael considered perfect weather for his liking. As he headed out to one of the newer neighborhoods to check the progress on two new cabins that were being built, he looked around at what he and the others had set in motion a few years back, marveling at how it had all come together so quickly. He knew there were many more things ahead of them, some good, some not so good, but for now it was going well.

He was approaching the machine shop when he heard loud voices, then cursing and yelling. He hurried his pace and walked through one of the bay doors to find Bill and Ted squared off, throwing punches at each other. Bill's shirt was torn almost in half and blood was dripping from his face. Ted's left eye was swollen.

Michael yelled for them to stop, and while Bill started to back off at the sound of his voice, Ted kept coming at him. Michael yelled again to no avail. Ted kept swinging. Bill was ducking and trying to move away.

Michael pulled the handgun he almost always carried, flicked off the safety and fired two shots in rapid succession into the dirt floor. Ted looked up and stopped swinging.

"Enough!" Michael yelled. "Enough! Back off, take a breather and calm yourselves down, both of you!"

Bill rubbed blood from his chin and backed off more. Ted continued to stare at him, the wildness in his eyes stoked and burning.

"Ted!" Michael said loudly. "Breathe! Move away and calm down."

Ted flipped him the finger and walked out of the building.

Michael turned to Bill. "Are you okay?"

"Yeah, I'm fine."

"You want to tell me what the hell is going on?"

"Man, that guy is out of his fucking mind!" Bill said, huffing to catch his breath. "Out of his fucking mind!"

Michael questioned him for specifics.

"He's always going all gloom and doom about everything - the survivalist shit - so that wasn't anything different. He started in while we were working on that tractor and I dared to say that things here were shaping up pretty damn good, better than he and I thought it would be before y'all started arriving. Well, that just seemed to set him off real bad. He starts going on about how this place was run so poorly until Lizbeth started getting things organized, how, in his opinion, she should be in charge. I told him that wasn't true, that you guys were doing great and it was like a switch got thrown and he comes at me. Son of a bitch! He caught me off guard, tagged me hard with the first one. I don't think he laid another good one on me after that. I'll tell you, he's big, but he sucks at fighting…though he'd probably kill you if he got you in a bear hug."

"Do me a favor: unless you have to be working here right now, go find something else to do. I'll give him some time to cool down, find him and talk to him. Your jaw looks pretty swollen to me. Move it around a bit. Hurt? It doesn't look broken. Maybe you should go see Doc Watts just to be sure. And if you see Ted, head the other way, will you? Thanks."

Michael saw a crowd of onlookers as he headed out of the machine shop. He walked quickly to Ted and Lizbeth's cabin, saw a shadow through the shades and knew the man was inside. A knock on the door produced no response. He knocked again and called Ted's name.

"When you're ready to talk, Ted, I'll be out back the main building."

It was over an hour before Ted showed up.

"You got something to say to me?"

"Sit down," Michael said, extending his hand toward the nearest chair.

"I'll stand."

Michael knew what he was trying to do: refusing to sit to show his objections and resistance to talking; using the high ground to intimidate.

"Suit yourself," Michael said, showing no fear. "What went on today?"

"Got into a fight."

"Over what?"

Ted stared him down. "Over nothing. None of your business. It's between me and him."

Michael stood up and stared back. "Whatever you two need to do to stay away from each other, do it. Happens again, you're out. Are we clear?"

Ted turned and walked away.

<hr>

Michael relayed what had gone on. The only surprise the group felt was that it had taken so long for Ted to go off on someone. There had been other squabbles among residents, even a weak punchy-wrestling match or two that had all been resolved easily and ended with handshakes. But this was different. Ted was overly serious, wound tight. As one of the first people of Berk Shire, he had held a distinction, an honor, almost, in the eyes of many of the later residents. He knew things they didn't; he was brought in *because* he knew things most people didn't. He was the one who taught them survival skills, hunting techniques, foraging tricks. As news of this fight traveled - and it would - some, maybe more, would start seeing a loose cannon walking around. The world was already falling apart. Berk Shire had been holding it together, offering a strong sense of safety to those who lived here. The colony had to stay strong as the outside grew weak.

"So we're agreed? He goes off one more time on anyone, he moves on?" Michael asked.

"He leaves, Lizbeth'll probably go with him," Bob said.

"Two birds," Marcy said.

<hr>

Marcy took Mica Martin out for some fresh air. He was in the carry-harness Heather had gotten her the previous Christmas, his tiny feet dangling over her shrinking belly. A small satchel slung over one shoulder bumped gently against her hip. She drifted lazily down one of the walking trails off the main building. It was a favorite of hers, richly scented by thick patches of cedars and the gently decaying leaves and pine needles on the ground. She liked being away from the busyness of the compound, liked the stillness of the forest. She hoped Mica Martin would come to love this as much as she did.

She rounded a bend in the path and saw one of the benches Bill had put together out of pieces of split pine logs left over from one of the cabins being built. The seat had been sanded glass-smooth. The ten millimeter handgun she had holstered on her belt poked her in the side as she sat down. She shifted it slightly.

Mica Martin looked up at her from the harness, made a wet gurgling sound. She smiled, rubbed his back lightly and cooed to him. He imitated her smile, gurgled again.

She reached into the satchel and pulled out an apple. She bit into it, put her head back a little, drew in the aroma of the fruit and savored the taste.

"Hey, I'm hungry, too," a voice said quietly.

She looked around, saw no one. It had sounded like someone had whispered directly into her ear. She looked at the baby, who smiled and waved his arms a bit.

"You're beautiful." The whisper seemed even quieter this time, but still as close.

She looked around again. A slight look of worry crossed her face as she put her hand on her hand gun.

"Relax, Marcy. Turn around and look straight down the path back towards the main building," the voice said, "and at the first curve, go to ten o'clock and back about fifty yards. That's right - by the big red pine."

Marcy followed the instructions, strained her eyes into the woods and finally saw Michael standing there holding a small silvery tube that was pointed at her.

"Hi, beautiful," he said in her ear. He put the tube into his shirt pocket and started walking towards her. As he approached, he saw that she was not all that happy.

"Sorry, I didn't mean to scare you," he said as he got close.

"Well, you didn't scare me, but I was getting a bit concerned. What is that thing?"

"PCD - pinpoint communication device. It can broadcast a voice to a small area up to two hundred yards away. It can be narrowed down to a single person, if desired."

"Well, if you hadn't revealed yourself, I would probably have started to wonder if I was hearing voices in my head or if Mica Martin had early onset ESP."

He bent down and kissed her, then kissed the baby's forehead.

Marcy took a bite out of her apple and handed it to Michael, who did the same. "When'd you get that toy?" she asked.

He handed the apple back to her. "A couple of weeks ago, mixed in with one of the many packages that arrived. Saw it online on a security site, thought it might come in handy calling across a field or something, rather than trying to get someone's attention by yelling, so I ordered a couple. And I'm thinking it might be a good idea not to let anyone know we've got them."

"So you can go and pull that shit on someone else?" she asked.

"Well, no. I don't think I'll do that again. I'm just thinking it might come in handy for other things."

"Like what?"

"I don't know…maybe if there was a sniper or something like that. Make him think someone's near him, make him paranoid. Like that."

Mica Martin let out a quiet *ooooo* sound. Marcy looked at him. "That's right: your daddy's always thinking ahead. Yes he is, you little cutey."

———))(((———

Every person in Berk Shire participated in the fall harvest. Some picked, some sorted; others hauled and delivered. Still others shucked and peeled and cut and canned or froze. Seeds were dried, saved and labeled for use in one of the greenhouses for seedlings the following spring.

The now annual pumpkin carving contest was held the week of Halloween. Fresh pumpkin pies were made for the colony's harvest dinner's dessert. Hunting parties went out on a regular basis, sometimes yielding nothing, other times bringing in small or large game. Neighbors familiar with the area showed some of the residents of Berk Shire productive fishing spots for trout and salmon. One of them invited a group over to learn how to make sausage in his old fashioned machine. Wayne orchestrated the building of a smokehouse so that fish and meats might be cured. He showed them how to use corn cobs and applewood for the sweetest flavor when smoking ham or bacon.

Money started to mean less and less as the fall rolled on, until it was deemed by many to be without value. The local economy responded by quickly moving to a system of trade and barter. Will and Clint had shipped in their stores of gold, which served Berk Shire well as the dollar's precipitous drop continued.

Riots were reported in more and more places. Protests happened only here and there. The mobs that had formed were now only about looting and stealing food or goods like comline monitors that would soon have no meaning or use.

Media channels disappeared. More and more it was the government communications centers that delivered the news, bad at best, devastating at worst. Their attempts to put a positive spin on things fell flatter and flatter. Websites became inaccessible as servers shut down from lack of maintenance or funds or people to operate them.

The group at Berk Shire downloaded information as quickly as they could, much of it survival-based, but also programs for the arts, cooking, and history and literature. It would be stored on the Konectables as well as being printed out at a later date using the cases and cases of archival paper in storage. Redundancy became the prudent norm.

Bob continued trying to get the government issued computers up and running, but without any luck. Upon hitting the on button, he kept getting the same message over and over, the now too familiar, blandly pleasant female voice repeatedly saying three words only: *Please stand by.*

Early in November, Theo and George arrived with two other cars and two box trucks following. Theo had dismantled his office and hired one of the few moving companies still in business to bring the equipment to Berk Shire. He had also brought his office staff with him: assistant, receptionist. A hygienist, a friend of the receptionist, accompanied them. Each of their boyfriends, girlfriends or spouses was either in long term care or dead.

The gathering for Thanksgiving had swollen to over a hundred and ninety people. Tables and chairs were trucked in from the cabins and set up in the great room to accommodate the entire group. All contributed to the meal in one way or another, cooking, baking, serving or cleaning up.

Michael looked at the crowd, then turned to Marcy. "For all my looking ahead, I never really considered holiday get-togethers, and certainly not of this size."

"Hey, you thought of a lot of things none of the rest of us did, but you can't think of it all," she responded. "We're probably going to have to close the gates soon. I know none of us wants to, but we can't keep up much longer. We're outgrowing ourselves too quickly. We need to meet soon, figure it out and set limits."

"You're right," he said. "I hate to say it, but we're going to have to start turning people away, and that is so against what I wanted to achieve here."

———«◉»———

The group met and looked at projections of people coming in, putting that information up against the available supplies. Thirty-eight cabins had been built and filled, with the last dozen being larger than the original ones. That used more of the timber stock they'd acquired. There was enough timber left to add an additional twenty or so cabins, some smaller, some larger, but none could be constructed until the ground unfroze sometime after the middle of March. When the owner of the timber company called Michael to tell his best and only customer that he had decided to pack it in, Michael purchased most of his equipment, including two tractor trailer rigs and a set up for a small sawmill. Without an outside source of timber, they would have to start their own logging operation.

All but four of the bedrooms in the main building were occupied. Those four were left open for guests. The dormitory set up in the basement could only support another ten or twelve people before becoming overrun. Food supply was in very good shape, especially with all twenty greenhouses adding daily to the stock.

It was decided that a colony meeting would be called.

All of this was explained to the one hundred and twenty-seven members of Berk Shire who gathered in the great room of the main building. They were asked to please curtail invitations to others still in the city areas.

Michael saw a hand go up in the back of the room.

"I have two family members and their child I'd like to invite. What if I were to put them up in my cabin? Would that be okay?" the woman asked.

Another hand went up. "My wife and I would be willing to open up our spare bedroom to another couple. Would that help?"

There were quite a number of people who vocalized their agreement with those suggestions.

Michael looked at the other members of the core group, who each shrugged, indicating they thought it was acceptable. "How many people here would be willing to do that, open up their homes to others on a temporary basis, meaning sometime between now and next May or June?" He took a count. "That would allow twenty-five or so more. That would be fine. But I will ask that any of you who are inviting others to join us to please let us know before you do so. We do not want to go past that twenty-five person mark. Are we agreed? All in favor say aye." He listened. "All opposed?" There were none in opposition.

"Then it's passed." He heard the words as they slid effortlessly from his lips. Berk Shire, in its entirety, had just had its first full member meeting and vote.

After the people had left the meeting, John asked Michael why he hadn't included the additional ten to twelve spots open in the dorm.

"We're going to get some stragglers."

"Stragglers?"

"People who sort of wander in, like the Talbots. They weren't headed here, but circumstances brought them here."

<hr>

The wedding, held in the early evening, was a well-planned affair. Michael and Marcy wrote their own vows. A Justice of the Peace from town performed the ceremony. Both had requested short and sweet. Heather stood with Marcy, John with Michael. Mica Martin, held by Chrissy, remained blissfully asleep through the whole thing.

As planned as the wedding was, the reception that followed was anything but. The organized chaos started as soon after the ceremony as it took to set the great room up for the party. The dining room was used for the buffet and bar. Four rotating shifts of volunteers manned the kitchen and wait staff duties, so that none missed the party completely.

Recorded music blasted through speakers for dancing. There were quite a number of musicians in the crowd. They gathered together, talked through a list of songs, and found enough common ground to put together a long set of rock or Irish or country music. Michael sat in for a few songs on piano, even singing one or two. It was the kind of event the neighboring area had never before witnessed, much less participated in.

The party melted seamlessly into the New Year's Eve celebration, which lasted well into the night. Though some got a little drunk, all were well-behaved. At the stroke of midnight, there was much hugging and kissing. Michael and Marcy made the rounds, wishing all the best in the coming year to anyone they met.

"Happy New Year, Ted," Michael said, offering his hand. Ted grunted something, but did not take his hand. "Lizbeth, Happy New Year," he said, moving to give her a kiss on the cheek.

Lizbeth was stuffed very tightly into a red cocktail dress, a mass of cleavage spilling out the top. She grabbed his face in both hands and kissed him full on the lips, holding on too long. He broke away from her.

"I wasn't done!" she yelled, a heavy slur in her voice.

Michael took Marcy's arm and started to walk away.

"Come back here, you bastard!"

Ted grabbed her arm and tried to direct her to the dining room.

"Paws off, Big Foot!"

She went to slap Ted, but he caught her hand inches away from his face. He held her hand there, gave her a look, then let go. She smoothed her dress down, glared at him and stormed out of the room. Ted looked back at the crowd and saw quite a few people staring at him. The angry look on his face deepened as he followed her out the door.

"She's going to blow this place apart if she keeps going like that," Marcy said.

Michael wiped his lips with the back of his hand. "I'll talk to her tomorrow when she's sober."

"No," Marcy said. "We'll all talk to her."

The conversation did not go well. At first, Lizbeth feigned not remembering what had transpired, then seemed to recall some of it. In a monotone, she said it wouldn't happen again, but showed no sign of owning what she'd done.

"I've kept this place organized, showed you how to manage people, even told you how to set up your defenses, and what do I get? I get spoken to like I'm a child. So I drank a little too much. Big deal. Everybody does that now and then."

"We are asking you to rein in the drinking, Lizbeth," Heather said. "You get going, you end up causing a scene. This is not the first time it's happened, but it needs to be the last."

Michael spoke up. "Lizbeth, you have been a big help here, and we all appreciate what you've done, but I think you need to decide how you want to move forward. If you want to stay in Berk Shire, you're going to have to change the behavior we're talking about. My suggestion is that you take a few days to think about what you want to do. Today is Tuesday. Why don't we meet again on Friday morning and talk about what you've decided to do."

"Are you asking me to leave?" Lizbeth asked, getting a little defensive.

"I'm asking you to consider if this is the place you want to call home, and if it is, are you willing to work on the drinking issue," Michael said. "I believe we're done here. We'll meet again Friday at 9:00 a.m."

She got up from her chair, looked briefly at each person in the room, then walked out without a word, leaving behind the acrid smell of disdain hanging in the air. The group sat in silence for a few moments.

"She's outlived her usefulness and welcome, as far as I'm concerned," Heather said.

"I'm hoping she packs it in," John said.

"Be careful what you wish for," Michael said.

"What do you mean?" John asked.

"Keep your friends close; keep your enemies closer," he answered.

"Oh...yeah...remember the chess games," John added.

<hr />

The group reassembled Friday morning for the meeting. Over the noise of chit-chat they heard fast footsteps approaching. Bill rushed into the room.

"They're gone! They took Ted's truck and stole Gabe Hoskins' heavy duty pickup. Left her Mercedes parked by their cabin."

Michael cursed, stood up and looked at Bill. "Check the powder room; I'll do the guns."

They hurried from the room, headed in opposite directions. The entire group, except Bob, followed Michael, who pressed his fingers on the biometric lock, opened the door and looked around. He walked quickly up and down the racks and shelves, counting to himself.

LARRY AUSTIN

"Shit!" he yelled, hurrying past the group, back to the hallway.

"How many?" Bill asked.

"At least thirty rifles, one of the air guns, a dozen handguns, maybe more. How much ammo?"

"Enough to fight a small war!"

Bob came running out of another storage room cursing and swearing. "They took two of the survival computers and ten Konectables."

"I'll bet he took bows, arrows, camo and fishing gear, tools," Michael said. "Shit! How could I have been so stupid as to not change the security access?"

"They must have been stockpiling the heavy stuff out in the back fields' area," Bill said, "then taken Gabe's truck late last night sometime. He always leaves it facing out, so no backup beepers. Ted leaves his the same way."

Michael herded them back into the conference room. "Let's think through what this means," he said.

"I think we should post sentries at the entrance," Bob said. The concern in his voice was matched by the look on his face. "I can organize enough shifts so that no one has to stay out there in the cold more than two hours at a time."

"I agree," Michael said, "but we should post at the back fields' entrance, too."

"And patrols throughout the village," Bill said.

"And shoot on sight...to kill," Marcy said.

They all looked at her.

"What?" she asked. "It's the only way to be sure. They just ripped us off big time and took a shit-load of guns. You think Ted's going to be kind and responsible if he starts firing on us?"

"She's right," Michael said. "Ted's loaded for bear. Pass out two-way headsets and put me on a shift. We also need to spread the word. Let's bring a few people in and get the news out about what's happening. They may never come back, but we need to be prepared in case they do."

"But she knows our defenses," Marcy pointed out.

"Shit! You're right. Okay, we need to figure that out and come up with other plans. Doubtful they'd come through the main road."

Bill was the one who spoke the unthinkable. "My money's on him taking pot shots at us, not necessarily to kill, but to keep us in a state of high alert, constantly looking over our shoulders. Mind you, I'd say he's capable of killing. The way she wraps her legs around him…well, let's just say he's willing to do what's asked of him. Before that fight, he told me he's just crazy in love with her, doesn't seem to mind taking the bad with the good, so who knows what he'll do."

Michael thought for a minute. "Bill, if you were a sniper, where would you set up for maximum effect?"

"Let's you and me take a walk outside, Michael, and figure that out. Goes without saying, we take rifles and pistols with us. Let's get into snow camo."

<hr />

Sentries were posted by the entrance, but were set up in hidden spots, dug in behind snow banks. A post was also set up at the dirt road leading into the fields at the far end of the property. The guard was changed every two hours to keep the sentries from getting too cold. Each shift checked in every fifteen minutes with the communications post that had been hastily set up in one of the basement rooms.

On the fourth night after Lizbeth and Ted had left, a man and a woman pulled up to take over at the back fields' post. They parked their SUV and walked to meet the guards.

"All right, guys, you can head back and get warm," the woman said.

"You bring hot coffee with you, Georgia?" the one man asked. "Temperature's dropping. You're going to need something warm."

She nodded. Her companion, Bernie, walked up next to them, held up two white blankets and a large thermos, said hello. He suddenly dropped everything and grabbed his arm.

"What's wrong?" she asked.

"My arm...it's like I got stung by a bee." He stepped into the beam of the headlights, looked at his coat, saw a rip in it. "What the...?"

Before he could finish, one of the sentries coming off duty yelled and grabbed his leg.

"Down! Down!" Georgia screamed. She scampered back to her vehicle, shut down the lights.

The others had crawled over to the car and were crouched down behind it.

"What the hell is it?" Bernie asked.

"Stan, Dave, keep a look out. Bernie, take off your jacket. Let me see," she said. She looked at the blood on Bernie's shirtsleeve. "Michael said they stole an air gun." She tapped the side of her headset and called in that they were under fire.

In less than ten minutes, Bob and two others pulled up in a van. One of the men drove the two wounded people back to the main building. Bob shined a portable flood light in the direction they thought the pellets had come from.

Michael drove his truck slowly along the stretch of road just outside the back fields' entrance, with Bill shining a high-intensity, handheld flood lamp back and forth along the road. Its beam of light threw close to one hundred feet into the woods. A second vehicle followed closely behind, shining its light onto the other side of the road. They both stopped a quarter mile down the road.

"Didn't really expect to find them, did you?" Bill asked.

"Guess not," Michael answered. He asked the people in the second truck to keep patrolling the same stretch for another hour, then return to the building. "Let's talk to Georgia and her crowd, see what went on."

She filled them in on what she knew, which was almost nothing. The guard was doubled to four. Each was given a night scope. Portable floodlights were brought in and kept on all night.

The following day Bill and a dozen others scoured the area within a half mile of the back fields' entrance, but found no trace that anyone had been in there. Bill told Michael that Ted had probably done that at Lizbeth's suggestion, as a way of putting some fear into their hearts. Michael thought that was likely true, but added that he thought it was Ted's way of saying fuck you and goodbye.

"Let's hope you're right," Bill said.

The core group sat in the great room of the main lodge. A typical evening, they chatted with each other, fussed over Mica Martin and sipped hot chocolate. Bob was playing with one of the government issued computers, a nightly ritual he went through to check if the annoyingly pleasant female voice had changed her tune. Unlike previous nights, the message had changed. The voice now simply repeated two words: *Stand by. Stand by. Stand by. Stand by.* This message, such as it was, repeated every five seconds.

"Hey, guys, something's happening here," he said. They gathered around him, staring at the small screen.

Stand by. Stand by. Stand. Silence. The screen flickered to life. An image of the President of the United States appeared. Dark circles under her eyes shone through a layer of makeup. Yvonne Taylor was a black woman of thirty-eight, who, at thirty-two, had become the youngest vice president elected, just one year after the minimum age had been reduced by amendment. She looked scared, exhausted, crushed. She had been the vice president for the first two years of the president's term. His suicide, shortly after his wife had died from the illness, moved her up into the driver's seat. Elections had been suspended a year after that on the grounds that any further change in administration would be too disruptive while the battle with the disease continued.

Taylor cleared her throat, tried in vain to project something approaching presidential composure, and started speaking. "This computer you are now watching was issued by the federal government to be used in the event that the unthinkable happened. We are no longer able to govern this once great nation. There are too few people left to man communications, maintain equipment, run the government, or protect the country. I am shocked to have to say this to you, but you are now on your own.

"This message was pre-recorded and downloaded into your computer on the first of January, 2041, in anticipation of this day. A fail-safe switch was set to trip and activate this device when, for whatever reason, the government was forced to shut down. Programmed into this device is a search program. When turned on, it will automatically connect you to specially equipped satellites that contain information that can help you survive. That information includes how to fish, hunt and trap animals, clean and cook what you catch, how to grow food, forage for food in the woods and fields, build shelter, make fire, and much, much more."

She drew in a breath. Letting it out, she tried to hide her anxiety.

"The state of the rest of the world is no different. Some foreign governments may survive a little longer, but they will eventually fall and anarchy will prevail, just as it has come to prevail in many of this country's major cities over the past few months. Without enough manpower to maintain order, there is no longer anything we can do to stop this, so we have prepared these devices in the hope that they will help the people who are left to survive and maybe even thrive some day. And perhaps, sometime in the future, you will resurrect this government." A tear slid slowly from her left eye. "Good luck to you, and may God help us all." The camera stayed on for a few seconds. She looked beyond it and said, "Turn it off, please!"

The screen went blank.

Michael checked his Konectable. "The 'net's gone. Nothing, no signal."

"Cells are down, too" Heather said. "Dead. It's like everything just shut off all at the same time."

They looked around at each other, all wondering what to do. Michael broke the silence. "Sound the bell for a gathering. Quickly. Let's get everyone together."

The meeting started thirty minutes later. Michael made the announcement. Even though they had come to Berk Shire because they had believed this day would come, all sat silently in shock at the news of its arrival. They looked around at each other as the information sank in. Tears streaked the faces of many in the room.

Michael looked around, sensed the despair. He broke the silence. "People! We all knew this would happen one day, and that day has now come. We have prepared for many months, some of us for years, learned all sorts of survival skills, built shelters that are comfortable. We have come together as a community, a colony that works together for the common goal of surviving what has now transpired."

He looked around the crowd. "We have many memories to look back on, as the life we knew moves on." He raised his voice up. "But now is the time not only to reflect back but to also look forward as we forge ahead to meet this challenge together! WE WILL STAND STRONG, TOGETHER! WE WILL SURVIVE, TOGETHER! AND WE WILL THRIVE TOGETHER IN THIS PLACE WE CALL BERK SHIRE!"

The crowd stood as one, clapping their hands and whistling their approval. Someone started up a chant of *Berk Shire! Berk Shire!* The entire group joined in.

Marcy stood up, holding Mica Martin in her arms, and moved next to Michael. "Good job," she said. The baby, wide awake, looked at the crowd and smiled.

⸻ ✹ ⸻

Bob and Marcy spent the next few days exploring what was available via the new devices. They turned on a few of the other computers, got President Taylor's message again. Both quickly concluded that what the government had put together was not going to be easy to use.

"It's a mess," Bob said. "It's like the person who programmed it was just learning code. I can't begin to tell you how disorganized it is! The search feature sucks! It's like a five year old put it together. Well, maybe that's not being too kind to the five year olds of the world. It's like they put it together in a mad rush, without any thought, any logic, and then nobody checked to see if it actually made sense."

"I'll tell you what I think happened," Marcy said. "I think they were way more focused on getting as much info into the databases as possible than they were focused on how well it worked. Info came in much faster than they could catalog it."

"Government S.O.P.," Michael said. "Can you two figure it out?"

"Yes, but the bigger question is how many years it will take to figure out. Anyone who has one may starve to death before they get any useful information from it. We can't move the data - no programming for that - it's all satellite to RAM. That's it. So we're stuck with how it does what it does. I can start an index on one of the 'tabs, basically create a directory on one to understand the directory of the other. We'll have to keep cross referencing whenever we need info. What a pain in the ass!"

Michael pointed out that they had been downloading information for the past year and a half. "So we may be a little better prepared than many. Keep working on it."

Marcy rolled her eyes, pushed her computer away and got up. She took Michael's hand and tugged him toward the door. "I need to walk," she said, "and I'd love to get some hot cider or something."

They headed upstairs to the kitchen. She asked him how Heather was doing with the baby. He said she was basking in the job.

"She just loves it. I'll bet she and Bob start trying pretty soon."

"I know she wants kids down the road," Marcy said. "I wonder if Bob's able."

<hr />

Bob explained his frustration with not being able to print out from the survival computer, and asked if they could look around the colony for a computer hardware expert who might be able to hook up a printer port.

"I don't really want to make these devices known to anyone else for the time being," Michael said. "It could be dangerous. A lot of people might want to use them, which could lead to breakage. We've also only got eighteen left and, considering that the government built them, we have no idea how long they'll actually last. Others might decide they should have one and *that* could cause problems."

"Gotcha," Bob said. "Makes sense."

"There's so much we don't know," Michael mused.

"And don't have! If John were here, he'd be on about needing agave to make tequila."

"Working on it," Michael said. "I believe that when things start to settle down, people are going to start trucking stuff in from all over, looking to trade."

"I hope you're right. There's an awful lot I'd miss that comes from other places."

"Goes for all of us," Michael said. "For what it's worth, it's starting to snow pretty hard. You figure out how to get weather on those things?"

"That's one of the only things we've been able to decipher," Bob said. "Can't find how to grow anything, but we'll know the weather will be just fine for crops. I wondered why they were doing this via satellites. To me it would have made more sense just to load the information onto the hard drives, but weather needs to be in real time." He brought up the weather program and pulled up a satellite image of the sky above them.

Marcy, sitting nearby, kept moving her fingers over the screen, tapping every now and then.

"Big storm," Bob said.

"There's a part of the program set up to give the likely forecast in our area," Marcy said. "The computer locks into the area in which it's being used and then filters it through a predictive analytics program. At least they did that right. Cool, here's a five-day. Twenty to twenty-five inches likely starting later today and lasting through late tomorrow evening, then a twenty-four hour break before the next front comes through and drops another foot. Shit, that is a big set of storms. We should probably spread the word and prepare."

Michael nodded and left the room. He put on his parka, hat and gloves and went out the back door toward Bill's cabin, alerted him to the amount of snow that would be coming down and asked what needed to be done.

"Down at Wayne's...get the animals into their pens, some feed on the henhouse floor, cows to the barnyard so we have access to them for milking - hurts them when they don't get milked. We should also position the plowing vehicles around the neighborhood so plowing's easier. We'll want to be plowing every path we'll need every two or three hours, so we'll need night coverage. Let's assign drivers and routes. The best move is to stay ahead of the snow. Let's start knocking on doors and tell those on the crews to meet in the machine shop ASAP so we can make a plan."

A half hour later, Bill was giving out assignments while Michael spoke to the people at Wayne's farm on a two-way hand held radio. The crew of twenty-five Berk Shire workers moved out. Tractors and backhoes were moved into position. The three trucks that had been set up for plowing were moved to the front and rear of the main building for use on the roads leading into the compound and behind it into the neighborhood areas. A separate crew was instructed to go to each of the cabins and alert the residents as to what was going on. Those who did not have shovels were instructed to pick one up at the machine shop. Extra firewood was brought inside the newer cabins that did not yet have electric heat installed.

As Michael walked back to the main house, he felt the same excitement he'd felt as a little kid when a hard snow started falling. It was the gateway to an adventure. He savored this feeling with his whole being. Gradually he started to realize the feeling was not just about the snow, but about what they all were doing. It was like something he had fantasized about when he was eight or nine, being on his own out in a storm, having to survive on his own, find food, make fire, fend against wild animals. Except…this was for real.

"Hey," he said quietly as he entered the bedroom.

Marcy, who was lying in bed, smiled and told him to get into his pajamas and join her. He propped a pillow up against the headboard and climbed in next to her, gave her a kiss.

The bed faced the window on the front of the building. The curtains were open. She shut off the light on the nightstand. The snow, falling heavily, was shimmering in the beam from the nearest outside security light. Every now and then a gust of wind whipped it sideways before letting it drop straight down again.

"Isn't it beautiful?" she asked, slipping her hand into his.

"It's incredible," he said. "And the best part is that there's no school tomorrow!"

She laughed. "Yeah, right: like you're going to have the day off."

"I've got the 8:00 shift on a plow and that's it."

She nodded in the direction of the baby. "Our little alarm clock will go off sometime around 6:00, so you'll be up in plenty of time. And I'll be happy to fix you a big breakfast after I give him his."

"Ready for lights out?" he asked, getting up to close the curtains.

—————«❍»—————

The first storm dumped almost thirty inches of snow on the area. It was powdery and light, a boon to those shoveling and plowing. Michael drove one of the smaller plowing vehicles through his four designated neighborhoods. He honked his horn at the kids playing in the snow, as they tried to make snowballs without any luck. Some of them tossed handfuls of the powder at him as he went by.

As he finished his two-hour shift, he parked his plow and called Marcy on the two-way, letting her know he'd be back at the main building in a few minutes. When he arrived, she escorted him into the great room to a chair by the roaring fire. She had a mug of hot cider waiting for him.

"So now you've got the rest of the day off?" she asked.

"I guess it'll be as close to a day off as I will ever...."

His two-way crackled to life. "Bill here, Michael. Just wanted you to know that one of the plows went down just outside the Hillsdale neighborhood. Over."

"Can you fix it? Over."

"I can't. Not here, anyway. I'm going to have to haul it in to the machine shop. I've got Jasper going back there now to get a tow strap. Over."

Michael looked at Marcy and rolled his eyes. "Okay. Out."

"I'm guessing it won't be much of a day...." Marcy said.

The two-way crackled again. "Michael, Jerry here. We might have a big problem in the Meadowlark section. I think you might want to come out here now. Over."

"Roger that, Jerry. Out," he said. He looked at Marcy, chugged down his cider, kissed her and the baby and put his parka back on. "So much for a snow day."

"Hey, you wanted to build a colony," she said.

"I'll call you when I'm done."

"Do what you've got to do. We're not going anywhere."

<hr/>

Early February brought another kind of storm. Two vans pulled onto the main street of Warren, turned around and parked in the middle of the road. Ten men got out, some holding hunting rifles, some with handguns. They quickly split up into twos and started entering the closest stores, including Bert's general store. Bert was emptying the last of the boxes of food stuffs from the last delivery a week before things had shut down. He looked up just as the men entered. One was about five-eight, with dark hair, the other around six foot and balding in the middle of his scalp. Neither had shaved or showered in at least a week. Their smell was as nasty as their look.

"Face down on the floor, motherfucker!" the dark haired one screamed, waving a 10mm pistol in Bert's face.

"Yes, sir," Bert said in a loud voice, dropping down flat.

"Why are you yelling?"

"I'm pretty deaf. Don't know how loud...."

"Shut up! You got boxes behind that counter?"

"Some. Some bags, too."

"You got any ammo?"

"No, sir. Been a helluva run on that the last month or so."

"Start loading up, Jackson. You move, pal and you're dead! You hear me?"

"Yes, sir," Bert said loudly. "Not moving."

Jackson started stripping the shelves, jamming things messily into the half dozen boxes he'd found.

"Storeroom?" the other asked.

"Empty. This is the last of it," Bert said, the volume of his voice still up.

"Where is it? I wanna check."

"Downstairs. Nothing there."

"Where's the entrance?"

"Outside...out back. But I'm telling you, there's nothing…." He was practically yelling.

"Shut the fuck up!" the man yelled back. "You move, Jackson here shoots. Got it?"

"Yes, sir. I'm not moving."

The man walked through the side door to the alley and headed to the back corner of the building. Bert put his ear against the floor, heard footsteps going down the stairs. He hoped Jimmy would be sensible, not put up a fight. When the sound on the stairs stopped, he heard a slight thump followed by a voice yelling *Shit*!

Jackson heard it, too. He waited a few seconds, then yelled, "Barry? You all right?"

"Yeah," came back a muffled voice.

A few minutes later a car horn sounded and they both heard footsteps on the basement stairs.

"Barry! Hurry up! Time to go!" Jackson yelled. The man heard footsteps approaching the side door and turned just in time to see the flash coming out of a double barreled shotgun. He went down, blood pouring out his chest.

Jimmy looked at the scene in front of him. A look of shock came over his face. The enormity of what he had done crashed over him.

Stunned, he just stood there, frozen.

Bert lay there for only a second before jumping up, knowing that the others in Jackson's group would probably be coming through the door any second. He saw Jimmy's face.

"Jimmy! JIMMY!!! LOOK AT ME! NOW!" he screamed. Jimmy shook his head sharply at the sound of Bert's voice. His eyes focused. "We've got to go. Now!"

Jimmy tossed him the shotgun and a box of shells, stepped out the door and grabbed a second twelve gauge he'd brought up from the basement.

"Let's go," Bert said as he ran into the alley and headed to the back. He turned right. They ran along the back alley toward the end of the row of buildings. "They're gonna head back out the way they came in, Jimmy. Fire one barrel at the lead van's windshield, the other at the second van. Then fall back and reload as quickly as you can. When they start coming out of the vans, I'll let 'em have it with both barrels. Toss me your rifle and reload mine. Stay back! I don't want you getting hurt!"

"Got it," Jimmy said. He emptied his box of shells into his shirt and pants pockets and pushed Barry's 10mm handgun a little further into his waistband.

"Okay, I can hear them. Here they come. Ready. Not yet…a little longer. Now!"

Jimmy stepped out and squeezed one trigger; the buckshot shattered the windshield of the first van. It skidded to a halt. The second van was about twenty feet back. He let them have the other barrel, then fell back behind the corner of the end building and reloaded.

Bert waited until he heard the van door open, stepped forward just slightly and fired both barrels. They switched guns. Bert fired a second time. The thieves started firing in their direction.

Bert stepped back, looked at Jimmy. "You ready? Kneel down; you'll be a smaller target. If they're side by side, you take the one on the left. And one barrel at a time."

They heard men running towards them, then the sound of gun-fire that was from further away. Two men ran into view of the alley opening, firing pistols. Bert and Jimmy fired at the same time. Both men went down. They waited for the next bunch, but they didn't come. Bert heard a building door slam shut.

"Stay here," Bert said. He knelt down and stuck his head around the corner. He saw five men hunkered down by the second van, fir-ing toward the other side of the street. Bert realized that some of the other townsfolk had joined in the shootout. He opened his gun, popped out both shells, put two more in. He saw Jimmy do-ing the same.

Then it dawned on him what the shutting door meant.

"Cover our asses," he said to the boy, pointing to the back end of the alley. "One or two might be coming that way."

Bert stepped out slightly from his cover and fired one barrel at the men by the right end of the van. He saw one go down and an-other grab his arm as buckshot ripped into him. As he brought the shotgun to bear on another man, he heard Jimmy fire both barrels. He turned and saw a second man aiming at the boy. He fired the second barrel and watched the man get flipped around by the power of the blast, finally hitting the ground.

"He's still twitching, Jimmy. Hit him again, now!"

Jimmy pulled the 10mm from his waistband and fired two shots, both hitting their mark.

"Reload, fast! There might be more that way!"

Suddenly there was silence. Bert waited a few seconds before poking his head around the corner of the building. He saw four men he knew walking towards the van from across the street, their rifles aimed at the men. The two outsiders had their hands behind their heads. Bert saw that each man had a gun in his hand.

"MATTHEW!" he screamed at the top of his lungs, hoping his

friends across the street would listen. "GET DOWN NOW!"

He tried to move so that his neighbors were out of his line of fire. The four residents started to drop. As they did, both men brought their handguns over their shoulders. Bert fired his first barrel. One man fell to the ground. The other turned. Bert pulled the second trigger. The hammer flicked forward, but the gun didn't fire. The man drew down on him.

"Shit," Bert muttered under his breath.

Four shots rang out. The man's arm dropped as he fired his pistol, its bullet pounding into the ground. Bert turned to see Jimmy standing behind him, 10mm in hand, the tip of the gun smoking.

He walked over to the boy, asked him if he were all right, got no answer. Jimmy stood there for a few seconds, gun still aimed at the dead man. Bert gently took the pistol from his hands, put the safety on and dropped it and his shotgun to the ground. He put one arm on Jimmy's shoulder, then the other. The boy stared blankly at him from somewhere else, a look of shock covering his face. His eyes started to focus. His face scrunched up as he started to sob. Bert held him and let him cry.

Despite all attempts to reach the world outside the compound by way of any communications devices, there was no response, no emergency broadcast system spewing out instructions so that people would know what to do, no comline news programs showing what was going on, no experts telling how things would go, no cell phone connections. There were certainly people out there, but there was no way to talk to them.

The townies, as they called themselves, became an integral part of Berk Shire. Food and supplies were shared so that no one went hungry. Many expressed their desire to move into the safety of the compound, but expansion limits had been set. A meeting in mid-February, with most of the people from town, became a time for ideas to be discussed on how to bring them into the fold as quickly as possible. Houses would be dismantled and cannibalized to make new buildings. The local well-digger would start sinking new wells throughout the area to accommodate the new residents' needs. Michael's original five hundred acre farm grew to over six thousand as the adjacent farms were assimilated into the new colony.

————)((•))(————

Jimmy drove into the compound in his shiny new truck and sought out Michael. He handed him a five pound bag of yellow cubanelle pepper seeds.

"Bert got this in just before things shut down. Figured you'd want to get some seedlings started."

"Jimmy, I appreciate it, but I'm betting you didn't drive all the way out here just to deliver a bag of seeds. What's up?"

The boy dropped his head down, shuffled his feet a bit. "I've never really done this before, never really had to, but times are different now, so here goes. You once told me that if there was ever anything you could do for me that I should ask."

Michael smiled and said, "Ask."

"Could Bert and me move in here soon? He's hasn't been himself since those men came into town. He's not saying anything outright, but I know he's getting worried that more outsiders are going to start coming through the area. He talks about it a lot and he says it ain't gonna be good."

Michael put his hand on Jimmy's shoulder. "We have an opening upstairs. Can the two of you room together until we can get a cabin ready?"

Jimmy finally looked up at Michael and smiled. "No problem. Thanks, Michael. Thanks a lot. I really appreciate this. I know it's a big favor to ask, and I'm sorry, but I know Bert would be shy about asking."

"Well, I'm glad you weren't shy about taking me up on my offer for a favor. Now, would you like to join me, Marcy and Mica Martin for lunch? She's in the kitchen heating up a big pot of chicken soup."

Michael took him into the kitchen to wash up. Jimmy greeted Marcy. Mica Martin, playing on the floor a little ways away from her, looked up and flashed a wet smile at the teen. He got up, did his drunken sailor walk over to them, faced Jimmy and put his arms out to be picked up.

Jimmy looked at Michael, who nodded his okay. He scooped Mica up into his arms and gave him a big hug, then held him out a bit.

"You are getting so big, Mica Martin! So big!"

"You know Jimmy," Marcy said.

"Eemy."

"Joining us?" she asked.

"If that's okay," Jimmy said, blushing a little.

"Of course it is. Wash up. It's almost ready. Michael, would you set another place?"

Michael announced Jimmy's plan. They talked about what he'd like to be a part of in Berk Shire, explored some of the things he might get into. The teen seemed drawn to the business end of the colony, but let them know he would also work in the fields or greenhouses if they wanted. He was eager to please and eager to get started, said he hoped he and Bert could be in the week after next, maybe sooner.

He spent an hour or so after lunch playing with Mica Martin. As he was putting on his coat to leave, the child started to cry.

"Don't worry, I'll be back real soon, and then we can play more."

He gave Mica a hug, kissed him on the forehead and handed him off to Marcy. "I don't know if you need a sitter, but I'd be happy to help out with him. It's kinda fun. I used to entertain the little kids who came into the store with their parents, you know, when they were talking to Bert."

"Well, he certainly likes you a lot, and I think you're very good with him," Marcy said, touching the sleeve of his coat. "We'd be happy to have you spend time with him. There's so much going on here that getting a break now and then would be quite welcome."

"Deal," Jimmy said.

"He is so sweet," she said to Michael after he'd left.

———=«()»=———

First contact from the outside world came in the form of a military All Personnel Carrier which arrived at the entrance to Berk Shire the first week of March. The sentries, who had become a regular fixture over the winter, alerted the communications person at the main building, who sounded the two bell warning. Each person in the compound knew his or her assignment and moved into position quickly.

The APC pulled up to the front door of the main building. Twelve soldiers in full combat gear got out, positioned themselves to cover multiple directions, weapons at the ready. One pulled out a small, but powerful bullhorn and demanded the leader show himself.

The small front door opened slowly, allowing Michael, unarmed, to walk out to face these men. He stood just outside the doorway for a moment before approaching the one who appeared to be in charge. The man was about five-eight, had a few day's growth on his face and an intensity in his eyes. He looked at the man's face, figured he was maybe all of twenty-two or -three. He checked out the stripes on the man's uniform, then moved about ten feet from him.

"Sergeant," he said, bowing his head slightly. "What can I do for you?"

The man stared at Michael for a few long moments before answering. "We have been ordered to secure this area, including all buildings, supplies and equipment for government use, sir!"

Michael stared at the man for a few moments before responding. "And where did these orders come from, Sergeant?"

"My commander, sir. We have been ordered to...."

"And where is your commander at this time, Sergeant?"

The man shifted from one foot to the other. "Back at the command center, sir."

"And the command center is where, exactly?"

"We have been ordered...."

"I'm going to raise my right hand up, Sergeant. Is that okay with you?"

The man just stared. Michael slowly raised his right hand over his head. Four of the soldiers raised their weapons at him.

"Sergeant, if one of your men shoots me or my hand drops without a certain amount of fingers having been extended for a certain amount of time, all of you will be cut down before I hit the ground. Hidden in the area around you, I have ten men with assault rifles similar to yours and five more with bolt-action thirty-thirties with hunting scopes."

Three of the other soldiers raised their weapons at Michael. The other four started to look around them, pointing their weapons in different directions.

"I don't believe you have any men hiding around here, sir. I think you're just one person with a few others inside and you're bluffing."

Michael looked directly at the sergeant and smiled. "Then I guess we're playing poker and you're calling my bluff. Tell you what: how about I up the ante, Sergeant. I'll tell you where one of my men is hiding and I'll call *your* play. Look to your left, about nine o'clock. Okay, now look back into the woods about a hundred feet. You'll see a bunch of pines tightly grouped together, but one of them is a lot thicker than the others. What do you see tight to the side of the tree? That's right: a man in white camo with one of those bolt action babies pointed in your direction. That's Bill from Wyoming. Cowboy, hunter, crackerjack shot. And most likely, his aim is now on you."

The sergeant stared at the man next to the tree, saw his aim was true. His eyes shifted back and forth as he tried to think of what the right move was. Despite the chill in the air, beads of sweat started to form on his forehead.

"So you've got one man with a rifle. There are twelve of us," he said.

"Sergeant, I could go on revealing other rifles pointed at you and your men, but my arm is getting awfully tired, and I still don't have any fingers extended to signal my people what to do. You want to go on playing poker, you go right ahead," Michael said very calmly. "I'm going to lower my arm, and that signals them to shoot. Now I could get all dramatic and give you a count of three, but I'm really much too tired to do that. Are you ready?" He started to move his arm down slightly.

"Wait!" the sergeant yelled.

"For what?" Michael asked, holding his arm steady.

The sergeant's mouth opened but he didn't answer. It was clear he had no next move in mind.

"Sergeant, let me ask you a question. When was the last time you had a decent meal and a warm place to sleep?" Michael asked in a smooth, soothing voice.

"Huh?"

"It really is a simple question: when was the last time you had a decent meal and a warm place to sleep?"

The man looked around at his men, his eyes still wild. The sweat that had formed on his forehead started to drip off his brow. "Uh...uh...about a week ago, sir."

"Look at me, Sergeant," Michael directed. "Take a breath and try to relax a bit. Would you like to join us for dinner? We're having beef stew with lots of vegetables, and we're also having cornbread - made from scratch and freshly baked. You can also have a hot shower if you'd like."

The look on the man's face was one of seriousness about the food and confusion about the offer. His mouth opened slightly, his tongue showed just inside his lips. It moved slightly as if he was tasting the stew.

"I'm serious, Sergeant. You and your men are welcome to join us for dinner. How about you tell your men to stand down and I'll tell mine the same thing."

His eyes welled up. He didn't move.

"This is a new situation for all of us," Michael said. "It's confusing and chaotic and we're all in survival mode, but we have no interest in violence or confrontation. You don't have to trick us into giving you food, and you certainly don't have to take it at gunpoint. Please, join us for dinner. We'll all sit down like rational people and break bread - freshly baked cornbread - just like it used to be. What do you say?"

A single tear dropped from one eye, ran down his cheek. He looked at his men and nodded. They lowered their weapons.

Michael extended five fingers, held his arm there for a few moments, turning in various directions, then lowered it slowly. "Come on inside and get warm. I will ask that you leave your weapons in the outer room. Come on in. You are welcome here."

The sergeant stood frozen where he was. Michael walked over to him and extended his hand. "I'm Michael Macalister."

The man slowly raised his hand and shook Michael's. He sniffled a few times, then said, "Sergeant...uh, Robert Cox."

"Pleased to meet you, Robert. Follow me…all of you." Michael turned and led the way to the entry foyer.

The men put their weapons on the floor there, then followed him in through the small door. As they entered the living room they turned and looked all around. They didn't expect what they saw. There were twenty or so people there looking back at them, ten with weapons raised.

Michael gave the signal for them to lower their guns. "Sound the bell to stand down. These men will be our guests for whatever time they choose to stay. How far are we from dinner? About an hour? Robert, why don't you and your men take off whatever gear you want to take off, then wash the road off of you. John? Bob? Could you get them what they need? Show them to the basement showers. Thanks. Gentlemen, when you're cleaned up, come join us for a drink before dinner."

When the men had left the room, Marcy came over to him and gave him a hug. "I'm so glad you're all right! Next time let someone else do that, damn it."

"Sorry, but it had to be me."

"Well, I guess I know that. Anyway, you were amazing. You didn't even flinch when they aimed at you," she said.

"And now I'm shaking like a leaf," he said, holding up a hand.

"Come on, I'll buy the first round," she said, grabbing him by the arm and leading him into the dining room.

The soldiers had stripped off all their military hardware, but remained in their combat fatigues. They were of various heights and complexions. All were in top shape, and all had taken the opportunity to shower and shave. Some seemed a little suspicious of the situation, while others relaxed into it.

Robert introduced his men. Michael introduced the people who were in the dining room. He led them to the table in the corner that held the various types of beverages available. He also told them there was beer in the kitchen refrigerator just inside the swinging doors.

Michael, Bob and John brought food in from the kitchen and set it up on the long dining table. He told the soldiers it would be served family style and that they were welcome to help themselves to whatever and however much they wanted.

"So tell us what happened to you guys," Michael said.

"We lost contact with command all of sudden, about six weeks ago. We were told it might happen and had been given previous instructions to return to base ASAP," Robert explained. "We headed back, took us two full days. A bunch of roads were blocked from accidents and abandoned vehicles. We had to go through the main section of Peabody. It was the shortest way there. That's when we hit the first mob. They came at us, not a big deal because the APC is heavy, built to take a lot of shit. But they surrounded us, like bees swarming a hive. We didn't want to hurt any of them, but they wouldn't let up. Then we started taking fire and I was thinking this is bad. So I got on the loudspeaker and told them we were moving forward whether they got out of the way or not. Must've run over damn near a dozen of them. After that we kept the pedal to the metal." He took a breath and a gulp of beer.

"The base was five miles outside of town. We got there and it was pretty much empty except for a few men, mostly drunk out of their minds. Two were reasonable and joined up with us. They told us the federal government had shut down, like, just stopped being. Didn't make much sense to us. I mean, we were waiting for orders, man."

"Orders that never came," Michael said.

"Word was another mob was on the other side of the base headed our way. They'd gotten into storage and had guns and grenade launchers, shoulder packs - you know, the serious shit that could take us out, so we just hightailed it as fast as we could. Didn't even stay long enough to stock up on MREs or anything."

"MREs?" Heather asked.

"Oh: meals ready to eat. Freeze dried shit. Actually pretty tasty. I mean, not like this, ma'am. This is real home cooking," he said, spooning in a mouthful of stew.

"I saw a couple of men way back, like a hundred yards or so, running after us. I think they were friendlies, but we couldn't stop. If we got hit with one of those grenades, we'd've been hurting something awful."

He went on to explain that they had headed away from the city. They put it to a vote and decided that the more remote the place, the better. One of the men knew this area a bit, had had a friend in Stoughton, some hundred miles away. The glitch in their plan was that they had almost no equipment to cook with and no refrigeration. They tried asking for food at some of the houses they passed, but a lot of people said they only had enough for themselves. A few gave them some bread or cooked meat, some invited them in for a meal, but mostly they got turned away. That's when they came up with *going official.*

"We did the show of strength thing, like someone was still in control out there. We found that most people wanted to believe the government's still running the show. It was like they felt safe with us there. Then I'd pretend we'd gotten new orders and we'd move on."

"And you ended up here," John said.

"We really didn't know what else to do, sir. We're not criminals or anything. We're just good people in a bad situation. But things will be okay again when the government reorganizes and gets things started again."

The others looked at Michael, deferring to him to respond. Michael took a sip of his drink. "It is very unlikely the government will re-form itself, Robert. Very, very unlikely."

Robert looked at Michael in disbelief, then at the rest of the people at the table. His eyes showed something between fear and confusion. "Wait…you're saying it's over?"

Michael nodded his head slightly. "Sorry, but yes."

"So what happens now?"

"A period of chaos, anarchy, mobs, groups that run around trying to take what they need. Right now, it all comes down to survival, and people will do whatever they need to do to survive - steal, kill, band together if it makes sense…maybe even if it doesn't. People had gotten pretty dependent on knowing that if they couldn't figure it out, the government would step in and make it work. Someone would tell them what to do. Bottom line is we're all on our own now."

"But this place…I mean, it's so organized…you knew what to do when we showed up."

Michael explained how Berk Shire was put together piece by piece, organized by a small bunch who kept trying to think ahead. He gave credit to the others, talking about what each of them had brought to the table and how bringing others in made them stronger and more secure.

John cleared his throat loudly. The table faced him.

"What Michael isn't telling you is that he saw all this happening way before any of us ever thought of it as a possibility. He was already buying land, building this place before any of us signed on to join him. He has led us in a quest to make survival more likely, and certainly more comfortable," he said, raising his glass in salute.

The soldiers were invited to stay the night and were set up in the dormitory in the basement. They got clean bedding, pillows and cots, and were told they had free run of the compound, though it was suggested they take Bob or John with them if they strayed from the main building much. Michael told them that until word got around that they were guests, the other residents might be a little distrustful.

Michael called the group together before bed to discuss the merits of inviting the soldiers to stay on. He pointed out that they offered a skill set not yet known in Berk Shire, a skill set that could be the backbone of a defense program. He also reminded the others of the ten or twelve spots that had been left open for any surprise guests.

In the morning, just after breakfast, the core group met with the soldiers and put forth the offer. The unit was given a chance to talk it over privately amongst themselves. After ten or fifteen minutes, they returned to the dining area and accepted. With one exception, they were all smiling. The exception was a man of Native American descent.

Michael pulled Robert aside and said, "That man there doesn't seem too happy about the decision to stay."

Robert informed Michael that Bobby Ray had never smiled the entire time he had known him, but they could tell he was happy with the decision. He added that they all felt like they had a purpose again.

<hr />

By mid-spring, over two hundred acres had been plowed and planted. Many more hens were put in with the roosters, larger pens were built. Another bull was allowed to grow, and more of the milkers were allowed to go into heat, keeping the old bull very busy. Wayne's herd of lambs was increased greatly, with new ones being born every few weeks. None would be taken for food until the herd had doubled in size. The wool was sheared and spun to be used for weaving material. More parties were sent out hunting and fishing, bringing in deer, rabbits, trout and salmon. Bobby Ray asked to be part of these groups and always seemed to come back with game.

Care was taken to move around to different streams and lakes and hunting grounds.

Conservation was an appreciated factor. They had watched the oceans get over-fished in the past century, with more and more fish having to be produced by way of aquaculture as the wild fisheries had collapsed. They were determined not to repeat the same mistakes.

In May a large area was dug out for a pond. It was cut out from an area close enough to be convenient, but far enough away from the cabins to compensate for the noise that would be created. A few groups were sent out to surrounding lakes and ponds to capture frogs and bring in lily pads, as well as catfish. This was inspired by something they had stumbled upon on the survival computer that touted the nutrition frogs legs could provide. Catfish was already a known source of protein, and the two seemed to work well together in a pond setting. It was estimated that the pond would start producing food the following spring.

Parties were sent out in vehicles to search out potential new hunting grounds and waters. Each was given enough weaponry to defend themselves. These weapons were kept out of sight so as not to upset any people met along the road. Protocols were developed by the soldiers to help insure the safety of those exploring. One was to have a soldier, dressed in civilian clothes, with every expedition. Another was not talking about Berk Shire, only referring to it as a small group of people trying to survive together.

None of the explorers encountered any hostility. Those they met on the road included farmers and people of small towns who had good survival skills to start with, and although they encountered small groups that had banded together in compounds that had been built, none came close to the size of Berk Shire. All were registered on a Konectable with directions and approximate coordinates. As usual, Michael was planning ahead, thinking about trade opportunities that might arise when things settled down.

In the beginning of July, on a warm morning, Heather and Bob asked if Marcy and Michael would please join them for a short walk.

The couple led them to a path that was much less traveled than others. There was some chitchat, but there was a slight charge to Heather's and Bob's energy.

"So, I guess we're alone enough to put it out there," Heather said. "We have been so happy taking care of Mica Martin since the beginning. We'd always talked about having kids, but between his career and mine, we kept managing to put it off. And, well…Bob, why don't you take it from here."

Bob looked at the sky for a few seconds before speaking. "We want to have a baby, but Heather tested me and it's not going to happen. I can't. So…so…"

Heather put her hand on Bob's arm. "I'm just going to spit it out," she said, looking at Michael. "We want to know if you'd consider being the donor." She turned to Marcy. "But it has to be all right with both of you. It has the potential to be a little weird, but, hell, we're in a pretty weird situation anyhow, making it up as we go along. And I really don't want the donor to be someone I don't know. We're not exactly set up for in vitro conception, and just scooping sperm in isn't so reliable, so our best bet is the old fashioned way."

Both Michael and Marcy stopped in their tracks, mouths slightly agape. She looked at him. He looked back, searching for some clue as to what she was thinking. She gave him a slight smile, then a peck on the lips.

"Maybe I'm jumping ahead here, but we're honored," she said, slipping her arm around Michael's waist. "However, I have to know if you're both really on board with this, not just one of you."

Bob spoke first. "We've talked about this for over a month, going back and forth. Our main concern is that our relationship with you guys stays the same. I guess *we're* concerned that *you* both be on board."

Marcy smiled and laughed a bit. "I remember when I first went to Michael about getting pregnant. It seemed so out there, and we talked about our concerns for our relationship getting messed up, but it didn't…obviously. Give us a little time to talk it over, make sure we're both all right with this."

<hr />

Two weeks later, Michael and Heather sat together in one of the last spare bedrooms, going through the same awkwardness he and Marcy had experienced. They clinked their glasses and downed their drinks, the second in about ten minutes.

"This is so weird," she said.

"And our respective spouses are out on the veranda having a drink together," Michael said. "I wonder what they're talking about."

"Don't know and don't care," Heather said. "We've got a job to do, that's it. I'm not concerned about having an orgasm. I just want you to inseminate me. So if you'll go in the bathroom and get yourself ready, I'll hop into bed and do the same. Agreed? All right, then, I'll give you a call when I'm ready."

A few minutes later she called to him. He walked into the room naked to find her lying on the bed, her nightgown hiked slightly above her waist. She looked at his flaccid penis.

"A little too clinical?" she asked. "Sorry."

"Me, too," Michael said, looking down.

She smiled and put a finger to her lips, stood up, slipped out of her nightgown and tossed it to the side. She motioned him onto the bed and pushed him onto his back. She kissed him lightly on the cheek and said he should never tell anyone, then kissed her way down his body. When he was hard, she pulled him on top of her and guided him in.

"It's okay to touch me, if you want…if that…helps," she whispered into his ear, softly running her hands down his back and over his ass.

He dressed, went back to his room to find it empty, and got into the shower. A few minutes later, Marcy pulled the shower curtain back and stepped in. They said nothing, just looked at each other for a moment. He pulled her to him and kissed her deeply. She shut the water off and grabbed his hand, urging him onto their bed. They made love quickly, but passionately.

"Oh my god!" she said, catching her breath. "I'll have to send you out like that more often."

Two weeks later Heather and Bob told them she was pregnant, due in late April. Michael saw that Bob was experiencing very mixed emotions. He shook Bob's hand, then pulled him in and wrapped his arms around him.

"Thanks," Bob said.

"Sorry it had to be this way, man," Michael said back quietly.

Marcy stood in front of Michael in a pair of cut off denims, a light top and a pair of sneakers. She had her baseball cap on and held another out to him.

"You're taking the afternoon off," Marcy said to Michael. "Me, you and Mica Martin are going to take a nice Sunday afternoon ride out into the fields - and not the ones that are planted. Now put on the hat and get in the truck. I'm driving."

"But…."

"The only butt I want is yours on the truck seat! Get in! Now! The cooler's packed and we're going. That's it! Not open to discussion."

He stood there, knowing that no matter what he said, he was going to lose this battle of wills. She checked Mica's car seat safety belts, got into the driver's side and pointed to the passenger seat.

"All right," he said, "but not the whole afternoon. I've got a lot to do."

"Do you ever *not* have a lot to do? Get in!"

He did. She drove, heading through the neighborhoods, past the nearest fields of corn and wheat and peppers.

"Where are you taking me?" he asked.

"You'll see when we get there," she said, a little smirk on her face.

They entered a ten-acre open field that had been cleared and leveled flat. From the edge of the field, he could only see what looked like a few small piles of something off-white, scattered here and there, four pieces, to be exact. Each was only a few inches tall and maybe a foot around. As they got closer, he saw they were arranged in a square. Closer still, he realized he was looking at a baseball diamond.

A minute after they stopped, he heard vehicles coming up behind them and turned to see about twenty-five or so, led by Will and Chrissy in one of his SUVs. Groups of people started getting out of the vehicles and walking toward the diamond area. Clint and Will ended up in the middle of the crowd. Large canvas sacks were dropped and opened.

Will spoke up. "I'd like to welcome you all to the first New World Series, being held this year in lovely Berk Shire, Massachusetts, home of the brave. We are going to play six innings. Marcy has volunteered to be the home plate umpire. Where are the other umps? Take your spots, please. Our second official order of business is going to be choosing up sides. Clint will be the captain of one team, the Yankees; I'll take the other, the Sox. Michael, would you step forward, please.

That's right, step this way. I have in my hand an ordinary coin, heads on one side, tails on the other. The winner gets first choice; the loser gets to bat first. Would you do the honors of flipping the coin to see which captain chooses first? Call it in the air, Clint."

Clint called heads.

"Tails!" Will said. "I choose…" He looked around the group twice. "Chrissy!"

Anyone who wanted to play was put on a team, kids and adults alike, and all were promised time on the field. Clint and Will distributed gloves. Bats were leaned up against one truck. Balls were thrown around and hit for a warm up period before the game was started, with the Yankees batting first.

Michael looked at Marcy. "You little sneak! You set this all up without me knowing about it?"

"You're so damned busy working all the time, it was easy to pull this off. Plus I had a little help from the pros," she said, pointing to Will and Clint.

Will's pitching turned out to be horrendous, sloppy and very inaccurate. Michael asked him what was wrong.

"I'm so used to throwing the ball at ninety-five miles per hour; I have no control when I throw this slowly!"

Jimmy shined in his duties at second base, and managed to hit more than a few long balls. On his third at bat, he took a swing and connected big time. The ball bounced between the center and left field players. He made it all the way to third base before the ball came in. The next batter hit a grounder. The shortstop dove for the ball, landed on the ground, got up fairly quickly and fired the ball home. Jimmy slid into the plate just as the ball got there. Marcy hesitated for a moment before declaring him safe.

The game went on for over two and a half hours. The players did their best, gave the little kids lots of chances and breaks without letting on. There were strikeouts and a lot of infield hits, arguments, real and fake, with the umpires. Some of the people were able to hit the ball fairly deep, causing fielders to run and dive. The ball was caught. The ball was dropped. The ball was thrown wildly over the heads of basemen, or fell pitifully short of their reach.

In the bottom of the sixth inning, with two outs, the score was eight to seven, with Will's team behind and at bat. Michael took a small lead off first base. Bill was up with two strikes. He connected with the next pitch and hit a fly deep into left center field. Michael took off, running full tilt. Clint scooped the ball off the ground and cocked his arm back just as Michael rounded third, heading for home. Clint let the ball fly, rocketing it toward the catcher. Michael went into a slide, feet aimed directly at the plate. He felt the catcher's mitt touch his leg just as he felt his toes touch the base.

Everyone looked at Marcy for her determination. She thrust her fist across her body to one side and yelled, "You're out!"

"Whadaya mean, I'm out?" he yelled. "I was safe by a mile!"

"Out!!!" she yelled, louder than him. Then she leaned in and smiled. "I love you," she said softly.

He put his arms up in the air as if to protest. The crowd grew quiet. Then he leaned in toward her, put his arms around her and hugged her. "This was so much fun," he whispered into her ear. "Thank you, thank you, thank you! I really needed this." He kissed her. The crowd cheered.

A large picnic followed, with food and drink set out on tailgates. Blankets were spread for those who wanted to sit, while others ate standing up or walking around, huddling into small groups. Many people rubbed their muscles as they ate their food, or stretched out legs to ward off cramps. The game was rehashed. Most talked about having this become an annual event.

The first incident on the road occurred on a warm and cloudy mid-September day. Robert had gone out in a small silver van on a westerly heading with two other residents, looking for potential fishing spots along the Chickley River. They came around a long bend to a straight section of road. Seeing a small sedan pulled over a hundred yards away, they slowed down to a crawl, then came to a stop. They could see a few people behind the car, all crouched down except one. A small puff of smoke registered with Robert as gunfire. Further away they saw other tiny clouds of smoke appearing from behind bushes off to the side of the road. Using a set of high powered binoculars, Robert surveyed the situation.

"Either one of you really good at driving this thing backwards?" he asked.

"Janet's probably better than I am," Dave Hannon said.

"Okay, Janet, you'll be driving. Here's the situation as far as I can tell. There are two adults and two young kids behind the vehicle. At least two bad guys are up the road about a hundred feet further. The bad guys have the parents and kids pinned down. I'm going to move into the woods and flank the bad guys. I'll give you two clicks on the two-way," he said, strapping on a headset and grabbing an assault rifle. "I'll start firing at the bad guys, you start driving to the family. Get them in this vehicle and back it up as fast as you can, back to here. Got it?"

He slung the rifle and checked the handgun that was always at his side.

"Dave, you also want to keep a pistol and an extra clip handy. If the bad guys start shooting at you, just start firing in their direction. Doesn't matter if you hit anything or not, just shoot in their direction. That'll get them to hunker down a bit. I'll try to take them out. Okay, here we go," he said as he exited the car.

Robert slid out the side door and moved quickly into the trees. Dave put on a headset, followed the man with his eyes, losing him to the woods a few moments later. The tiny speaker in his ear crackled to life.

"Just testing," Robert said quietly.

"I hear you."

"Remember: two clicks like this." The device clicked twice, then went silent.

Janet picked up the binoculars. "Shit, those poor kids. The oldest can't be more than seven. The mother's got them on the ground, just about lying on top of them."

They waited for what seemed like an incredibly long time. Nothing changed in front of them. Dave jumped when the headset clicked twice. He heard repeating fire and knew Robert was shooting. He signaled Janet to move.

She put her foot on the accelerator, then slammed it down hard. The torque of the electric motor spun the wheels and brought them quickly up to fifty. Dave moved to the side door panel and partially opened it. As she got the van behind and slightly off to the other vehicle's driver's side, Dave yelled out for them to get into the van. The woman pushed the kids in, then jumped in herself. The father fired twice, was hit and went down on one knee, a look of absolute disbelief on his face. Dave hopped out and yanked him into the van. The man was hit in the chest, slightly to the upper left side of his heart. He looked at his wife, reached for her hand.

His voice gurgled as he said *I love you all* to his wife. Blood seeped from his chest as the life drained from his eyes.

Dave slammed the door shut. "Go! Go! Go!" he yelled.

Janet turned around to look out the back window. A bullet pinged off the van. She slammed her foot down again, and, moving in reverse, drove them back a safe distance.

"Anyone else hit?" she asked, putting the van in park and climbing into the back.

The woman seemed to meet her gaze, but there was no

connection, only a look of utter shock in her eyes. Her breathing was rapid, shallow.

"Ma'am," Janet said, trying to get the woman to focus. There was no response. Jan got right into her face and screamed, "Look at me! Now!"

The woman gave a small, but quick jerk of her head and focused on her. Tears started pouring down her face. Janet reached out and held her, then extended her arms out to the kids and pulled them in.

Dave got out of the van and listened. There were no shots being fired. He tapped the earpiece twice, then listened. Nothing. He clicked twice again. Nothing.

"I'm going up to find Robert," he said.

"Dave, no! Wait for him! Stay here!"

"Something's wrong. He's not answering the two-way." He climbed back into the van, grabbed an assault rifle and two extra clips. He flicked the switch to automatic, checked the safety, slung the rifle and pulled out his handgun.

"Fire up another two-way, Janet. I'll call when I know what's going on. And get your pistol out, just I case. And if it's not Robert or me coming down the road toward you, take off! You hear me?" She nodded.

He started jogging down the road toward the other vehicle. As he approached, he moved into a crouching position, just as Robert had instructed him to do in combat class. He stayed behind the other vehicle for a few moments, listening. Nothing. He got ready to move into the road and immediately felt his heart rate pick up until it felt like his chest was going to explode. Taking in a couple of deep breaths and holding his handgun out in front of him, he stepped out, keeping his body low, moving slowly forward, his eyes darting back and forth at the woods ahead of him.

About seventy-five feet down the road, he saw multiple scrape marks on the pines, telling him this was where it had gone down. He moved off the road and into the trees. Not too far ahead he saw two people, one lying on the ground in an unnatural position. The other was slumped against a tree, his chest covered with blood. The man's eyes were open, but Dave couldn't tell if they were following him or not. He raised his pistol, aiming at the man's chest, just like he'd been shown in training. He could hear Robert's voice in his head: *If it's a known bad guy and he so much as flinches, shoot and put three or four rounds in him.*

His heart thumped as he got within twenty feet. The eyes seemed to be watching him. There was a handgun in the man's hand, pointing toward the ground.

"Drop it or I'll shoot!" Dave yelled. "Drop it now!" He knew it was a bad guy, wasn't sure if he was alive, so he fired five shots, three hitting the man.

"It's all right; he's dead."

Startled, Dave turned in one rapid motion toward the voice and aimed.

"Whoa! It's me!"

Robert was also slumped against a tree, maybe thirty feet away. He was holding a piece of blood-soaked khaki material against his leg. The two-way headset lay by his side, twisted and broken. "Took one, but I got 'em both."

Dave holstered his gun, tapped his ear piece once. "Janet? About seventy, eighty feet down from the sedan. Quickly! Robert's been hit." He turned to the soldier. "What should I do?"

"See that little plastic pouch on the side of my belt? Open it and get the piece of strapping that's in there. Yeah, that's it. Now take this cloth and keep a lot of pressure on the wound."

Robert worked to fasten the Velcro strapping around his leg above the wound. "That should at least slow down the bleeding for now. It's a vein that got hit - artery would pulse - but I'm going to need some work ASAP," he said. "I'm hoping one of the docs back home can fix me up. How'd everyone else make out?"

"The man died, the woman and kids are fine. Well, not fine, but not shot."

They heard a horn beep. "Do you remember the fireman's carry, Dave? Good, 'cause that's what you're going to have to do. Let's leave all our finery here for now. Come back for that after you get me in the truck."

With Janet pushing as much speed as was safe, they arrived back at the compound about an hour later. Michael, Bill, Bob, John, Heather and Marcy, alerted by radio, were waiting by the rear basement entrance with a stretcher. Michael, Bob and John took Robert in immediately. Bill attended to the man's remains, while Marcy took the woman and children inside.

Robert was moved into the treatment room where Marcy had had her baby. A computer was hooked up to a large monitor. A surgical guide program was up and running. The picture showed an exploded view of the bones, musculature and vasculature of a leg.

"We're going to give you an injection that will put you out for a few hours," Heather said. "Then we'll fix you up."

"Anytime you're ready," Robert said. His voice was thin, his words slightly slurred. He had lost a lot of blood and was approaching the edges of incoherence.

John administered the shot through the line dripping a universal blood substitute into his arm.

"John, keep a close watch on his pressure and heart rate and let us know if anything changes more than a few points. Heather, the only surgical experience I had was in rotation way back when, so you are point person on this one."

"Out of my area of expertise, but I've done enough GYN surgery to think I might be able to pull this off. Glad you saw fit to put in a laser cutter. At my supervisor's insistence, I tried one of the old fashioned scalpels once. Whoa! Talk about blood! Okay, here we go," she said, pressing the button of the laser and cutting into the leg tissue to open the wound area up a bit more. The laser cauterized the incision margins immediately.

"I'm going to release the tourniquet and get some flow back to the leg, then we're going to flush it and you're going to swab your brains out. Next time we'll tighten up the 'tourney and try to shed some light on the subject," she said to Michael.

As she undid the tourniquet slightly, blood started to flow out of the wound again. She allowed this for a few moments, then told Michael to put pressure on the wound. She watched as the color returned to Robert's leg, then tightened the strap up again. Michael swabbed with large pieces of cloth, throwing them on the floor as they became saturated.

"Right. There's the vein. Medium sized." She set clamps on either side of it. "I'm going to have to cut out the damaged area first, then sew in a piece of the artificial stuff. Let's match up for size before I start cutting, and I'm going to need at least two dozen interior sutures, just to be sure. Why don't you set those up?"

Three hours later Heather finished up the last exterior suture. They worked to bring Robert out of the anesthesia, slowly administering small amounts of stimulant, waiting for him to come back a little closer to consciousness without becoming fully conscious. A bag of antibiotics, mixed from powder, was hooked up to the line and the drip was adjusted. When they were satisfied he was stable, they scrubbed out, leaving John to monitor the man. Heather stood by the sink for a moment, holding onto its edge to stop herself from swaying, then vomited into it. Michael approached her, but she waved him off.

"Nerves and hormonal fluctuations," she said. "I'll be fine. If I wasn't pregnant, I'd say let's go get drunk. That was brutal. That's the first of many, I'm sure. We need a surgeon or three. In the meantime, we'd better start studying up big time, because we're it! Theo should get involved, too, and doctors Watts and Pierce. We need to train assistants, as well."

<hr />

The woman, Barbara Murray, sat in the basement conference room with Michael and Marcy. Five-eight and on the leaner side, she rested her chin on both hands, her fingers extending up onto her cheeks. Her hazel eyes were red from crying, her hair, a wavy brown, stuck out in all directions. A half-empty glass of water was set to her right.

"What am I going to do?" she asked. "How am I going to get by without Ed? He was my whole life." She started crying again, dabbed at her eyes with the handkerchief Michael had given her.

Marcy placed her hand near Barbara's, and the woman's fingers reached out slightly, not quite touching anything. Marcy slid her hand next to hers and the woman grabbed on tight. She looked at Marcy through her tears, then put her head on Marcy's shoulder and sobbed. They gave her time to cry before talking with her.

"For now," Michael said, "you stay here and take all the time you need. When you're ready you can figure out what you want to do."

"What about Ed?"

Michael glanced at Marcy. There had been no deaths at Berk Shire. Berk Shire had been about focusing on surviving, seeking to maintain life. There had been no discussions about how to deal with this unwanted, but inevitable new visitor.

"We'll talk about that tomorrow," Marcy said softly. "Right now let's get you and your children settled into one of the rooms upstairs." She gently urged Barbara up and got her walking toward the stairs. "Michael, get the others together, would you? I'll be back in a half hour or so."

The group convened a little while later, sitting in the same room.

Michael raised the issue of what to do with those who died. He, John and Marcy knew all too well the implications of burying bodies - even the immune - that might still contain some form of the deadly virus. There could be ground water contamination sometime in the future, putting Berk Shire's water supply at risk, or contamination into the food supply straight from the soil. From seeming death, the little bastard had sprung back to life and wiped out the better part of the population of the world. And who knew what else from that disease could be lying dormant in a body? If a contamination did occur, there was the possibility some variant might just finish the job.

"Cremation is the only way to be sure," Michael said, "so we're going to have to make a policy decision. Some won't like it much, but we can't take the risks."

"So what do we do about some sort of funeral service?" Bob asked. "The local minister left three months ago to stay with relatives in Vermont."

They all looked at Michael. "I guess I'll work on putting something together."

⸻⸻ ((◊)) ⸻⸻

The baseball field was chosen as the site for the cremation. Because it was already cleared, sparks from the funeral pyre were very unlikely to make it into any woods where a blaze might be started. The last thing they needed was a wildfire they were ill equipped to handle.

The body was fully wrapped in cloth soaked in grain alcohol. Well-seasoned pine was mixed with hardwoods and used for the fire, so the flames would initially burn very quickly, but then remain hot enough to reduce the body to cinders.

Most of Berk Shire showed up, even though no one except

Barbara and her children knew the man being cremated. It was a sign of unity and respect. Life had always been fragile and fleeting, but now seemed more so than ever.

Michael did his best not to make his words too impersonal, putting the death in the context of the times, mentioning things that Barbara had told him about Ed, his caring as a husband and father, his wonderful sense of humor. John, guitar in hand, accompanied Gemma, a woman of Irish descent who sang a centuries old song called *The Green Fields of France*, about men who had died at war and were buried far from their homes.

The fire consumed the body, leaving only ashes and fragments of bone among the glowing embers that remained after the blaze. Many of the people attending cried, not out of sadness for someone they'd lost, but for the woman and children left behind. They knew that although this was the first funeral in the colony, death would certainly be a more frequent caller in the days to come. They also cried for the loss they felt in their own lives, the way of things they'd been forced to leave behind, the way of things past.

Person after person shuffled past Barbara and her children, some only speaking a few words of condolence, some shaking her hand gently, some embracing her and letting her know they would help take care of her so that life would go on for what was left of her family.

—◦《◉》◦—

The fall harvest was the biggest and best ever. Michael's forethought about a large commercial grade kitchen paid off. There were a full twenty-five people working comfortably in there. One crop at a time was dealt with. Assembly lines were set up to speed the work. The kitchen was running at a frenetic pace from sunrise until well after sunset. One stove was temporarily given over for breakfasts, lunches and dinners, but otherwise all were in use constantly. At times, people sang while they worked or chatted in small or larger groups. Other times, word games were played as they sliced and diced and cooked.

The problem was storage. There were enough canning options, mason and pickle jars, along with plasteel containers that sealed out air. It was space they were lacking in which to store these canned goods. The basement rooms had been mostly turned into offices and medical treatment rooms as the operation of Berk Shire had grown.

In the end, as much of the food as could be, was divided up and trucked out to the individual neighborhoods for storage and usage. Pantries were constructed underground for cooler storing.

There were now over fifty cabins built, with more under construction. They had run out of electric powered stoves and were now importing them in from the townies' houses that had more than one unit. The photovoltaic cells that created the power started to become in short supply. Bob, knowing the day would come soon when power could no longer be installed in the newly built cabins, came up with designs of wood-fired stoves and ovens that could be built from stones that had been gathered from the newly plowed fields.

The group realized that Berk Shire was being overrun and was in danger of running out of building supplies. Fortunately food was not an issue. Most of the hybridized crops they grew produced two harvests a year. Raising chickens, sheep, hogs, frogs, cows, catfish and rabbits would keep them going without having to over-harvest deer and wild turkeys or any of the smaller game available.

"So how do we tell a family that shows up they can't stay?" Marcy asked the group as she finished nursing Mica Martin.

"It's against everything I had in mind when I thought of doing this. For all my looking ahead, I never saw this coming. We've got just over one hundred and fifty residents and that really is the current limit," Michael said, sipping lemon verbena tea.

"Well," John said, scratching his head, "People will keep showing up, and it's not like we have anywhere to send them."

Michael looked up at the ceiling, his eyes darting back and forth. He smacked his hand on the table, making the others jump. "Wait a minute. What about the other colonies we've been charting? There are what, fourteen or fifteen of them within a two hundred miles radius. Maybe they'd be able to accept new residents."

"Why would they? They're probably overwhelmed as much as we are," John said.

"Five new members who can work the fields produce way more than they can eat," Bob said. "This might work. Besides, we're producing so much food now that we could sweeten the pot a little, at least in the beginning."

"There's only one way to find out," Michael responded. "How about three or four of us go find out? We can take a handful of the soldiers along so we'll be pretty safe…and take the APC. It's well armored against rifle and small arms fire, and there's enough room in it to store food and maybe some gifts for our fellow colony members."

<hr />

They stood in front of the main building. Mica Martin squirmed to get loose, but Marcy held fast. "I really wish you'd let the others do this."

He kissed her on the forehead and ran his hand over Mica's head. "This is something I have to do, something I want to do. Besides trying to solve one problem, I'll see what the other colonies have, maybe start setting up some trading deals."

"Well, just don't invite them all over for Thanksgiving," she said, leaning in to kiss him on the lips.

He kissed her back, then kissed the baby. "I won't."

A tear slid from Marcy's eye. "I guess I'm worried that you won't come back. Don't take any risks out there."

"We'll be fine. Figure we'll be back in about two and a half weeks, two if the roads aren't in too bad a condition and we can make good time. But definitely in time for the annual pumpkin carving, so don't get worried. You have the itinerary, and we'll be following it, and if we meet people on the road heading this way, we'll ask them to stop in and let you know we're okay." He looked at Marcy, Heather, Bob, John and Bill. "You guys hold it all together. I'll be back." He turned to Robert, who was balanced on crutches. "I know you'd like to be going. Maybe next time."

He nodded to the soldiers who had been waiting outside the APC. They climbed in. Michael put one foot in the vehicle, then looked back at Marcy and the baby, smiled and waved. "Let's move it out," he said as he slid inside.

Wayne and Bert had been asked to join the crew. It was felt that because they had lived in the region all their lives they might be more acceptable to the leaders of the colonies they'd be visiting. Wayne had agreed on the condition that he not have to make any speeches.

Five soldiers rounded out the crew, with Smiling Bobby Ray, as Michael had jokingly started calling him, leading the defense team. Bobby Ray, the Native American, had actually smiled ever so slightly the first time he'd heard Michael use that name, said he liked it. Trained as Special Ops, he was considered the sharpshooter of the bunch, and his tracking skills were, as Robert put it, *the stuff legends are made out of*. His main function in the unit had been as a sniper and tracker, but he was also a corporal, so he had leadership skills as well.

A man named Johnson - he wouldn't tell anyone his first name, and his unit was sworn to secrecy - was driving, pushing the vehicle up to a steady fifty miles per hour. While the vehicle was capable of seventy-five, safety was the bigger factor.

Michael looked at the condition of the road. There were no major potholes, but cracks could be seen in many places. With fewer and fewer people to maintain the roads over the past few years, the surfaces were now exhibiting the first real signs of deterioration. Frost heaves from the past winter showed, mostly at the more vulnerable edges of the roadway. The gravel medium running down the middle of the four lanes was grossly overgrown. There were only glimpses of the plasteel guardrail cutting through the center. He wondered how long it would be before the damage of neglect made the roads unusable. There was only enough gravelly shoulder on either side to accommodate a single vehicle, but speeds above twenty or so would become impossible. That would probably impair trade...*if* it ever started up.

It took a little over two hours to reach the first colony, a farm the residents there had taken to calling Morgansville, named after the man who owned the land. Jake Morgan was a farmer working a four hundred acre spread. Because they were kind people, he and his wife, Betsy, both in their early-thirties, had started taking in a few stragglers here and there. The stragglers ended up numbering over forty.

The Morgans were noted in the Konectable listing as friendly people, but were very on guard when the crew first got out of the APC. All the residents who were present were carrying either handguns or rifles, though no one was holding his weapon in a threatening way.

Michael looked at the man who was standing most forward. He was close to six foot tall with longish, wavy brown hair. His build was husky without being overweight, and his eyes showed some suspicion, but they were not hardened. He fit the description in the Konectable.

Michael approached him. "Jake Morgan? I'm Dr. Michael Macalister."

Morgan nodded and shook Michael's hand. "How do you know my name?"

Michael answered his question and asked if there was some place they could talk.

Morgan pointed to the house fifty feet away. It was two stories high, with four windows across the ground floor level only. The
clapboard front was painted a light green, with no peel showing. An
eight foot wide farmer's porch ran the length of the building.

Michael looked at Smiling Bobby Ray and held his hand up at
lower chest level, indicating he should keep his men by the vehicle.
Wayne and Bert followed him onto the porch, where Morgan was
pulling white Adirondack chairs into a semi-circle.

Morgan's wife and one other man sat down with them. The
farmer introduced them. Betsy, at five-nine, was only a few inches
shorter than her husband, wearing jeans and a light flannel shirt. Her
dark brown hair was pulled back under a blue polka-dotted bandana.
She was not thin, nor was she heavy, but easily held the extra weight
of someone who worked hard and ate well. She was good looking in
a weathered sort of way, with friendly brown eyes that showed her
excitement at having people from outside of their area on her porch.

The man sitting with them, Jake's foreman, Tim Johanson, was
cordial enough, but had a serious manner about him. He was tall and
slim, older than the Morgans by more than twenty years, with long
graying hair pulled into a pony tail. A thick mustache curved down
to fairly tailored points a full inch below each side of his mouth.
He removed his straw cowboy hat as he sat down. He was quiet, an
observer who looked and listened and seemed to be taking in more
than most would.

Michael introduced Wayne first, telling Morgan that Wayne
still owned twenty-five hundred acres where they had started out
from. He then introduced Bert as the founder and former owner of
Colby's General store in Warren.

Morgan looked them over, shook their hands, then came back
to Michael. "So you figured if you brought along two guys closer to
me than you, that I'd relax right into whatever conversation you're

meaning to have."

Michael smiled and without missing a beat said, "I figured I'd bring along two of the friends I made when I bought property from Wayne a few years back. Whether or not you settle into the conversation I'd like to have is going to depend on how you feel about what I have to say."

Morgan stared at him for a moment, then broke into a wide smile and gave a single, hearty laugh. "Betsy, would you mind bringing us some of that cider we just pressed? Thanks." He turned back to Michael, then nodded in the direction of the APC. "And the goon squad?"

"They're soldiers who came to us after the government ceased operating. I assume you know about that."

Jake looked at him and smiled. "Yeah, I've been able to maintain a little contact with some outside this area."

"Well, they were lost without any contact with their commanders and had no idea what was going on. After a somewhat rocky introduction, we invited them in for dinner. The following day we invited them to stay on at Berk Shire if they wanted to, and they have been with us ever since. As you've probably surmised, one of their main functions is security. I do hope you know we have no hostile intent, despite driving up in an armored military vehicle. One of our exploration teams ran into some problems a few weeks back, leaving one of our guys wounded, another good guy and two bad guys dead. So when we thought about coming out to talk to you and some of the other colonies that have been started, we figured we'd be a little safer in that."

Morgan looked over at the vehicle, then back at Michael. "That's what I'd've done... *if* I was fool enough to go around visiting in these times."

"Wasn't so much a question of being foolish, but more of trying to be considerate of others."

"How so?"

"We're neighbors," Michael said. "Thought we should get acquainted and thought we might talk over a little possible business."

"I think that's the right friendly thing to do," Betsy said, arriving with a tray of glasses and a pitcher of cider. She poured and gave the glasses to her husband to hand out. When everyone had a glass, he raised his up to the others. "All right then, to our neighbors to the east." Everyone drank. "So tell me some more about this Berk Shire place."

Michael took a long sip of cider and gave him a very condensed history of the colony. "Our policy has been to invite all comers to stay, but we are now at about the maximum limits we can handle. Our curiosity is whether we can refer people to Morgansville," he said without much fanfare.

A sly smile came across Morgan's mouth. "And why would we want to accommodate you on that?"

Michael explained what they had figured out, that one person could do enough work in the fields to supply four or five people with food.

"Got enough food and enough people."

"Mechanics? Got enough of them to fix the equipment?"

"Plenty."

"How about doctors? Got enough of them?"

Morgan thought for a moment. "Now you've got my attention."

"We have two primary care doctors, and myself - I'm an infectious disease specialist."

"I watched the comline when it was still up and running. I know who you are," Jake said. "Go on."

"...and I'm now training in primary care and field surgery. We also have an OB/GYN. We could start doing visits a few times a year," Michael said. "Or you could come get me. I'm only a few hours away. Or we could start training someone here to do the basic stuff."

"Training and some visits would be good."

"The OB/GYN could teach you about birthing babies."

"I probably wouldn't be the best one to train, but my Betsy would take to that, maybe one of the other women, too. Funny, there haven't been any pregnancies since we started taking people in. Know anything about that?"

Michael explained what they had discovered and that he or one of the other doctors could test all the men in the future. He did not explain how they had started dealing with the infertility at Berk Shire. They moved on to talking about how the medical visits might come about and about how many people they might be able to take in. Michael also broached the subject of setting up some trading. They talked about that a little, but only touched on what each might be willing to trade.

"Tell you what I miss," Jake said. "I miss bourbon. Had my last sip...well, must be at least a year ago. Knew I should have stocked up more, but the price kept going up. Being a dyed-in-the-wool Yankee, I was damned if was going to pay that kind of premium. Course, that line of thought seems a little silly in retrospect."

In the end, they stayed for lunch before moving on. Morgan promised to make a visit to Berk Shire sometime before the snows started.

Back on the road, they got off the main highway about fifty miles down from Morgansville, onto a local two lane road. Smaller frost heaves from the previous winter freeze and spring thaw had, for the most part, not been repaired. The larger ones had been dug out and simply filled with gravel which had been oiled down a bit. Johnson couldn't push the vehicle much over twenty-five.

While the GPS system was useless now that the Internet uplink was inoperative, all the original directional information had been downloaded into a Konectable. This showed where they were headed, but did not give real time information. Bert, who had visited relatives in the area a few decades back, remembered some of the landmarks and tried his best to verify where they were.

Michael looked at the bright colors coming up in the maple, oak and birch trees. Memories flooded in of the one time he and Sherilyn had taken a brief weekend getaway and gone to Vermont to go leaf-peeping. Unwanted passengers - feelings of sadness and regret - tagged along with the images. He thought about trying to push them away, but decided it was better to face them directly, to savor them, even, bittersweet and all.

This was his third fall living in the area, and though he had always noted the colors, it had been more of a perfunctory nod to the change in season. He had not taken the time to soak in the grandeur of the show nature had up and running. There had always been something to do, something to fix or figure out, something to plan. *Something!*

He realized he'd been in overdrive for the last few years putting Berk Shire together. But it was there before all that. His work. He had gotten all too caught up in what he was doing, in his reputation as the go-to doctor for patients with rare diseases no one else could figure out, or his work as a researcher, always looking for the next new thing, the better way, that he somehow almost always managed to find. He'd let himself start to believe all the buzz and hype about himself that he'd read or heard, got off on being interviewed for this journal or that comline program. But the seventy-five plus hour weeks had meant less time with Sherilyn, and being so driven had brought him to not look forward to vacations or time off for celebrations. They were interruptions, unwanted, unneeded. By the time he'd started to relax, the vacation was just about over. He'd lived his work, was his work...just like his father.

Sorry, he muttered under his breath, speaking to his dead wife.

Another memory insinuated itself in his mind: he had made those same promises to Sherilyn that his father had made over and over, telling him they would go to a game *soon*, go fishing *soon*, spend more time together *soon. I promise!*

He promised himself he would take more time to enjoy what was around him. He looked out the window and promised himself that he would not make that promise an empty one, that he *would* spend more time with Marcy and Mica Martin starting as soon as they got back from this trip.

And then he realized that he'd just put it off again. The promise was to start paying more attention *now.* The colors were vivid *now!* He turned to take in the beauty that was right in front of his face. *Be in the moment,* Marcy had said. *That's when life happens.*

The day had given way to dusk by the time they reached the next colony, Jackie's Place. Jackie was listed as in his mid-seventies and having lost his wife to the illness about seven years earlier. She had been one of the first to contract the disease in this area. His dairy farm was a little over seven hundred acres, with fifty milkers. There were twenty-one colonists listed in the Konectable, including Jackie.

The entranceway to the farm was relatively short at about one hundred feet. At Michael's request, Johnson had given a couple of light, friendly toots on the horn as they approached the house. They were met by an older man, presumably Jackie, who stood in the door-way, lever-action rifle held diagonally across his chest. Three other men moved closer to the vehicle's side, each with a semi-automatic handgun raised and ready.

Michael exited the APC first, hands held outward at mid-chest height. The man in the doorway shined a large spotlight in his face.

"State your business right quick," he said.

"My name is Dr. Michael Macalister. I'm from a neighboring colony about a hundred and fifty miles away from here, near the town of Warren. Just looking to chat a bit. I have seven other men in the vehicle, five of them soldiers from the U.S. Army."

The man looked at Michael, then moved his spotlight toward the APC. "They have weapons?" he asked.

"They do, and I'll be happy to ask them to leave everything in the vehicle, if that's your wish."

"It is. Bring 'em out one by one and do it slowly so I can see each one. Tell 'em hands where I can see 'em."

Michael called back into the vehicle, asked Wayne to step out. As each man came out, Michael introduced him by name and asked them all to line up single file next to him.

"Tell the soldiers to sit down in a circle where my men can keep an eye on them, then you and the two others come closer."

Michael did as he was told. When they had gotten about five feet from the porch of the house, two other men came out and frisked them for weapons.

Wayne looked up at the man. "Seems like you've had some trouble already, the way you're treating us."

"Had a bunch of young 'uns - three of 'em - show up two weeks ago. One of 'em started talking to me on the porch, asking if we needed any help. When I told him we were all set, he asked if we could spare any food and water. Just as I was starting to feel a bit sorry for 'em, he pulls a pistol out and sticks it in my face. My dog picked up on the aggression and came walking forward, teeth bared, growling - real friendly shepherd, but he's got a nasty looking set of teeth and he don't like anyone who don't like me. The kid turned and shot him. Killed the damn dog! When he went to turn back in my direction, I damn near knocked his brains out with my right fist. He went down with one hit. I picked up his pistol, drew down on the other two, told 'em to grab their friend and get the hell off my land. I been waiting for 'em to come for their payback ever since."

"We had a couple of people out exploring a few weeks back," Michael said. "They ran into a shootout on the highway. Two guys had pinned down a father, mother and two small kids, working to jack their car. The father had a gun and was defending his family. One of our soldiers was with the exploration team, slinked through the woods and distracted the two bad guys while the other two drove down and got the family to safety. Well, not the father. He got shot and killed. The soldier ended up killing both bad guys, but he took a bad hit in the leg. There's definitely more of that coming in the days ahead."

"I'd say you got that right. I'm Jackie Johnson," the old man said, extending his hand. "You boys seem all right. You're welcome to join us for supper, such as it is. I've got enough room for you three. The soldiers will have to eat with the others in the next building. Let me show you where you can wash up."

Joining them at the table were three couples, one of whom had a girl of nine or ten. Introductions were made and some polite table talk ensued. Supper itself was simple, a thick savory soup of mostly vegetables with a little bit of meat - probably rabbit or squirrel - mixed in. There was fresh bread and cider, as well.

The conversation quickly moved to the state of the country. "Or whatever it is now. Guess it's not the United States of anything at the moment," Jackie said. "You figure the government will ever get cooking again and bring us all back together?"

"*The* government, no," Michael said. "Some form of government, maybe. I think it's going to be every man for himself - no gender bias intended, ladies - for quite some time. That's more or less why we're making the rounds to some of the groups that have formed. You met some of my people a while back. They were just touching base to see who was where in the neighborhood, the neighborhood being about two hundred or so square miles."

"I remember them. Right friendly, asked a lot of question but didn't give much back in the way of answers. I guess we probably stonewalled each other more than anything. They said their main purpose was just figuring out where others were. Nothing bad had happened to us yet, so we didn't think much of it."

Michael explained what he was looking for. Everyone at the

table deferred to Jackie whenever Michael asked a question or posed an issue. Jackie would not commit to taking any newcomers in, but he also didn't say no. He was most interested in setting up some sort of trading, wanted to know what kinds of seeds Michael might have that he didn't have. They learned that each had something the other could use, and though no formal agreements were set up, Michael invited him and a few others to visit sooner rather than later for an exchange of an equal amount of seeds of various crops.

"You boys are welcome to stay the night, have a good breakfast before you head out. We have one building with no one in it, bunch of beds, fireplace. No running water and the toilet is an outhouse about eighty or ninety feet away, but we can give you a couple of jars to get through the night or you can just step outside. You got some bedding with you? We don't have much of that to spare."

"We'll get our stuff out of the APC. Thanks for your hospitality, Jackie. When you come visit, plan on staying a few days, if you'd like, so we can return the favor," Michael said.

The following morning, after a breakfast of eggs and spoon biscuits, the entourage took off for the next colony, a place called Bergen's Field. The colony sat on a small lake, a feeder stream constantly pumping in a fresh supply of cold mountain water. The notes in the Konectable said the group did some farming and a lot of fishing. The people were a large group of Irish descent who had banded together back in Boston, pooled their resources and bought up property a year or so later than Michael.

"It should be just ahead," Michael said, going over the directions in the Konectable. "Three pines growing together next to a large boulder. There. Take a right."

The side road was more of a dirt path than anything else, unmarked, somewhat overgrown with grass. At places, two ruts on either side of a six-inch mound was all it consisted of, making them glad the APC had good ground clearance. It seemed to go on forever before breaking through large grassy fields. At the end of the fields they saw a row of cabins and off in the distance a quarter mile or so, patches of water behind a larger building.

A large black wolfhound greeted them with a few loud woofs before going about its business. Moving slowly down the lane between the cabins, they saw two women, each carrying a basket of wash. Three children, eight or nine years old, followed. Michael got out of the APC and walked a few steps toward them.

"I'm Michael Macalister."

The women both had longish brown hair, were of average height. One was thin, the other slightly overweight. Both wore jeans. Fall-weight jackets mostly covered their white shirts.

"I'm Sinead," the one said, a slight accent to her voice, "and this is Rosemary. Are you looking for anyone in particular or are you lost? We mostly get the lost back here."

"We're not lost," he said, "and we're looking for anyone who might be in a position of authority. We're from a neighboring colony near the town of Warren."

Sinead smiled warmly, showing no fear of the group. "Well, the person you'd be wanting to speak with is Matty O. He's been the leader ever since we set out from the city."

"Where might we find him?"

"Go down to the town hall and park your truck, or whatever it is. Start walking to the lake, go right along the shore until you come to the stream, not too far down," Rosemary said. "Then follow that stream up about a half mile. He'll be somewhere thereabouts."

"Thank you for your help."

"You're quite welcome. I expect we'll be seeing you for dinner tonight. We all eat in the hall."

"Maybe so," Michael said, climbing back in the APC.

They found the stream, headed up the near side. The water was clear and gave off a fresh, clean smell. The stream bed was mostly hand-sized rocks and large pebbles with an occasional small boulder breaking up the flow. The bank sloped down to the water's edge in spots, while in other places it sat three or four feet above, giving trout and salmon ideal hiding spots. An agreeable cedar scent drifted through the air. Birch and small, feathery white pines were mixed in, giving the area a very calm and pleasant feel.

They approached a group of men working the water, some in it, some on the land.

One of the men looked up, said something to the others. None of them stopped what they were doing until Michael was within speaking distance.

The one in the water closest to them waded out onto dry land. He put down his fly rod, wiped his hands on his pants and came right up to them. He looked as if he was waiting to turn thirty. Five-six and sporting a full head of jet black hair, his facial features were thin and slightly angular.

He nodded. "Matthew O'Neill," he said.

"Michael Macalister."

"Mac, huh…well, it's a Scots version of an Irish name, so you've got to have some Irish blood in ya, and that's close enough for me."

"Well, on occasion, I went to a place called The Black Rose in Boston, if that helps," Michael said.

"I know the place well…miss it a lot. Always had good music." He stuck out his hand. "Friends call me Matty. Sinead and Rosemary send you out here?"

"They did."

"So what can I do for you and your bunch, Michael?"

"We're from a colony some ways away, near Warren. Do you know the town?"

"I remember stopping there on one of our first trips out here, when we were getting set up a few years back. Small place, if I recall.

Little café with good food."

"That's the place. We're about twenty miles west of there in place we call Berk Shire. We're touching base with other colonies, finding out who's who and talking about possibly setting up some trading."

A few of the others had banded together behind Matty. They weren't threatening, but their body language conveyed that they were ready for action, if needed. "It's all right, lads, they're friendly enough."

"You have some trouble with outsiders?" Wayne asked.

"Not much, but a bit. Had a small group come through a few months back, looking for work and food, stole some things from us. We caught them, took our stuff back, and, uh, uh…well, let's just say we made our point with them in a way that'll make them think twice before coming back. And you?"

"We also had a couple steal from us, but they had been living with us for some time," Michael said.

"Didn't catch them, did you?"

"No, but we're hoping they don't come back either."

"I'm going to suggest we leave the rest of our business until a little later. We need to catch a few more so we can have a good supper. Speaking of which, you're welcome to join us tonight, if you've a mind. It'll be simple, but tasty, that I can tell you."

"Thank you. We'd be happy to. Could we help catch a few?"

"You familiar with fly fishing?" Matty asked.

"Haven't had much of a chance to do any in recent days, but, sure."

Matty looked back at one of his men. "Sean, would you be so kind as to set these fellows up with a rig and a stringer? Thanks." He turned back to Michael. "Sorry, we don't have any more waders. The water's a bit cold, so you may have to switch turns a bit to stay warm. Take a few towels with you. We're using a dry hopper and a wet nymph. Go about fifty paces down stream, get out into the water about six or seven feet from shore, cast out another twelve feet or so, let it dead-drift, mend when you have to to keep it looking natural to the fish. They're mostly hitting the nymph, so keep your eye on the hopper to let you know what's happening below. We're only keeping them twelve inches or more. Luck to you, lads."

Michael polled his men as they walked downstream. Of the others, only Wayne and Bert had ever fly fished before. He stripped off to his underwear and waded into the water.

"Oh, yeah! That's refreshing!" he said, hoping his body would adjust to the cold.

It took him a few casts to get the hang of it again, then a few more before he hooked into a fish. Wayne yelled at him to keep the rod tip up. The soldiers watched as he pulled in a seventeen inch brown trout and walked to shore to put it on the stringer.

Wayne, standing in his boxers, took the rod and waded out, cursing as the cold water hit his balls. He went slowly so as not to misstep. His skill at fly fishing was immediately evident. He pulled out a twenty-five foot length of line, smoothly brought the rod back and forth a few times before letting the flies drift down the current. His second cast yielded a twenty inch rainbow.

"Yours is definitely bigger, Wayne," Michael said.

"Not something that's usually said about an old man," Wayne responded.

An hour went by before Matty whistled loudly and waved them upstream, inviting them to lunch. They produced a sack with bread, mustard, mutton slices, and two jugs.

"This one," Matty said, pointing to one jug, "is water from our town well. Clean and sweet as can be. And this other one…well, let's just say it's got a bit of a kick to it."

"Yeah, a bit," one of his boys said dryly. His friends laughed.

Matty poured a cup and handed it to Michael. "The tradition is this: any newcomers we're to call friends must take a swig and swallow it. No spitting it out. Just a swig. Doesn't have to be a mouthful or anything. It's kind of an initiation, a rite of passage to being accepted by us. Agreed?"

Michael nodded and bought the cup to his lips. The high octane fumes wafting up seemed to singe his sinuses, made him want to cringe. He took more than a sip, but less than a shot, swallowed and waited. He felt his face heat up as the feeling of fire grew, first in his throat, then in the pit of his belly.

Matty smiled, more of a smirk than anything.

Bert took the cup, had the same reaction, but held it together. Wayne went next, showed little distress, if any. One by one, the soldiers took their swig. Some coughed a little, others turned beet red.

Bobby Ray took the cup last, looked in it, passed it back to Matty for more. Matty filled it halfway, handed it back. Bobby Ray sniffed it, held it up to the sky as if offering a prayer, closed his eyes and brought it to his lips. He drained it, looked at Matty and smiled ever so slightly.

"Jesus, Mary and Joseph," he said, looking around at his men. "You might want to lay back, there, man. When that hits you, you'll end up flat on yer arse!"

"My daddy made stronger," Bobby Ray said, handing the cup back.

"Okay, then," Matty said, a look of disbelief on his face. "Let's eat."

—◦◦◦—

Michael, Wayne and Bert were given a tour of the operation of Bergen's Field, the barns, stables, some of the closer fields. Wayne asked about their distillery, but Matty gave only vague and evasive answers, doing so in such a friendly way that Wayne didn't push. All he found out was that their moonshine was corn based.

Matty was much more open about their smokehouse, and Wayne talked about the one they'd set up in Berk Shire. They discussed the finer points of what woods gave what flavors to the various meats. Matty was very interested in Wayne's use of corncobs for ham and bacon.

"I see you got mules," Wayne said. "You set out to do that?"

"No. It came about because of a broken fence, which I think the donkey did on purpose. Mare in heat got him thinking and kicking, they got cozy and that's what we got. Then we decided to keep it going. Mules are strong, powerful animals. Fast, too. Got a reputation for being stubborn, and they can be a might willful at times, but they pretty much do what they're trained to do if you know how to keep 'em in line."

After the tour, Michael, Wayne and Bert spent time before dinner with Matty and a few of the other people of Bergen's Field, sitting at a long picnic table by the lake. They talked about the kinds of things each needed or had for possible trade. Again, the thing that most interested Matty was having medical services. He agreed to consider taking on some additional people, but said he'd prefer those of Irish descent. Nothing was decided or agreed upon, except that Matty and whatever company he wanted to bring to visit Berk Shire would be most welcome.

At Matty's direction, one of the men went out into the cabin area, returned a few minutes later with a woman in tow. She was in her late-twenties, pretty and petite, with long auburn hair tied together and draped over one shoulder.

"This is Caitlin, our resident medical provider," Matty said.

She looked at Michael for a moment, stuck out her hand. "Dr. Macalister," she said.

"Do we know each other?" Michael asked, shaking her hand and gesturing to a seat.

"No, but I know your work. You lectured at MGH when I was just out of school and at my first position there. I certainly know you from the comline and the 'net, and a lot of us followed your work very closely on the numbing cold virus."

"Well, it's a pleasure to meet you, Caitlin. What did you do at

MGH?"

"Nurse practitioner…ER. Whatever came in, we took care of it."

"So you're taking care of things here, now."

"Best I can," she said. "But I'll tell you, I have a thousand questions for you about all the stuff I don't know."

Matty stood up, announced that the group was going to leave the two of them alone so they could talk shop. "But don't worry, we'll ring the dinner bell."

Caitlin and Michael talked for a half hour before she raised the subject of fertility. "I thought it was strange that no one was getting pregnant. The women seemed to be going through their cycles, and God knows there was a lot of…togetherness, if you catch my drift. So I asked a few guys I knew pretty well if I could test them, and after I saw the results, I tested the rest. Not a one is fertile. When the few kids we have grow up, that'll be it. Did you find the same thing in Berk Shire?"

"I've only tested myself and a few others in the core group. Only one of us is fertile," Michael said.

"Well if he's here, I like to introduce him to a few of the women, myself included. We'd just love to have some babies messing about."

Michael felt himself blush a little.

"And there's the bell for dinner, so I guess you're safe for now," she said, touching his arm ever so slightly.

The Berk Shire group was formed into a greeting line just inside the town hall doorway and introduced to the fifty-two members of Bergen's Field before dinner started. There was much handshaking and many *welcome*s offered. Michael found himself feeling quite comfortable with these people.

As described on the stream, the meal was simple and tasty. Trout was breaded and fried. String beans and colcannon, a concoction of potatoes and cabbage were the sides. The moonshine that was served was watered down and had been infused with juniper berries, giving it a taste something like gin.

As the meal wound down, Wayne excused himself and left the building. He returned a few minutes later with a gallon jug of his apple jack. He took an empty water pitcher and filled it, handed it to Matty, who poured a bit out and passed it on. When any who wanted had poured a cup, Wayne stood up.

"I would like to propose a toast!" he said loudly enough for all to hear. "To our new friends at Bergen's Field! May this be the start of a long and fruitful relationship!" He raised his glass, took a swig. The others in the room followed suit.

Matty then stood. "And now I'd like to propose a toast. To our new friends and trading partners from Berk Shire!" They drank. Matty leaned over to Wayne. "This is wonderful stuff. I must have the recipe."

"When you come visit us, I promise to show you my still and how to make it."

The remains of the meal were cleared, the tables pushed against the wall. Drums, acoustic guitars, a button accordion, Uilleann pipes, fiddles and tin whistles were brought out and played. Songs were sung, stories were told and dances were danced.

Caitlin, who had sat quietly through the beginning of the music, worked her way around the floor and approached Michael, asked him for a dance. He shrugged, told her he had no idea what he was doing.

"Just follow me, I'll guide you," she said. "And don't worry if you step on my feet a time or two. You'll get the hang of it."

She led him into the crowd, into a group with three other couples, put her arm around his waist and started dancing. He stumbled a bit at first, trying to imitate her steps, went forward when he should have gone backwards and bumped into her a few times, but caught on quickly.

"You're doing great!" she yelled to him. "Don't stop!"

They danced the next three numbers. Michael realized his heart was beating fast and he was a little out of breath. Caitlin saw this and pulled him aside.

"Time for a drink," she said, grabbing a pitcher and pouring them each some of the strong stuff, watering it down by half.

The party went just past midnight. Everyone joined in cleaning and rearranging the tables and chairs. Matty thumped his hand on a table to get the room's attention.

"I'm assuming you can't all sleep in that vehicle of yours, least not comfortably, so let's see what we can do. John and Mary? You've got room for one, don't you? Good. Seamus? One? Lizzy? One?" He continued on, ending with Michael. "Caitlin? Could you put the good doctor up? Great. I'll see you all in the morning for breakfast, then."

The walk to Caitlin's cabin was brightly lit by a nearly full moon. A not unpleasant fall weather chill was in the air, dry and crisp. She pulled her shawl a little tighter around her shoulders as they approached her cabin. Once inside the door, she lit two candles, handed him one, then showed him to her second bedroom.

"I'll be back in a few minutes with some white willow bark extract and a big glass of water to keep you from being hung over," she said, closing the door as she left.

He held the candle up in the air, looked around the room. It was sparsely appointed with a chair, double-sized bed, clothes rack, nightstand and dresser. Putting the candle on the nightstand, he sat on the edge of the bed and took his boots and socks off, then untucked his shirt.

There was a knock on the door. "Are you decent?" she called in, pushing the door in slightly.

"Come on in."

She had changed into a long, white nightgown that laced partially up the front. Her hair, free of the piece of ribbon, flowed down over her shoulders. She approached him with a tray on which sat her candle, a large glass of water and a small vial. Putting it down on the night stand, she twisted an eyedropper off the vial, filled it twice, squirting it into the water. She instructed him to finish the entire contents of the glass. When he had set it back down he looked up and thanked her. She didn't move.

"I know you're the one tested all right," she said, "and maybe I'm being quite forward, but times have changed and we must change with them or die off." She untied the top of her nightgown, slipped it off her shoulders and let it fall around her waist. "I'm hoping you'll say yes."

He kept his eyes focused on hers and reached out and took her hands. "Caitlin, I am truly honored, but I have a wife and son back home. My wife has shared me with another there, but that was different."

"How?" she asked. "She knows this type of thing must happen if we are to survive. How is that different from now?"

"She knew. I had her blessing."

Caitlin stepped back and pulled her nightgown back up, holding it with one hand. "You're an honorable man, Michael, and I respect that. I truly do. I can't say I'm not disappointed. On top of wanting a baby, it's been a while since I've been with anyone. But promise me this: will you talk to your wife about our need and consider returning at some time in the future?"

He smiled. "I will do that," he said. "I can't promise anything, but maybe if you came with Matty when he visits, and time your visit with your cycle, perhaps it might happen then."

She moved close to him again, leaned in and gave him a peck on the cheek. "I'll do that and hope my prayers are answered."

<hr />

In the next few weeks they visited a total of twelve more colonies. Some were quite small, with less than a dozen people, but most averaged between twenty-five and fifty. All were at least mildly receptive to the idea of taking on a few more people *if* there was something in it for them, though limits were set as to how many. The idea of Michael, John, Heather and Theo giving medical training to some of the residents was most appealing. Trade talks came up with some interesting and useful barter items put on the table. Some of the colonies gave some food to take away with them, while others had so little that Michael left some of their supplies to help out.

The group returned with a Konectable full of information and promises from most of the colonies to visit Berk Shire anywhere from soon to next spring. Michael briefed the others on their successes and talked about the ideas that had been floated. They discussed what they needed or wanted. Chrissy and Jim promised to put together projections of what they had to spare. This would be measured against what they would likely gain.

A meeting of the Berk Shire residents was called to inform them of the results of the trip and to set parameters for what was not to be talked about with any visitors, mainly the arsenal. At the end of the meeting it was announced that the second jack-o-lantern carving contest would be held in two nights. Residents were encouraged to go to the picking fields to get their pumpkins.

Back in their bedroom, Marcy put Mica Martin down in the crib. She rocked him gently while Michael sat nearby. When she was satisfied the boy was asleep, she sat down on the couch next to him and took his hand.

"I continue to be so amazed at what you're accomplishing," she said. "First this whole thing; now, alliances and trade routes. If nothing stops you, you're going to put together a whole new country."

Michael heard her words, then the echo of his own from the trip. He smiled at her and leaned in and kissed her. He told her about

Caitlin's request and his denial.

Marcy looked into his eyes. "You could have said yes and I would probably have been okay with that," she said, "but I'm glad you said you needed to ask me first. We should get around to testing all the guys here. You can't be the only one. Then we'll have to rotate you all around to keep from having too many first cousins running around and getting married."

"Maybe over the winter we'll get everyone checked out."

"So I have one last question," Marcy said.

"What's that?"

"What do *I* have to do to sweet talk you into bed?" she asked.

"You just did." He kissed her again.

<hr/>

The following day Michael called a meeting of the core group. He told them they needed an Office of Trade set up, and he was nominating Bert for the job. Bert tried to beg off at first, but saw the rest of the group were all in favor of him heading it up. He said he'd accept on one condition, that Jimmy be his second in command. They all agreed that that was an acceptable term. A small room in the basement was cleaned out and set up for them to use. They were given their own computer and were hooked into the wireless servers. Bob offered to help them set up a program to meet their needs, but Jimmy said he'd be fine doing that.

Jake and Betsy Morgan did come to visit two weeks after Halloween. Michael and Marcy met them at the front of the main building. Jake said he'd left Tim in charge, and proceeded to proudly display the weapons he and Betsy had brought, including two twelve-gauge pump action shotguns, and two double-barreled ones sawed off halfway to scatter shot widely at close range. They'd kept them by their sides for the trip. The rifle rack hugging the back window of their pickup truck held two lever action Winchesters. On either side of her waist, Betsy sported a holstered pair of matching semi-automatic handguns. Jake had a large caliber six-shooter tucked into his belt.

"Betsy's a damn good shot, more than comfortable with any of these bad boys. I figure anyone wants to mess with her is in big trouble. Someone starts shooting at us, I'm pretty much just along for the ride," Jake said.

Michael introduced Marcy and invited them in.

Jake looked around the living room and up at the supporting log structure, whistled, commented on the size, then turned to Michael. "Nice place you got here, and I want to hear all about it, but if you don't mind - and I hope I'm not being too pushy here - ever since you told me about having some bourbon around, I have had a powerful hankering for it. It's been over a year since I ran out."

"Guess that's what really got the conversation going when you two met," Marcy said with a smile. "Right this way, Jake. I'll show you to the bar. Betsy, what would you like?"

She looked at Marcy, cocked her head to one side as if she didn't know if she should ask. Marcy encouraged her to ask for anything. "Worst thing'll happen is I'll say we don't have any."

"Would you by any stroke of luck have...tea?"

"Let's go into the kitchen and see what we can find."

Michael and Marcy took them on a tour of the compound and some of the nearer fields, which were still being plowed under for the winter. Jake was impressed with the frog and catfish pond.

Betsy thought the cabins were laid out in a neighborly way. "It's like a little town springing up in the middle of nowhere," she said.

"You were quite the fortune teller, Michael," Jake said. "And the planning you did...well let's just say you did the work of a dozen people to get this place going."

Michael smiled and thanked him, then told him of the core

group of people who also participated in the organization and running of the place.

All thirty seats at the dinner table were taken that evening. Jake enjoyed more bourbon with ice before the meal, and was introduced to some of the people Michael had spoken to him about at their meeting in Morgansville.

"You remember Bert? Well, our visit around the countryside sparked a lot of interest in people wanting to start trading, so Bert, ably assisted by Jimmy, here, is now our head of trading operations. This is Chrissy, and this is Jim. They know pretty much all of what we have in the way of people, equipment, and items for trade. Between the four of them, we'll know what we can offer and what we need," Michael said.

The dinner spread included venison with a robust gravy, mashed white and sweet potatoes, corn and peas thawed out from the freezer, freshly churned butter and freshly baked cornbread. Apple and pumpkin pies were served for dessert along with decaff coffee and a blackberry liqueur they had learned to make using grain alcohol as a base. Jake opted for more bourbon.

"So what is it you need from us?" Jake asked.

"You've got sugar pumpkins. We've only got the big variety. And you've got broccoli. We don't."

Jake thought for a moment. "You've got peppers. We don't. Three kinds, if I'm remembering our earlier conversation correctly. And I'm impressed with all your beehives, too, so I wouldn't mind having some bees to get started, but you'd have to show us how to build and maintain the hives."

"Can you spare enough sugar pumpkin and broccoli seed to get me started on about an acre each? I'll give you enough for one-half acre each of the three different pepper seeds and a nuclear colony of bees. And before you leave, I'll give you the plans for building a hive so you can give the bees a home next spring when it's okay to move them."

Jake hesitated for a moment before offering one of the old ham radios he had lying around. "I've got six of them, but two are broken. Don't suppose you'd have anyone who'd know anything about ancient technology? I've got a load of spare parts and some diagrams that make no sense to me."

"I believe we have an electrical engineer somewhere in our midst. You bring them over and I'll have her take a look. In the meantime, we'll be able to communicate. There's a bit to taking care of bees, so our people can give your people suggestions and advice."

Jake extended his hand. The first inter-colony trade in the new era had taken place without lawyers, contracts or money. Michael sealed the deal by shaking Jake's hand.

The following morning when Jake and Betsy were loading up their vehicle, Michael handed him a bottle of bourbon and shook his hand. Jake promised Michael he would send someone over with the ham radios and spare parts. Marcy gave Betsy a jar full of loose tea and received a big hug in return.

Michael slipped his arm around Marcy's waist. "We are so good together making nice with the neighbors," he said after they'd left.

Other than the usual chaos of working to fit all the residents into the great room for Thanksgiving, the day went off without a hitch. The following day trees were cut for Christmas, one tall, large one for the main building, and smaller ones for any who wanted to set one up in their cabins. Plans were made for the coming snows, where to put the various pieces of equipment set up for plowing so that the cabins and the animals were accessible. Firewood was distributed to those who needed it. The business of keeping Berk Shire running smoothly was settling into a routine.

An open invitation went out to the residents for a Christmas Eve get together. Some came, while others chose to spend the evening in their homes with family. A fire was kept roaring in the main hearth. Food was set out buffet style, with all attending contributing their specialty to the spread.

Midway through the evening, Michael was informed that someone was banging loudly on the front door. He grabbed Robert and Bob. Each went to a side room to get handguns before going to the door. As they approached, they heard a frantic thumping. They looked in the monitor, and through the frosted lens saw a slightly blurry image of a small group of people clinging to each other. Michael counted four heads. They drew their guns as he opened the small outer door.

A man, woman and two children stood huddled together, a thin blanket wrapped over their collective shoulders. Michael motioned them into the secured foyer and closed the door. The man, shivering almost uncontrollably, peeled back the hood of his dark green jacket. Ice crystals that had formed on his mustache slowly started to melt.

"We need help," he said in a weak, trembling voice.

The woman, her arms wrapped around both children, looked at Michael. She was crying.

"Come in. Bob, go get Marcy and Heather...and some thermal blankets."

He led the family inside. Their jackets had not been heavy enough to keep them warm against the outside temperatures. The children had mittens that didn't seem thick enough to adequately protect their hands. Tears were streaming down both kids' faces.

Heather arrived first, quickly followed by Marcy and Bob, who was carrying a bag. They helped the family out of their jackets and wrapped them in heat-reflecting blankets. As they walked them across the living room toward the fireplace, the din of conversation in the room slowly dropped to silence. Marcy said in a loud voice to no one in particular, that they needed something warm to drink, ASAP. Four people moved quickly to the hot cider bowl and filled mugs.

The man started to talk, but Michael put his hand up. "Get warm first…all of you."

The man was in his mid-thirties, the woman a little younger. He was of average height and thin, with jet black hair and a long, full mustache trailing over his upper lip. Michael recognized the scared, confused look in his brown eyes, the same look Robert had had upon his arrival.

The woman, slightly shorter and heavier than the man, had unkempt brown hair with eyes the same color. She looked beaten down, close to giving up. Their children, a boy about seven, a girl around nine, were very thin. It was clear they hadn't eaten much in the past few days…or maybe weeks.

After a few minutes, when they were warming up, Heather pulled the mother and children aside and started asking simple questions to assess their medical condition. Marcy left the group to get hot soup and bread set up at a table off to one side.

"Thank you for opening that door," the man said.

Michael extended his hand. "I'm Michael Macalister."

"Joe Walker. That's my wife, Jean; my son Sam, daughter Jeanette."

"What happened?" Michael asked.

The man sipped from what was left of his cider. "Our car broke down a ways back…maybe two and a half, three miles. Heater wouldn't work. Had no way to start a fire, so I figured we had to start walking, hoped we'd find something. Didn't seem so cold when we started out, but jeez, the temperature seemed to drop quickly. We kept telling the children we'd find a place soon, but nothing. Then I smelled smoke - from your fireplace - and knew we were close to someone."

"Where were you headed?"

"Burlington - up in Vermont. Got a cousin there, I think. Haven't seen him in about ten years, haven't even spoken to him since then, but he always said if we had no place to go, we could go there."

"Let me see your hands," Michael said.

"Why?"

"I'm a doctor. So is the woman talking with your wife and kids. I just want to check you your fingers for any signs of frostbite. Nope, you're good. Come on over to the table my wife's setting up for you and get you something hot to eat."

As the family was eating, the residents started cleaning up. It was clear the party was over. Marcy and Heather made sure the children had all they wanted to eat and drink, then went to get warm pajamas out of storage for them.

Michael talked with the parents a little longer, then suggested they might want to rest. He showed them all to the upstairs. Bob had already moved two portable beds into an open bedroom so the family could all stay together for the night. Heather had said it would be better for the children to be with their parents at least this first night.

When Michael returned to the living room, Marcy was waiting for him.

"Did you check on Mica Martin?" he asked.

"Yes. Ginny said she's fine watching him a little longer, and besides, John's with her. He's going to walk her back to her cabin when we relieve her. I think he's sweet on her."

"I think you're right. Good for them. Little nightcap?"

"Wouldn't mind," she said, settling onto a love seat.

He came back in a minute with two cordial glasses, handed her one as he sat down next to her.

"The snow's started," she said. "For all the problems with that government computer, predicting the weather's pretty accurate."

"And that means the roads are going to be impassable for at least the next week, maybe more."

She snuggled into him. "And that means we're going to have guests for a while."

————)(◍)(————

Marcy and Chrissy were both up extra early on Christmas morning. They moved through the various storerooms in the basement, searching out items they thought might be nice gifts for the Walker children so they wouldn't feel left out when presents were exchanged. Chrissy's ability to remember where almost everything was helped them pull things together quickly. Fresh clothes for all four were also gathered up.

Michael explained to Joe that the storm, which had dumped over a foot of snow on the ground overnight, would make getting to their vehicle difficult at best. He added that the next storm would be coming through in a few days and that that would make it very unlikely they would be able to get on the road again anytime soon.

"Not like the old days when the town or county was out plowing all night," Michael said.

"Well, thank you for your hospitality. I don't think there's any way I can ever repay you for that. We don't have much in the car, sort of grabbed whatever we could quickly when we left home. It's mostly clothes, some pots and pans, a few photo albums."

"Where were you coming from?"

Joe talked about driving up from Plymouth. He said the area had been fairly civil when things started to go bad in Boston, and he'd taken the road around the city to avoid trouble.

"But there seemed to be trouble everywhere. At one point Route 128 was barricaded off. There were all kinds of people standing in front of the barricades, a big bonfire blazing. I realized it was a mob and they were probably going to take everything we had, so I turned

— 206 —

around quickly, went the wrong way and got off at the last exit. We ended up going directly through Boston, which turned out pretty good. It was a ghost town. We had to drive around a lot of abandoned vehicles. That was easy. It was trying to get past the smell. I can't even describe it other than to say I have never, ever smelled anything as disgusting."

"Decomposing bodies," Michael said. "So why'd you want to leave Plymouth?"

"There wasn't enough of anything anymore. The town government tried to keep things going, rationing what food there was, organizing people to grow things. A lot of us started fishing, but the area's pretty well fished out. Clams - there were plenty of clams at first, then that got fished out. We'd take trips to the Cape. People there were friendly at first, but then they got real territorial. I guess I can understand that. It all just started to fall apart, little by little by little. We decided to get out before it got really bad."

Jean and the kids walked down the stairs. The kids looked the Christmas tree up and down, ending with the presents wrapped in colored cloth. They started to move towards it, but their mother pulled them back. Michael said good morning and told them they would have breakfast first.

"I believe we're having pancakes with maple syrup, bacon, and some fruit compote - like a mushy fruit cocktail. And then...." He hesitated for a long pause, raised his head with a slight tilt, a smile in his eyes, and added, "...and then we'll see what's what under the tree. I think there might even be some things for the two of you," he said, winking at them.

Marcy sat next to Jean. The two children were between their parents. Jean dished out one pancake for each of the kids, then took a half of one for herself. She put one strip of bacon on each of the kids' plates, but took none for herself. Joe, too, had taken only one pancake and one strip of bacon. Marcy watched as the kids gobbled up their food, while Jean picked at hers very slowly.

"Would you like some more," Marcy asked the children. Each looked at their mother, who gave a subtle shake of her head. "Jean, would you give me a hand in the kitchen for a moment?"

They walked into the next room where Marcy asked why the kids weren't allowed to take more food when they were obviously hungry.

"We don't want to take much from people who may not have enough for themselves," the woman answered, her head turned down slightly.

Marcy took her arm and gently guided her to the nearest refrigerator and opened the door. She then took her to the bank of freezers and opened the first one. Both were filled with food.

"Now come back to the table and take what you want and let the kids eat until they're full. It's okay. We have more then enough to keep ourselves going throughout the winter and probably all of next spring and summer, too."

Jean looked up at Marcy and started to cry. Marcy pulled her into her arms and hugged her. "It's okay. It really is okay. You're safe here."

When they returned to the table, Jean put more food on the kids' plates, then passed the dishes to Joe. She said quietly, "Its okay." He took two more pancakes and a few strips of bacon.

<hr />

A few days after Christmas, Bill and another man took a truck and brought Joe out to his vehicle. The windows had been smashed in and almost all of the family's possessions had been taken. One photo album lay on the floor of the snow-covered back seat, ripped apart. The vehicle was towed in and placed in the machine shop, where Bill said his people would see what they could do. He knew there was nothing he would be able to do, but said this simply to help keep some hope alive in the man until he could explain things to Michael. There were no spare windshields lying around. It was clear to him that little could be done except to cannibalize it for spare parts for other repairs.

"I suppose that sometime in the spring some of us could drive you up Burlington," Michael said, after informing Joe of the situation with his car, "but I'm wondering if your cousin would even still be there. We don't know the situation out there, and we also don't know how dangerous the roads will be between here and there."

"So what are we supposed to do?" Joe asked.

"I put it to a vote with the core group and we all agreed that you can stay here, or we can find you space at one of the nearby colonies when the weather warms up."

"Jean and I have talked about how nice things are here. I know the kids feel safer than they have in a long time, so if we could, staying here would be okay with us."

"Consider it done," Michael said. "Welcome to Berk Shire. Let's talk about what you used to do and how you can contribute here. Everyone here works at something, earns his or her keep. Even the kids pitch in."

<hr />

It was in mid-January when Joe and Jean came to Michael asking to talk to him about something. Both entered his office with heads down, looking guilty and ashamed. He asked what this was about. Joe said that it was a very hard thing they had to tell him, and he hesitated for a few moments before Michael suggested he just spit it out.

"There was a woman that was here for awhile. She calls herself Doctor Lizbeth."

Michael narrowed his eyes and felt his body tense up. He had wondered if she would ever show up in his life again. He suspected she would, but didn't know where or when it would happen.

"What has she got to do with anything?" he asked.

"She's leading a group - a big group - of people. She told us she knew where there was a lot of food and shelter and cars and trucks, animals and all. She said she had put this place together, but that a bunch of people she'd taken in had taken it away from her. Now they ran this place, pretending to be good people, but they weren't. She told us that the people pretended to be nice, but were taking all the best things for themselves and that they made everyone work hard so they didn't have to. She said she had a plan to take the place back and run it the way it should be run, for the benefit of the people."

Michael felt his temper start to rise, but suppressed it. "And she sent you here."

"She told us she'd prepare us to come here and look like we were really down on our luck. The car being broken into, that was all part of the plan to make us appear even more helpless. She even re-stricted what the kids ate for a few weeks to make them really thin."

"And why are you telling me this now?"

"Because we think she was lying to us, and we want to stay here."

"Do you know what her plan is?"

"She wanted us to check everything out and then sneak off in the middle of April. There's a radio of some sort about ten miles from here, hidden off the road. We were supposed to go to it and call her, let her know what was what here. Then she would attack."

Michael called a meeting of the group and relayed what he had been told. The others talked about having to be prepared for the at-tack from mid-April on and started tossing out ideas of how they might do this. The volume of the crosstalk made it next to impos-sible for anyone to hear anyone. Michael rapped his knuckles on the table to get their attention.

"We're focused on the attack coming sometime from mid-April

on, but we need to explore some other possibilities first," he said.

Marcy caught on quickly. "She told us that organization usually wins out over disorganization…something like that. She knows we're organized, so she would want to use that against us…."

"…and so she might get the Walkers to confess what they did in order to make us think that she will attack sometime in April," Michael said, finishing her thought.

"And she might want to attack us a little earlier, before we were fully prepared," Marcy said.

"When did the two of you move toward paranoia?" John asked, adding, "And I mean that in the most complimentary way possible."

Robert, who been had assigned the position of Head of Security shortly after being shot, had been sitting silently, quietly taking in all that was being said. When he spoke, his voice was matter-of-fact, without emotion. "When are we at our most vulnerable?"

"What do you mean?" Bob asked.

"When would it be the hardest to get everyone together or when would we be mostly together but not ready to fight?"

The group went into silent thought. It was Heather who spoke first.

"When we're spread out in the fields. Most everyone's engaged in the process, some plowing, some delivering seedlings, others planting them or sowing seeds."

"Or when we're asleep," Bob added.

"Or having some sort of group dinner or meeting," Wayne said.

They all looked at Robert and realized that, while they were out their element, he was steeped in his. He started laying out scenarios for each of the ideas that had been put on the table. He said that a nighttime attack was unlikely because it would be difficult to shoot with any accuracy.

"Unless they have night scopes. While you might have been able to get them on the Web, it's no longer working. The only place there's any stockpile of those is at military bases or agencies like the FBI or CIA, and even then, in limited supply. I think it's doubtful they've accessed anything like that. So my money's on a daytime attack, most likely in the early part of the morning, maybe right around daybreak."

He said he needed to think this through more thoroughly and told them he would put some plans together within a few days. He wanted to meet with his men and brainstorm.

Michael went back to the Walkers and asked them questions about weapons and location, but they seemed to know little other than that they had seen some rifles and handguns and only knew that the group was staying a hundred or so miles away on Route 2 just outside a place called Harwood.

"What were they living on?"

"They have a lot to eat, broke into a food warehouse that some people had locked up pretty good. They shot at us, but there weren't many of them."

"So you killed them?"

Joe hesitated. "I…didn't have a gun," he said, looking down.

"But the ones who did, killed those people."

More hesitation. "Yes."

Michael slowly shook his head.

"We were starving. They wouldn't share. I know it was wrong, but Dr. Lizbeth said it was the only thing we could do. It was kill or be killed: survival of the strongest."

"If the weather holds, tomorrow you're going to show us where that radio is hidden," he said, going to the door of his office and making it clear he wanted them out of his space. When he heard their footsteps on the basement stairs, he closed his door and leaned against it. "Son of a bitch! This is what it's coming to."

The following day, Joe was loaded into a truck and asked to take them to the radio. He guided them to the area, showed them the subtle marker on the side of the road. He moved into the woods and counted off paces. When he'd reached the end of his count, he started looking around a bit before pointing. They pulled away brush and leaves and found a dark brown box, two foot square. In it they found some water and a few MREs along with directions on how to set up and operate the radio.

Robert and Smiling Bobby Ray returned from scouting the area and reported they had only found animal tracks that were probably a few days old.

"Any other footprints that were here have been long covered up by the snows," Robert said, "as ours will be in a few days."

"Let's take this back to the compound and check it out," Michael said.

<hr />

The group agreed that the Walkers were not to be trusted. They might be telling the truth, but they also might not be. Robert had suggested some interrogation techniques that would likely provide results, but Michael did not want to move in that direction. He pointed out that the Walkers might truly not know more, that Lizbeth might have purposefully kept them in the dark for the security of her own plans.

Michael knew that Lizbeth's training in organizational psychology would give her an advantage in potentially confusing the leaders of Berk Shire, but he also knew that Robert's training might give them a tactical advantage.

Robert's various attack scenarios and potential defenses were laid out for the group to see. He said that the APC had about a dozen mid-range sensors that might be set up to give them some warning as to when Lizbeth's group was approaching.

"But they'll only send a signal about five miles, so that won't give us much time to get set," he said. "And there aren't enough of them to cover all around us. We're going to have to choose the most likely approaches and concentrate on them. To move a large group, they'd have to have a lot of vehicles or a couple of big units, like buses or tractor trailers. I'd venture to say that those would be pretty available out there."

Bob raised the possibility that they might send a pair of residents out in a scout vehicle beyond the range of the sensors, and that seemed reasonable, but they kept coming back to second guessing themselves. Wouldn't Lizbeth have already considered that? And if she'd figured out the government-issued computer, she'd also know when the weather would break and when the moon would be in what phase to give them light or offer them cover of darkness.

Robert kept working up ideas the group gave him. The resident electrical engineer, Maggie, a pretty, mid-twenties woman with café au lait skin and long, curly black hair, was brought in to see if the military sensors could be modified to send signals further. After four days of pulling one apart and attempting to tweak it into a more powerful mode, she told the group that they were what they were and could not be pushed any more. She added that she wanted to keep working with the sensors to see if she could come up with anything else.

The weather started to break a bit by the middle of February. The survival computer's weather program was very accurate out to about five days, and fairly accurate to ten. Beyond that the unit moved into a predictive analytic mode, tagging output as *most likely, but without guarantee*. The program showed no more snow storms, temperatures rising into the mid-forties.

Smiling Bobby Ray and another soldier named Jeff took off in a small, but fortified vehicle to do reconnaissance along the road to Harwood. Bobby Ray said he hoped to be back in about a week to a week and a half.

Maggie announced that she had come up with a way to modify the sensors so that one would transmit to another. Robert gave this thought and came up with the idea of staggering the devices to cover much more of the areas from which Lizbeth might approach.

"This would give us about twenty miles of warning, though we have to think of how much time that translates into. We might also think about digging up the roads some to slow them down if they're trying to get here quickly in vehicles," he told the group.

"But that will come back to bite us later when we want to travel out again," John pointed out.

"Yes and no," Bob cut in. "We also have the equipment to fix the roads later, only we'll be using gravel instead of poly-mac. So I'm all for cutting it up and forcing them onto their feet."

"I'd rather avoid that if at all possible. It will make extra work and hastened the ultimate demise of the roads," Michael said. "We could set up some obstructions in the roads, but really, all we're talking about is slowing them down a little, postponing the inevitable... and I'll bet they'll be very prepared for that sort of thing."

"We could put some snipers in the areas around them. We might draw their fire away, take a few out, maybe slow them down a bit," Robert said.

"But you know as well as I do that that would pretty much be a suicide mission against a shit load of armed people."

"I could take my men out...."

Michael looked at Robert and shook his head from side to side. "You're all worth a lot more here, helping to run the show."

The following day, Maggie and Robert took two teams out to set sensors up to cover the main road from the one direction. Bill joined them later to set sensors in the woods near the main pathways into the fields between Berk Shire and Wayne's farm.

Stacks of long logs were delivered to the inner edges of the fields most likely to be the scene of any skirmishes. Equipment was used to set up barricades through which Berk Shire residents could shoot. These blinds were set up so that the people could also retreat safely if overrun. It was decided that three rifles would be set for every person assigned to firing weapons, and that each blind would be manned by ten people. Two of those would continually move up and down their half of the line reloading the empty guns so that constant fire could be maintained.

Plans for defense were gone over numerous times with each of the groups that would be stationed in various places around the area closest to the main compound. A simple set of signals was created using the bell sound through the speaker. Captains were chosen, with each one assigned a lieutenant who would take over *in case*. Older children were drilled in bringing supplies to stations within the main building, especially the sniper blinds on the roof of the main building.

And always, Joe, Jean and their kids were kept from these meetings. They were brought into bogus meetings in the basement or simply placed in one of the outbuildings when necessary. It was made clear that the other residents were not to talk to them about any plans. It was also decided that when the time came, all four would be locked in one of the basement rooms. No one could be sure if they could be trusted.

The sensors went off one morning, a little over two weeks from when Jeff and Smiling Bobby Ray had left. A sentinel at the five mile marker, hidden in the woods, called in that it was the vehicle the two soldiers had taken for the reconnaissance mission. The vehicle zipped into the entranceway and skidded to a halt in front of the main building. Neither Smiling Bobby Ray nor Jeff got out of the car. Instead, two other men, dressed in combat fatigues, carrying side arms, stepped out. As Michael approached the men, both drew their handguns.

"Whoa, easy," Michael said, raising his hands up in the air.

One of the men was carrying a satchel. The other walked up to Michael and stuck his handgun at his forehead. "You don't tell me what to do!" he shouted. "I'm in control here!"

Michael took a deep breath. "You're here to deliver a message and I'm here to receive that message, so how about we do the message part and get this over with?"

"You want to fucking live, pal, you'll shut up and listen," the aggressive one said, raising his hand as if to strike Michael.

"You hit me, you die. You shoot me, you die," Michael said calmly, extending a single finger on each hand. "Look around you." The Berk Shire people stepped away from their cover but kept their rifles aimed at the men.

The aggressive one started pointing his pistol in one direction, then shifting to another, aiming at the people who had him in their sights.

"Fuckin' A, Ryan, there's a lot of them aiming at us!"

"If I don't put up a certain number of fingers before I drop my hands, you're dead. Lower your weapons or they'll take you out. Let's get to the message part. That's why you're here. Come on, lower them so nobody gets hurt."

The man holding the satchel lowered his weapon, but the aggressive one did not. He pointed it back at Michael's forehead.

"Did you come here to get killed? Was this supposed to be a suicide mission?" he calmly asked the man. "Or are you just supposed to deliver a message?"

"I'll fucking shoot you if you don't do what I say!"

Michael drew in another breath, let it go slowly. He looked directly into the man's eyes. "Go ahead," he said so quietly that only the aggressive one could hear. "If you want to die, go ahead and shoot me. I've now got seven fingers raised, which tells my people to aim to wound. You shoot, I'll die, and you'll be in incredible pain, and they'll just leave you here screaming in pain, dying little by little. So, go ahead. This isn't about who controls who. It's about delivering a message. Do you want to do your job or not?"

The aggressive one kept his gun pointed at Michael for a few moments, then slowly lowered it, holding it at his side.

"Now, what is the message?"

The one holding the satchel stepped forward and put it down halfway between him and Michael.

"If y'all're Michael, Dr. Lizbeth said that's for y'all," he said. His voice was gruff with a backwoods accent. Even though his eyes were fearful, Michael picked up a sense of conflict. He wondered if this man was a soldier or simply dressed as one.

"And if either of us doesn't return safely, your guy back with her will be tortured and killed. That's the message." He stepped back.

Michael held up three fingers for a few moments, signaling his people to keep their weapons aimed, but not to fire. He lowered his arm. He stepped forward and picked up the satchel. It was fairly heavy, weighing about fifteen pounds. He stepped back to his original position and put it down on the ground. He went to open it.

"Stop! Michael! Stop!" It was Robert's voice. "I'll open it…in case it's wired."

He stepped out from the tree that he had been hiding behind and walked out to the satchel, his handgun in its holster. He looked the bag over, picked it up, sniffed it, made a face indicating it smelled bad, then checked the bottom, running a finger over it. His finger came up reddish-brown. He told Michael to step back towards the building. He undid the catch on the satchel and slowly opened it up. A look of anger moved slowly over his face as he stared into the bag. In a very quick move, he came to his feet, drawing his gun and pointing it at the man who had held the bag. Both of them immediately raised their weapons, pointing one at him and one at Michael, who again raised his hands halfway up.

"Easy, Robert," he said, realizing what was in the bag. "Who?" he asked, not taking his eyes off the men.

"Jeff."

"So tell me, what's the rest of the message?" Michael asked very calmly.

"Dr. Lizbeth said y'all can do this the hard way or the easy way. The easy way is to pack up and leave. Y'all know what the hard way is. She said to tell y'all she has us very organized, all three hundred and fifty of us. She said to tell y'all we have the hardware to blow that front door of yours off its hinges. Our group formed around the military base a few hundred miles away, so we've got a lot of firepower. She said to tell y'all y'all're sure to lose, and everyone will be killed."

Michael raised two fingers. Men and women with rifles and handguns started moving in closer to the men, surrounding them slowly, coming with ten feet. All weapons were trained on them.

The one man continued to stare at Michael. The aggressive one turned from one side to the other, nervously pointing his weapon at various people.

"Your friend is getting a little twitchy," Michael whispered to the one staring at him. "Let me ask you, would you like to leave here alive?"

"We would."

"*We*…well, I'm only asking *you*," Michael said very quietly, locking into his gaze. He saw the man swallow hard.

"Yes, sir, that would be my preference."

Michael kept his voice soft and low, so that only the man nearest him could hear. "Then let me tell you what I've decided. I've decided to let you live, and for what it's worth, I give you my word on that. But there are conditions…actually only one condition. And for the gift of going on living, I'm going to ask you to lower your weapon and place it on the ground. If you choose not to do that and make one tiny move with the finger you have on the trigger, you will die instantly, and believe me, that one finger is the entire focus of my man, Robert, here, and now mine also," Michael said, locking his eyes onto the finger. "Put it down and live; continue holding it and die. Make your choice."

The man held his aim steady at Michael for a moment, then slowly lowered the gun. He placed it on the ground, still cocked. The aggressive one, seeing what his partner had done, started shifting back and forth, one foot to the other. He noisily sucked in a breath, letting it out even more loudly.

"Pick it back up, man. You know what Ted said: whatever you do, don't put your weapon down. Pick it up, man!" he said, his voice filling with panic.

"Ted ain't here, Billy. Put it down."

"But Ted told us...."

"Billy, put it down or this is going to go bad real quick."

Billy hesitated for a moment, then slowly put his weapon on the ground, too. Michael stepped forward and picked up both handguns, released the hammers and set the safeties.

"You got him, Robert?" Michael asked.

"He moves, he dies."

Michael approached the aggressive one. He asked the group to all move to one side. He looked the man in the eye. The man stared back, venom in his gaze, the smell of fear coming off his body.

"I'm going to ask both of you to get down on the ground, please, while I consult with Robert. Please, down," he said, his voice almost soothing. Both men dropped face down on the ground.

"Bobby Ray?" Michael asked, pulling Robert away from earshot of the men, but keeping his gun pointed at them.

"If he ain't dead already, he will be, and he knows it."

"Then we should send a message back, don't you think?"

"I'll be happy to do it," Robert said.

"I can't tell you I wouldn't prefer that, but if I'm going to lead...."

"Understood."

Michael told the others they should go inside, pointed to one man on the ground. Robert walked over to the one who had carried the bag, put a knee on his back and held the barrel of his gun to the back of the man's head.

Michael took a deep breath and forced himself into clinical mode. He started walking quickly back to the men on the ground. Without hesitation, he put his ten millimeter within two feet of the back of the aggressive one's neck and pulled the trigger. Blood splattered in all directions. He walked over and pulled Robert's knife out of the sheath in his waistband, went back to the body and finished what little severing the gun blast had not already accomplished.

"I've got this one, Robert," Michael said, moving close to the one still alive on the ground. He pointed his gun at the man. "You move one inch either way and you'll join your friend. You stay still and I'll keep my promise."

"Robert? Can you think of anything else to be done? No?"

Michael told the man who had held the satchel to stand up. The man looked at the headless body, the flow of blood still oozing from what was left of the neck. Michael saw the fear in his eyes ratchet up and felt glad his message was already sinking in.

"I have been a medical doctor for some time now, and my thing has always been healing people, keeping them alive. But now we are living in extraordinary times, so I'm adapting to what is. This place, Berk Shire - you've only seen a tiny bit of it. People who come here join as friends and colleagues. We work together to survive. No one is forced to stay or to work. We do so because we choose to.

"Before your Dr. Lizbeth moved on from here she was being spoken to about some pretty bad behavior. She was given a choice to change it, but she decided to leave, took her boyfriend Ted and stole a whole lot of stuff from us. She didn't start this place nor did she do anything other than help in moving it along.

"She is a very sick individual. She has you killing innocent people who are just trying to survive. Think about the people at the food warehouse. Give that some thought. Who threatened who? And she has now declared war on us with her message. You want to believe her, I can't stop you, but if you start thinking about things and decide it might not quite be the way she says it is, you may find yourself not being so comfortable in her mob, maybe even wanting to leave. And if Bobby Ray, the other soldier from here, is still alive - and we have our doubts - but if he is and you can find it in your heart to help him escape, you are welcome to come back and live here, work with us instead of fighting, and very possibly dying, in a battle that doesn't have to take place."

Michael drew in a long breath and let it out. "If she wins this battle and takes this place over, what do think she's going to do? Go out in the fields and work? She's going to make everyone else do it for her, just like she made someone else kill Jeff and cut off his head. She'll declare herself queen and all of you will bow to her bidding or else."

Michael picked the severed head up by the hair and told the man to follow him to the car. He popped open the trunk and tossed the head in. He took the man's gun, unloaded the clip, emptied the chamber, and threw that in the trunk, too.

"The message to Lizbeth is this: *At least I had the balls to do my own dirty work.*

"As for you, I kept my word and let you live. If you return with Bobby Ray, I will, once again, keep my word to you. Now leave this place and come back as enemy or as friend. Your choice."

He turned and walked back to the main building. As he approached the door, he realized his jacket and pants were covered in blood. He realized what he had just done, and he tried hard not to care.

Marcy met him at the inner door. The others in the room stared at him. Without saying a word, she took him by the arm and led him to their room upstairs. He appeared to be going into some sort of shock. His eyes glazed over. He didn't speak or make eye contact, and offered no resistance to being guided away.

In the bathroom she helped him out of his clothes, put him in the shower and washed off any blood she could see. She put him into a robe and looked at him.

"Michael," she said softly. No response. "Michael," she said a little louder. No response. "Michael!" she shouted, getting right up in his face.

His eyes fluttered a bit. He looked at her. She saw his eyes soften just a bit, then show fear, then soften again, then move to anger, then soften again. She put her arms on his shoulders and pulled him to her. He started to sob.

—————•《◊》•—————

The next day, he met with the group to talk about what had transpired. He listened as the others told him he did not need to justify his actions, but at the same time he could sense that they did want to know what had been going on in his head. He certainly wanted - *needed* - to talk about it. He explained about being given the satchel and went through the events one by one, bringing in his thoughts and feelings during the situation.

"I'm not quite sure when it clicked in my mind: this is war, and in war people often find themselves in circumstances in which they would otherwise never find themselves, and within those circumstances they sometimes do atrocious things." He stopped for a moment and felt himself trying to shut down to his emotions. "I regret what I did, but it was also a very necessary action." He stopped again and bowed his head. "I very much regret what I did, and I will live with that the rest of my life."

Tears streamed down his face. The others said nothing, silently bearing witness to his pain and feeling utterly helpless to do anything about it.

He sniffed hard, took a breath and looked at them. "In the coming weeks, some of you will also experience what I have in taking another human being's life. I pray that it won't happen, but I know it will if… no…when this battle comes to us. We each need to know that this is not the type of people we are, but the type of people we must be in order to defend ourselves. If we do not, they will take everything that means anything to us, including quite possibly, our very lives. In the end, there will be a lot of deaths on both sides. Is it avoidable? Yes. Will it be avoided? Unlikely. We will do what we have to do."

"God help us all," Bob said. He reached to the person on either side of him and took their hands. Each one, in turn, did the same.

<hr/>

Mica Martin drifted off to sleep as Michael gently rocked his crib. Marcy came out of the bathroom, fresh from a shower, wearing a thick robe, toweling off her hair. She stood next to Michael and looked down at the baby.

"So at peace," she said, rubbing Michael's shoulder.

He turned, took her into his arms and kissed her, then led her to the bed. He quickly got out of his clothes and climbed under the covers with her. He started kissing up and down her body, paying attention to every inch of it, softly, gently. When they were done, he held her in his arms and told her he loved her.

"I love you, too, and enough to know that something's going on in that mind of yours," she said.

"I want you to take Mica Martin over to Jake and Betsy's. Bob's asking Heather to go, also, and all the kids under fifteen will be going. I spoke to Jake on the radio and he says it's no problem. I don't want to risk having you or Mica here. It might be distracting."

Marcy's hackles went up a bit. "So now I'm a distraction?" she said somewhat loudly.

Michael put his finger to her lips. "You know that's not what I mean. We've got a child to think of. It's not just about you and me anymore. Hell, if we didn't have Mica, I'd want you right by my side. Not only are you a crack shot, you hold it together when the shit hits the fan."

She took a deep breath, closed her eyes for a moment and refocused. "Sorry. You're right. It's the best thing to do for Mica. Doesn't mean I'm going to like it, though."

"Didn't think you would."

"When do I leave?"

"Couple of days. We just don't know when Lizbeth's going to attack. Take the truck. Hell, I don't want it getting shot up anyway. I love that truck. I'll send a couple of soldiers with you in another vehicle to make sure you all get there safely, then they'll come back."

"I want two tens, my favorite lever action and a shit load of ammo in case anyone comes after us at Jake's. Deal?"

"Deal. Seal it with a kiss?"

Marcy, Heather and ten other mothers left with their children two days later, the trucks stocked with clothes, food, guns, ammunition and two bottles of bourbon. Bob put his arm on Michael's shoulder as they watched their women leave.

Barely three hours later the woman monitoring the sensors called Michael on a two-way handheld, telling him that the furthest one out had gone off. He contacted Robert, who met him in the monitoring room.

"How many?" Robert asked.

"One ping; no more. Short one, at that," the woman said.

"Single vehicle." He checked the wall clock. It was ten after eleven. "Let's time this out," he told Michael. "If the second sensor pings, I'll have an idea how fast the thing is moving."

"Could it be a bear or a deer?"

"Possibly, but if it is, it'll probably take an hour to reach the second one if it even heads in that direction. However, if it's a vehicle, the next ping should be within five to ten minutes, depending on how fast it's moving, so hang tight. You might want to call up top and make sure the outer defenses stay frosty."

The next ping occurred in less than five minutes.

"Sixty-five at least," Robert said. "It'll be here in about eight, nine minutes max. Let's go."

Michael called the guards on the main road and instructed them to put up the barricades just past the turnoff for Berk Shire's entrance. He wanted to know who this was and what they were doing in this area. As soon as they got through the front door, both pulled their pistols.

"Lock and load," Robert said, pumping a round into the chamber.

Michael's radio crackled to life. "Car turned in, moving at a good clip. Over."

"Copy that. Out," Michael said into his unit.

They did not recognize the vehicle. It was a small two-seater with darkly tinted windows. It came speeding down the driveway and screeched to a halt ten paces in front of Michael and Robert, who both pointed their weapons at the doors on either side.

The driver's door opened. Smiling Bobby Ray hopped out, only he was smiling even less that usual.

"Help me get him out of the car. He took one in the arm and he's bleeding badly."

The passenger turned out to be the man who had delivered the satchel. He was rushed into the building and downstairs to the operatory. John and Theo met them there.

"Make me up four units of universal blood and get set for possible surgery. Shit! Where's Heather when we need her?" Michael yelled.

He took scissors and cut the man's shirt open, then trimmed out the shoulder and sleeve. The arm had a makeshift tourniquet just above his bicep, and a blood-soaked bandage slightly below that. The skin below the tourniquet was a grayish-blue. The man was unconscious. He put a blood pressure monitor on his index finger.

"Bobby Ray, cut the rest of his shirt off. Pressure's low. John or Theo, start a line with saline and the universal…and push the universal. He's lost a lot of blood. Somebody get that computer program up and running with the surgery pictures in it. I need the left arm on the screen, stat, then both of you scrub in. Bobby Ray, I want you to hold this cloth over the wound and press hard. I'm going to release the tourniquet for a minute and get some blood flow back to the arm, then tighten it up again. Here we go."

He undid the tourniquet and waited until the man's arm turned pink again. He had Bobby Ray lift up the cloth. No pulsing, but a substantial flow. One of the larger veins! He instructed Bobby Ray to apply pressure again so that he could scrub in.

In the sterilization room, he peeled off his bloody shirt, then poured liquid antiseptic liberally on his hands and forearms, letting it soak while he waited for the sink to open up.

"Theo, you're going to assist. John, you'll do anesthesia, but very, very lightly. This guy is not stable. You know where the gowns are. Get three out. Okay, I'll be in in a minute."

The surgery lasted over four hours. Michael commented that he was glad he and Heather had studied up on the procedures and techniques needed for these types of wounds. John volunteered to stay with the patient until they could locate one of the primary care doctors.

Smiling Bobby Ray, who had washed up and hung around

outside the operatory, was invited to join them for a drink after they scrubbed out. He told them the man's name was Ryan. He was not a soldier, but had been a construction worker before things had changed.

"We did some talking when I was being held. He used to come by and chat for a few minutes. Sounds like a bit of a lost soul. Then late one night - more like the early, early morning - he came to the room I was in, told me to follow him, that he was going to help me escape. We walked by the guard, who was passed out on the floor. Said he brought him a bottle of beer with some heavy duty sleeping pills he'd traded his dinner for. Anyway, he had it all planned out, led me into this wet field of really tall marsh grass. There was this little shit car waiting on the other side. Just as we were hopping in, there was a shot and he was hit. He pulled a gun and started shooting back, told me to drive. Took off like a bat out of hell and kept watching in the rearview, but no one followed us. He put a towel on his arm, but started to get a little groggy as we were driving, so I pulled over and did the tourniquet."

"You did the right thing," Theo said. "He would have bled out otherwise."

"He going to make it?"

"We'll see," Michael said. "Tell me what you saw where you were."

Bobby Ray talked about being captured by a patrol of soldiers who were part of the group, led by one named Davis, who had been Special Forces. He said he suspected they had some sort of sensors set because he and Jeff had been extremely careful.

"Being walked into their camp, we saw probably three hundred twenty-five people, maybe more, some dressed in fatigues. I can't tell you how many actually were soldiers because I heard that a bunch of them had ransacked the base where we had been stationed, so a lot of the uniforms were stolen."

"How many women?" Michael asked.

"Fifty, maybe sixty."

"Kids?"

"Maybe twenty."

"Weapons?"

Bobby Ray thought about this. "I saw lots of assault rifles and tens, some shotguns, hunting rifles, six shooters, two RPGs for sure, maybe more."

"RP what?"

"Rocket propelled grenades. Pack a lot of punch. Don't know how many boxes of grenades they had with them. What else? One hundred millimeter rifle with a tripod, mounted on the back of a pickup truck. That sucker will go through a half inch of steel. Don't know how much ammo. One full bore, fifty millimeter machine gun and tripod. Two APCs - that means they probably have some plastic explosives - and four tractor-trailers. The tractors are hybrid, bio-diesel/electric combination, so if they're running on electric only, they'll be limited to about twenty-five miles per hour with a half-full trailer of people or more. However, they were holed up in a food distribution warehouse, so if there's vegetable oil, they'll run faster on that. Still, on these roads, we're talking forty, tops, for something that big."

Michael looked at Theo and whistled. "We're in trouble. We are in a shit load of trouble."

<hr />

Ryan stabilized by the next day and, though groggy from pain medication, was able to talk. Michael asked about Lizbeth's reaction to his return message. Ryan explained that initially she'd had no reaction, but he'd heard her get very angry a few minutes later when he'd left her office in the warehouse, said it sounded like she was throwing things.

Michael assembled the group to relay the news that they were outnumbered, though he wasn't exactly sure by how much, that Lizbeth had far more powerful weapons than they had, and that she could transport her people en masse.

John was the first to speak. "So basically, you're telling us we're fucked."

"In a straight out firefight, yes, unless we can come up with something that can even out the numbers and take out some of their firepower."

They stared at each other, no one speaking. Wayne finally threw out an idea.

"My granddaddy used to talk about a fire bomb of some sort, called it a *something* cocktail...masoltov or something like that."

Robert laughed. "Molotov cocktail. Some sort of flammable fuel in a capped bottle with a fuel-soaked rag threaded through the opening. You lit it, threw it, and when it hit anything and broke, it sent flames all around. Old school, but that might be very useful."

Bob brought up the grain alcohol they had been making over the past year or so. Chrissy piped in right away that they had over fifty gallons stored in an outbuilding. She also brought up that most of the canning jars were in use. John pointed out that they could dump out food and make up a few dozen without hurting storage too much.

Bobby Ray pointed out that they didn't want to start any fires in the woods. "We don't exactly have a lot of fire firing equipment."

Michael listened with half an ear. He kept rolling around Lizbeth's statement that organization - *for the most part* - wins out over disorganization. He finally spoke her words out loud to the group.

"So when would organization not win out over disorganization?" he asked the others.

They started brainstorming, throwing out idea after idea, a practice they had used many times in their frequent meetings in the beginning of Berk Shire. Chrissy, who was by far the most organized person at the meeting, posed a thought: "When organization gets confused by something."

"Stay with that," Michael asked, moving one hand in a circle in the air.

She thought for a moment, formulated an analogy. "Like if I walked into my office expecting to find things in exactly the same order in which I left them the night before, but something happened to change where everything was filed, I would be confused by that. I'd start wondering what happened and maybe even try to figure out why. But it would slow me down, confuse me. I'd have to start looking for things in order to start putting them back into the order I knew before - to reorient - and I'd be distracted from my regular work."

Michael smacked his hand down on the table hard. The others jumped. "That's it! So the question is: what is Lizbeth expecting to find?"

They immediately moved back into brainstorming mode, talking about the defenses she knew about that they had put in place, noting them as useless. A few minutes later Michael sat back in his chair and smiled widely.

"People, we have a lot of work to do in a very short period of time. Here's what I'm thinking."

<hr />

The residents of Berk Shire were broken into smaller groups and assigned various tasks. The Walkers were simply locked in a cabin with the windows covered over. One guard stayed with them at all times.

Michael oversaw the removal of all computer and filing equipment from the main building, moving it all into a hastily built shelter in the woods at the far reaches of the farm. Three of the freezers and refrigerators were removed and hooked into another set of new buildings, far away from the main areas. The minimal amount of photovoltaic panels needed were cannibalized from cabins, then installed to keep the equipment running. As much food as could be stored was moved into those units. Most of the remaining food was distributed to all the cabins that still had working refrigeration units.

The arsenal was emptied. Weapons and ammunition were distributed to a few areas around the property, hidden in makeshift storage containers. Crews quickly built more blinds out in the fields, smaller than the original ones. Finally, most of the farm equipment was moved to outer areas unlikely to be the focus of any action, and parts of the motors were dismantled to make them useless to Lizbeth's people, should they find any of it. Amongst the vehicles moved into hiding was the armored car they had built to disperse the enemy in a large scale attack. There were comments about how all that work had been for nothing. Robert pointed out that while it would have been useful with a not-so-well equipped mob, this one was extremely well-armed. One rocket grenade would pulverize it and anyone in it. Its usefulness would be short-lived, at best; its mission suicidal.

The last piece of preparation was explained to the residents at a meeting in the main building.

When it had been implemented, Michael said, "Robert; Bob - let's get to work and finish this up."

<hr />

The core group sat at the dining room table, finishing the dinner Michael and Chrissy had cooked. Because of the impending attack, each person there had agreed to have no more than two drinks over the course of dinner, before, during or after.

"Compliments to the chefs. That was damned good," Wayne said.

All now had a two-way headset with them at all times. The sensors were monitored by two people at all times, around the clock. In addition to the sentinels posted at the entranceway, two man patrols were also monitoring the easiest routes in through the woods and fields. A sentinel was hidden away in the woods within sight of each of the sensor arrays on the road leading in, starting with the second set. Robert had produced a personal night scope for each to use if darkness was an issue.

Michael found himself staying up later and getting up earlier. He felt a sense of weight shifting onto his shoulders. What he had started and put together was now entering a new phase, one he had considered, though not to this extent. He had expected that there would be some violence by individuals, maybe even small groups of ten to twenty people. But he had never expected an army of over three hundred to be in the picture. He hadn't thought people would get that organized. But from all the research he had done in his adult life, he knew there were always variables that he would not have considered. Lizbeth was one of them.

He spoke to Marcy every evening, shortly after dinner, and sometimes called her on the ham radio during the day just to tell her he missed her and to ask about Mica Martin. He missed seeing her every day, missed the sound of her voice, the smell of her hair and skin. He told her this and that he loved them both more than anything in the world. He told her this because he did not how much longer he would be able to tell her. He was now living in what would shortly become a war zone.

They chatted, talked about many different things, but he did not reveal any thoughts or plans on the upcoming battle or their defenses. He and Marcy had discussed this before she left. They were never to use each other's names and were only to refer to Mica Martin as the kid. Lizbeth also had radios and although the frequency she had listed on the instruction sheet for the Walkers was different, he assumed she was also monitoring other bands as well. He had no idea if she would start looking for Marcy to use her against him in the upcoming battle.

He heard John's voice echoing in his head: *When did the two of you get so paranoid?*

He realized he had changed almost as much as the country - no, the world - had. He was now expecting the worst from people, planning for it, getting devious in his thoughts. He had killed. That came back to him more frequently than he cared to admit, the images of *that* act taking center screen in both his dreams and his waking hours. Sometimes he could move away from it, sometimes he couldn't. He wondered if he would ever be able to forgive himself enough to put it to rest. He doubted it.

He was now prepared to kill more people, some from a distance, some up close, some by his own hand, some by the hands of others he would lead into battle.

Bob's words floated through his head: *God help us all.*

<hr />

As usual, Michael was up very early, before any of the others beyond the night crew of monitors and guards. From one of the last batches of tea left, he had brewed a large pot. He leaned against a countertop in the kitchen, sipping and thinking. He wondered if this was going to be the day Lizbeth attacked, or if it would simply be another ordinary day.

He chuckled out loud. *Ordinary!* He looked at the assault rifle and the shoulder bag full of ammunition and other goodies he had placed against the wall when he first entered the room. There had not been an ordinary day in his life since the numbing cold had appeared and he had been recruited to figure it all out. At first it had seemed ordinary to him, another disease to pull apart, figure out and cure, but it had gotten extraordinary very quickly and had never stopped climbing that ladder.

He realized that his definition of ordinary had morphed into something that would have been unrecognizable a few years back, something heavy at times, weighing him down, then turning into something uncontainable, uncontrollable, a dark looming storm cloud drifting through the back of his mind more often than not.

Chrissy and Bob walked into the kitchen. He offered them tea, and, knowing the others would be meandering in over the next ten or fifteen minutes, he started cracking eggs into a bowl for scrambling. Bob rummaged through the refrigerator and pulled out a container of bacon they had thawed out a few days earlier.

The talk was easy. *Breakfast talk*, they called it. Nothing heavy, nothing important. It had gotten harder and harder to keep things light even in the earlier parts of the day. They were waiting, knowing that sooner, rather than later, Michael's two-way handheld was going to crackle and life as they knew it would change yet again, only this time it would be a deadly change.

"When will the tea bushes in the greenhouse start producing?" John asked, as he poured himself a cup.

"Should be this year," Michael answered.

"I'd prefer coffee," Bob said to no one in particular.

"Jake's in contact with a grower in the mid-south. He's hopeful this guy will start shipping up here sometime in the summer, but we've got to come up with something he wants in trade. I'm hoping Jake can convince him to sell us a hundred or so bushes so we can grow our own."

They went back to eating in a silence that was neither comfortable nor uncomfortable, just unsettled.

"I know you don't want too much equipment out in the fields, Michael, but we've got to get more land plowed soon or we risk falling behind in the harvests," Chrissy said.

"Maybe we can send one tractor out and start...."

His two-way hissed to life. "Janet here. The furthest sensor just went off multiple times. Over."

Michael pushed a button. "How many? Over."

"Fifteen. I started the timer. I'll let you know in a few minutes. Out."

Michael looked at the others. "Leave the dishes," he said. "Hopefully we'll get to them later. Robert, give the signal. It's game time. Luck to us all."

Each picked up one of the rifles stacked neatly against the dining room wall and headed out. Michael grabbed the three mugs that still had tea in them and walked into the kitchen, placed them in a spectrawave oven and turned it on high for twenty seconds, sending the liquid in each to a boil. He returned the steaming mugs to the table, then sprinted downstairs to the radio and called Jake, who informed him that his wife was out in the barn finishing up milking the cows.

"It's happening. Tell her I love them both and take care of them for me. Over."

Jake's voice came back. "Will do. Keep your ass safe, you hear? Out."

He moved into the monitoring room. Janet looked at him and shook her head. The vehicles had not yet reached the second sensor, which meant they had either turned off the road, stopped, or were moving slowly. He told the second person in the room to go to his battle post, then sat down with Janet and waited.

Eleven minutes later the second sensor went off. Again, there were fifteen pings. Michael quickly did the math. The vehicles were moving in single file, at about thirty miles per hour.

"Robert? Over."

"I'm here. Over."

"ETA to outer areas is ten to fifteen minutes. To the main

entrance, a little more. Over."

"Got it. Out."

The sentinel at the second sensor called in his report. "Four tractor-trailers, two APCs, bunch of pickups. Two of the pickups have hardware on them, maybe machine guns. And the big trucks are...."

They heard a loud noise just before the radio went silent. Michael tried to reestablish contact, but didn't get any response. He looked at Janet. They both knew what that meant: first casualty.

They waited again. A little over ten minutes went by before the next pings started. Thirteen. The sentinel in that area called in. He reported three tractor trailers, two APCs, and eight pickups. His radio also went dead mid-sentence.

"Robert? Over."

"Yep? Over."

"One tractor trailer and one other vehicle have stopped at the outer fields. Over."

"Got it. Out."

Just before the third sensor, there was a small dirt road onto the property that would lead anyone taking it to the second set of fields. It ended at the animal pens. The animals had all been moved to a remote area and were being held in makeshift pens. Michael knew that hawks and coyotes and foxes would be after the chickens, but they hadn't had enough time to roof in those pens. He hoped that Wayne's Border Collies would fend off most of the predators.

The third sensor started pinging. The sentinel called in one tractor trailer, two APCs and five other vehicles. Before his radio went dead, they heard gunfire.

Michael called in to Robert, gave him the update. He turned to Janet, told her to move on to her post as quickly as possible, saying he'd handle it from here. She left the room with her rifle.

He forced himself to take regular, even breaths. He could not be calm, but he could keep himself from scrambling up the ramp into panic. He waited and breathed, waited and thought, focusing on running the plan through his head one last time, knowing that when the shit hit the fan, the plan might mean jack.

The pinging jolted him back to the room. His two-way crackled. The sentinel reported two APCs, one tractor-trailer, two pickups with hardware, and three....

He pressed the bell signal button four times in rapid succession, shut off and pocketed the hand held, put on a headset and called Robert as he was running up the basement stairs. He entered the living room and pressed the button that opened both the inner and outer sets of doors to the building. Jogging quickly through the building to the back door, he headed out, crossing the patio and going on to his post.

One APC arrived first, quickly followed by the pickup truck with the one-hundred millimeter rifle attached to its bed. Its driver slid it into position in front of the open doors, the rifle pointed directly in, ready to fire. The other pickup with the fifty caliber machine gun hidden behind a set of makeshift metal plates moved into position next to the first one.

As the cloud of dust started to settle, three pickups pulled up behind the APC, followed by a tractor-trailer. From the tractor-trailer, forty men appeared, weapons pointed at the front of the building and the sniper blinds on the roof line. Twenty more got out of the three pickups. Two of the men had RPGs pointed toward the front door. Six large men in full combat gear, including plasteel protective vests, got out from the last vehicle to enter, an APC. They formed a human barricade. Ted, in battle fatigues, got out first, looked around, then motioned inside the truck. Lizbeth, also wearing a plasteel vest over camouflage fatigues, stepped out, moving in behind her guards and next to Ted. Both of them had headsets on.

All had guns at the ready, only there was nothing to be ready for.

Lizbeth stared at the open doors, looking unsure how to act. She and Ted conferred briefly before he ordered a dozen men to enter the building and figure out what was going on. As they waited, over one hundred of their people started arriving by foot from the east side.

Ten minutes later the men exited the building and declared it totally empty. Ted looked at Lizbeth. Both were confused. This should have been the command center, the stronghold, the prize to be won. This is where the battle should have been raging from the start.

Lizbeth and Ted's ear pieces crackled to life. A voice quietly told them there was no one at the rear of the building. Ted started looking around, moving his eyes from one place to the other, searching for something that made sense: men hiding behind trees, blinds, anything. But there was nothing for him to see.

Lizbeth looked at him, searching for some sort of information that would help her proceed. He spoke to her briefly, then sent four two-man patrols out to reconnoiter the areas behind and around the main building. He suggested they go in and look around for themselves. She peeled off the vest and threw it to the nearest guard. The other five moved ahead of her, human shields.

Inside, they saw the living room set up as it had always been. They moved to the dining room and saw the dirty dishes sitting on the table. Ted picked up one of the half full mugs of tea and dipped his finger into the liquid.

"They were here not too long ago, within five minutes," he said. "These are still pretty hot."

Moving into the kitchen, they immediately saw the missing appliances. Opening the doors to the refrigerators and freezers still there, they found them fairly packed with food.

Their headsets clicked loudly, making her jump. Ted scowled

back at her as if asking her what she was so excited about.

"This is George. I'm by some sort of big building, southeast of the main one. There's a shit load of footprints around it and somebody tried to cover them up close to the building by dragging the area with something…maybe branches."

"Machine shop," Ted said to himself. He thought for a moment. "Where'd they come in from? What direction?"

"All over, man. Like they all rushed to this one place."

"Stay where you are and don't make any noise. Johnny, you there?"

"Out front."

"Bring the men, the APCs and the pickups to the rear of the building, then follow me."

They left through the back door, walked across the patio and onto the dirt road leading to the outbuildings. He assembled the men there, waited for the others to join him. He now had two hundred people at his back. He called to the other groups that were waiting by the edge of the fields to the east, telling them to hold position until he called back.

Ted found George kneeling down fifty feet from the front of the machine shop. The doors were closed, the window shutters down and locked. He had both pickups line up into position facing the main door, then positioned one of the men with an RPG in between the trucks.

"When I give the signal, I want the hundred millimeter and the RPG to fire at the doors. I want the front two lines, one standing, one kneeling down, to aim at the large door and the smaller doors to the right and left. When we blow this thing, start firing. They're going to start pouring out like cockroaches. Kill them all. Kill anything that moves. Everybody else, step back and off to the sides. Move! Now!" He kept waving them back with his arms, then gave them the signal to stop.

He moved back another fifty feet, taking Lizbeth by the arm, almost dragging her with him. She did little to resist until they stopped, then shook him off.

"I'll give the signal," she said.

"Be my guest. *You* be in charge," he said sarcastically.

"Ready!" she yelled raising her arm. She dropped it. "Fire!"

A second after the RPG hit and the one hundred millimeter fired, the entire front of the building exploded, sending sticks, stones and small and large pieces of timber flying at them. Many of the people in the rear of the group started running away, ducking and holding their hands over their heads.

When the dust settled, Ted and Lizbeth were looking at dead and dismembered bodies strewn all about the area. Many of those who had been standing further back had been hit by debris and were bruised, bleeding or in shock. The two pickup trucks had been crushed and covered by large timbers. Some people started firing their weapons.

"Fuck!" Ted yelled. He looked at Lizbeth and screamed, "Get in the APC! Now! Move it!" He turned to those who were left and yelled, "Take cover! Now!"

The group scattered, looking for trees and rocks to hide behind. Some hid behind the vehicles; others just crouched down and started nervously pointing their weapons in multiple directions, firing without settling on any particular target.

It took Ted a minute to figure out it was only his own people firing. "Cease fire!" he screamed. "CEASE FIRE!!"

They all waited, breathing hard, trying to be still and silent, waiting, waiting. There was only quiet: no firing, no movement, *no nothing*.

Lizbeth stepped back out into the open. Ted looked at her and spoke quietly, "You said you knew how they'd organize themselves; you told me *this is how it would go*, like you had a fucking clue. All your high and mighty fucking knowledge is just getting us killed."

"We still outnumber them more than two to one. We've still got the advantage," she said. "They want us all confused and angry - makes it harder to think clearly. You're doing exactly what they want. Take a breath. Calm down and think."

"Then where the fuck are they?"

She thought for a moment, then looked at him. "Where would the playing field be most level?"

He looked down, pursed his lips, thought. "The playing field... the playing field. Level playing field...that's it: the fields. But which ones?" He tapped his ear piece three times. "Judah, you there?"

"I'm here, boss."

"What do you see where you are?"

"There are these log walls, some thirty feet long, some smaller, ten, maybe twelve feet long."

"Any movement?"

"Nothing. No noise either."

"Sit tight."

"Gerry?"

"Yeah, Ted?"

"What do you see from your position?"

"Same thing as Judah. I've got two big ones, two small ones. No movement either...wait a minute. I think I saw...no...just an animal moving near one of them."

"Which direction are the backs of their walls facing?"

"Uh, sort of north."

"Judah?"

"Northeast, I guess. Yeah, northeast."

"Sit tight."

He moved Lizbeth into the APC, grabbed a Konectable and pulled up the map he had drawn of the area shortly after they'd left the compound over a year ago. They went over it to figure out how to access the areas behind the blinds. Looking at the map, they also realized they would have to go through a couple of the small neighborhoods, and that would slow them down.

"Maybe we should just go out the main entrance and use the back path to come up behind them," Lizbeth said.

"Take us a lot of time to do that, time we'd be giving them to prepare. So what are they trying to do?" he asked. "Could be they're trying to draw us to the fields knowing we have to go through the cabin areas. But then, they'd know we knew the layout and we'd probably think of that."

"Why don't we just fly through there?" she asked.

"'Cause I don't think either one of us has a fucking clue what to expect anymore. I'm sending out a bunch of patrols to make sure the area is clear before we go through."

He pulled out four Konectables that showed the maps he'd just looked at, then organized four patrols of four people each. After getting their instructions, the groups took off toward the cabins. A few minutes later the two-way came to life.

"Uh, Mike here. What I'm looking at is not what you put on the screen, man. I mean, in the beginning it was just like the map shows, but there're way more cabins than that now. What do you want me to do?"

"How many more cabins?" Ted asked.

"What I'm seeing is about fifteen, maybe more."

One of the other patrol leaders cut in. "Same here."

The last two groups reported the same. Ted thought for a moment before ordering them to split up and start searching the inside of each cabin.

He told the main group to form into groups of ten each, took a count of what he had left. He saw that many of them were scared, unsure of what was happening. Only seven of those nearby him were soldiers, four others, cops. He wondered how many other soldiers Michael had, and how well he had trained those who weren't. They probably had a fairly equal amount of guns and ammunition, but he still had an RPG left with seven more grenades. He could probably take out those log blinds pretty easily if he knew which ones they were hiding behind.

Fifteen minutes passed and he hadn't heard back from any of the patrols. He clicked his two-way to life and asked them to check in. None did. He called again and again got no response. He hadn't heard any firing, no yelling, no calls for help. He didn't remember any silencers when they were a part of Berk Shire. Maybe the soldiers had brought some in. Then it dawned on him. Part of Michael's cache of weapons included crossbows and compound bows, and he had talked about creating knockout gas when he'd built the foyer in the main building.

"Okay," he said, addressing his people, "we've got snipers around the cabins, but they're probably using arrows instead of bullets, or maybe some sort of gas. We're going to have to go through as a group. Keep it moving and keep your eyes to the sides of the cabins and the woods around there. I want to leave you ten people behind," he said, pointing to one group. "You're going to wait ten minutes, then follow us through. That way, if they come up behind us, you can take them out. Let's move."

——((•))——

Michael and the soldier named Johnson heard the backup beeper engage on an APC. They waited until the noise stopped, listened intently for the low hum of an electric motor. They heard a pair of vehicles whir into motion.

Each man held a canister made of plasteel. Johnson motioned that he would take the left side of the pathway. They moved forward quietly, and quickly slipped off the path to either side as soon as they saw a group of people hunkered down ahead of them. Each stuck a small re-breather in his mouth and clipped a little device to his nose that pinched his nostrils together so they wouldn't inhale the gas they were going to discharge.

When they were in position, Michael picked up a medium-sized stone and tossed it into the bushes to the side and just slightly ahead of the group. As all in the group turned in that direction, Michael and Johnson rolled the canisters into their midst. There was a slight popping sound, quickly followed by a large cloud of white fog. The people in the group went down almost instantly, before any knew what was happening.

Michael tapped his ear piece twice to summon the others in his patrol. The cleanup crew appeared and started dragging the unconscious bodies off the pathway, binding and gagging them and hiding them in the heavy brush that grew off to the sides.

He clicked again, three times, and waited for a response.

"One through six," a whispered voice said. "All clear ahead."

"Join up," he whispered back, then turned to Johnson. "The others just checked in. They got all of Lizbeth's patrols in cabin areas one through six - so all clear between them and the fields."

Before he and Johnson left, he gave instructions for the rest of his group to circle wide to the south and join up with the main body of Berk Shire people.

Ted told Lizbeth to take the first APC through with the doors closed, maybe draw their fire. The other one would follow the main group, doors open on both sides, ready for action. He moved to the front of the group and had his own guards walk around him. His eyes darted back and forth, searching for any sign of movement, anything that was out of place. Nothing. He kept moving forward and approached the first set of cabins. He had slung his rifle and held a ten millimeter pistol in each hand. He passed the first cabin, pointing his pistols into the space between that and the next one. Nothing.

Five cabins later he came to a more open space, with a few bench seats arranged in a semi-circle. He saw some of his men sitting on the benches.

"What the hell are you doing sitting there?" he called out. He kept moving. "Fuck!" he yelled as he got closer and realized that they were all dead, throats cut.

He ran back to the APC that carried Lizbeth. He looked at her angrily, pointed to the dead men, then stepped away and motioned for the entire group to form a circle around him. He gave instructions for the next leg of the trip. The squad leaders he had chosen each took their groups out of the circle. Ted looked behind, searching for the group he'd instructed to come up ten minutes after they'd started. *Nothing!* He briefly considered sending another few back but thought better of it. He was losing men slowly, but surely, and he didn't want the odds to get anywhere near even.

Lizbeth got out of the APC and walked next to him. "They are acting totally against what they were about when we were here. I didn't expect them to use the defenses we'd discussed, but this is totally out of character. Michael's thinking would be very methodical. This all seems hodge-podge to me."

"So what you're saying is you got *nothing*," Ted said. "What I'm seeing is that *we're* doing exactly what *they* want us to do, and that means we're in deep shit, *doctor!* So here's what you're going to do." He gave her instructions, then went over to one squad leader. "Davis," he said, "leave Jimsen in charge. You, Bucky and me are going to drop back and scout. I want whoever is sneaking around doing this shit." He held up his two-way. "Use your headsets only, go up ten cycles and scramble so we're not readable. One click means nothing; two, something; three, find me. You both know what Macalister looks like. Him we want alive. Anyone else, fuck 'em." Silencers on; I want to keep this quiet," Ted said, screwing one on his bolt action, another onto a pistol. "Lizbeth, you know the plan; you take them from here."

Ted and the two men dropped back, all heading in a southwesterly direction, disappearing into the woods.

"Squad leaders, move your groups out. Let's get these bastards!" Lizbeth yelled. She motioned her guards to pull in around her and let the main group of her people go first.

It took fifteen minutes for the squads all to be in place. The first one checked in, letting Lizbeth know they were standing behind a large blind, but no one was there. Each of the other groups reported the same thing. Lizbeth pulled out her Konectable and looked over the maps of the three fields being covered. She gave orders to each group, telling them to move around the perimeters of the fields looking for the enemy in the wooded areas.

Knowing it was safe to do so, she advanced forward to the middle of the tree line that edged up to the first field. She took binoculars out and looked over the ten acre spread and the woods around it. Nothing.

Gunfire erupted in the distance, lots of it. The enemy had been engaged.

"Squad two, here. We found 'em on the east end of field three. Must be a shit load, maybe all of 'em."

"All squads to field three," Lizbeth said into the two-way. "One through five, join up with two. Six through ten, flanking position on the south. Eleven through fifteen flank north. Sixteen through twenty, sweep wide south and come up behind the bastards. And sixteen through twenty, let me know when you're in position at their backs. No firing until I give the word. I don't want any friendly fire situations."

Sure of herself, a look of superiority slid across the smile she gave her guards as she started jogging toward field three. "Leave the APCs."

—»«O»«—

Ted moved through the woods, silently, doing what he knew to do. He slipped into predator mode, the wolf searching for prey. So far he'd found nothing, no shoe prints, no broken twigs on bushes, no scent. No indicators of human presence.

His headset had the sound turned way down, but he heard the quiet click, three times. Looking at the small monitor on his hand-held, he knew it was Davis. He picked up his pace, headed to the area where the man was tracking. He came up to the soldier and knelt down next to him. Bucky showed up a few seconds later.

Davis pointed two fingers at his eyes, two fingers up, then one finger forward. "One hundred yards at 11:00," he whispered.

Ted used a small high-powered monoscope to site the targets. "Macalister on the right, no hat."

"Bucky, drop back, circle wide to the north and keep looking. Ted, move up closer, get a bead on the other one. When you hear me click, pop him. I'll be behind Macalister when he turns around to see where the shot came from," Davis said, not waiting for a response before moving off to the left of their position.

Ted kept the scope on the targets to make sure they didn't hear any noise. When he was satisfied they were unaware, he started slinking from tree to tree, bush to bush. Fifty yards would give him a clear, sure shot. As he approached that distance, he looked for cover, found it, and moved behind a large rock about three feet high. He dropped to his knees, laid the barrel of his rifle on the rock and brought his target into the crosshairs of his scope.

Michael and Johnson were moving forward when they heard the crunch of a twig or leaf somewhere in front of them. They froze, crouched down a bit and searched the area. After two full minutes of looking, Johnson shrugged at Michael. They stood up. A second later, Michael heard a dull popping sound, looked at Johnson and saw a thick flow of blood coming out of his forehead. The man crumpled to the ground.

Michael crouched down and turned to look behind him, trying to see the sniper. He heard a metallic click and turned into the barrel of a pistol inches from his face. At the owner's motion, he dropped his rifle.

"On your knees, hands behind your head, fingers interlocked," the man commanded.

Ted came jogging up to them. He immediately took the handgun and ammunition belt from Michael's waist, slung it over his shoulder. He told Michael to stand up.

"So nice to see you again, Ted," Michael said.

Ted punched him in the stomach. "Keep your mouth shut. Davis, keep scouting. Catch up with Bucky. There may be others. I'll take him in."

The Berk Shire group was taking fire from three sides. They had good cover and plenty of ammunition. Each person firing a rifle had two others stacked up next to him or her. Ten of the group's members moved back and forth, reloading and restacking the rifles so that a constant barrage of fire rang out from their position.

When Robert had seen the reinforcements show up across from them, then watched a second group take up position to their south side, he knew another group would likely show up on their north side. In anticipation of the north side's flanking group, he redirected thirty-three people to that side of their position and assigned three to serve as reloading personnel. A stock of ammunition was moved to supply them, along with a box of grenades. Lizbeth's northern group came up shortly thereafter, took cover and started blasting away. Robert gave quiet orders to another group of fifteen.

He waited a few minutes, then moved through the ranks and told certain people to stop firing. He wanted to make it look like they were sustaining casualties. Little by little he reduced the number of those firing. He picked a few from each group to keep shooting, told the others to hunker down on the ground on his command and stay ready for the order to come back to life. Gradually, he got them down to only twenty firing, and told them to slow down the rate at which they shot their weapons.

Lizbeth's face twisted up into her *the queen is in control* smile as she heard less and less gunfire. Things were now going the way she wanted them to go, *the way this was supposed to go.* Ted would be proud. She ordered all squads to cease firing.

The voice of the squad leader behind the Berk Shire group came over the two-way. "Dr. Lizbeth? Over."

"Here. Over," she responded.

"Ready. Over."

She felt a surge of power jolt through her body as she said, "Do it!" She immediately heard rifle fire and turned to the guard nearest her. "They're toast!" She tapped her headset twice and told all squad leaders to get ready to charge the Berk Shire position.

The gunshots went on for a few minutes, before going quiet. "All squad leaders: move up! Move up!" She turned to her guards and told all but one of them to join the charge and take control when they overran the Berk Shire bastards.

From her position, she watched her people scurrying across the field from three sides. She spoke into the two-way. "Rear group, hold fire. The other squads are moving in. I repeat: hold fire. Respond. Then move up. Over."

"Understood. Out," a voice said back.

The groups approaching from all three sides were shouting in victory. They'd won, taken the prize. Berk Shire was theirs. They'd have a place to settle down, plenty of food and drink. They'd go back to a more normal life, living in houses with heat and stoves and toilets. They ran and they yelled. They were halfway across the field, within a hundred feet of the enemy, within a hundred feet of glorious triumph. They could see bodies on the ground behind the timbers, lots of bodies. Fifty feet. More bodies.

"So, Ted, how is it having all those mouths to feed?" Michael asked.

Ted said nothing.

"Lot of responsibility. Probably not what you signed up for. It's a lot easier to take care of yourself and one other person. But, hey, I know Lizbeth needs a lot of admirers, so it probably works well for her and...."

Ted pushed the end of his rifle sharply into Michael's shoulder. "Shut the fuck up and keep walking."

Michael looked forward and smirked.

The men who had been in the area behind the bunker came in, staying very low to the ground, just as they'd been instructed to do. They looked around, saw all the people face down on the ground.

"Mission accomplished," one said, smiling.

"Welcome back. Take your places so we can finish this thing up. Everybody ready? Now!" Robert yelled.

His people came off the ground firing. Clint and Will started lobbing grenades, placing them with almost surgical precision into the biggest clumps of charging people. Lizbeth's people stopped in their tracks, confused. The squad leaders urged them on, but many turned and ran.

"Group one, remain in position and keep firing!" Robert yelled at the top of his lungs. "Group two to the south edge, three to the north: Chase 'em down!"

He saw a large puff of smoke on the other side. "RPG! Down! Down! Down!"

Most dropped. The grenade exploded right in front of their cover, sending a cloud of dirt and rocks into the air. A second grenade landed a little further back, blowing out the rear side of the makeshift fort.

He looked to one side, saw Bobby Ray looking very intently through the scope of his rifle. Bobby Ray squeezed off a shot. There was an explosion on the other side as the man with the RPG was hit just as he was firing. The grenade struck the ground right in front of him, exploding and killing any within range.

"Everybody up! Two and three: move out!"

There was continued fire from the other side, but they were taken by surprise by the rising up of the dead. Some kneeled down and started firing, but many turned tail and ran back to where they had come from. By the time they reached the other side again, more than three quarters were dead or wounded on the ground.

Robert used his bullhorn to order his people to stop firing. He turned to the other side and called out, "It's over! Enough killing! It's over!"

A single gunshot rang out from the northernmost corner of the field. All eyes focused in that direction. Ted and Lizbeth walked out of the woods, Ted's rifle at the back of Michael's head.

"Listen up!" she shouted. "I'm only going to say this once! Put your weapons down, get on your knees, hands above your heads. Do it now or I'll put one into his leg!"

No one moved.

Lizbeth fired a shot into the ground near Michael's foot, then pointed it at his leg. "Now!" she screamed.

Robert told his people to drop their guns and do what she said.

"Come out into the center of the field, get on your knees, hands on top of your heads!" she yelled. "Now!"

Robert told them to comply.

"Turn off all two-ways and drop them."

They did.

Robert heard a distant, weak clicking sound behind him but didn't turn around. It was probably a two-way on one of the dead, maybe a straggler off in the woods trying to make contact. *Too late*, he thought. He hoped Lizbeth wouldn't kill them all, or if she did, that it would be quick and clean.

Lizbeth puffed out her chest as she looked over the field. She had won. She could now be in control of Berk Shire, Ted at her side. Now he would understand the power of her knowledge.

Yo, Elizabitch.

Lizbeth heard the voice, turned, but didn't see anyone. She looked at Ted. "Did you hear that?"

"Hear what? I didn't hear nothing."

Off to your left, Lizbitch, the voice said.

Lizbeth turned to see Marcy standing half-hidden behind a large tree, holding a small silvery tube. Marcy pointed the tube to the other side of the field for a moment, then put it down, pulled out her pistol. With two hands holding it steady, she aimed it at Lizbeth and walked a bit closer.

"Michael? You all right?" she asked.

"Never better. Why do you ask?"

Ted turned to see what was going on. As he did, a dozen men came out from the stand of trees and bushes behind Lizbeth's group, all of them aiming twelve-gauge shotguns at his men. Jake Morgan led them, his sawed-off pointing at the group. He knew he could take out seven or eight of them with one barrel.

"Put 'em down!" Jake said. "Put 'em down now and nobody gets hurt!"

Lizbeth looked back at her group. "Don't do it!" She turned to Jake. "*You* put your guns down or I'll kill him! I mean it!" she screamed, raising her gun at his head.

Marcy got a little closer. "Lizbeth, you shoot him and I will splatter your brains from here to next year."

Lizbeth jerked her head back toward Marcy. She moved her pistol closer to Michael's head. "You shoot me and my whole body will twitch, which means my finger will contract and pull the trigger, and then your precious Michael will be dead! It'll be just like you shot him. Besides, you can't possibly get both me and Ted, so your sweet fuck dies if you shoot. You lose!"

"Oh, yes, there's Ted, isn't there," Marcy said calmly, changing the aim of her pistol just a bit. She looked across the field, then back at Lizbeth. There was a crack and a bullet hit the finger Ted had on the trigger of his rifle, slicing off the tip. He dropped the gun and grabbed his hand. Marcy fired a split second later, hitting Lizbeth's gun, which went flying.

Lizbeth started moving quickly towards Marcy. She wanted blood. Marcy leveled her pistol at Lizbeth, hesitated for a moment, then abruptly dropped it on the ground. She braced to meet Lizbeth head on. Ted turned to intercept her. Michael leapt up and landed his feet on Ted's back, knocking him to the ground. In one smooth move, he got down on his knees, rolled back a bit and brought his bound hands in front of him, pulled the thin rope open with his teeth. Robert, who had moved closer to the action, picked up Ted's rifle and put the barrel a few inches from the man's face.

Lizbeth charged Marcy, a death scream on her lips. Marcy crouched slightly to meet the attack, deflecting Lizbeth's fist, countering with a right to her stomach. Lizbeth moved away, coughing,

SEER

doubled over, but quickly regained her composure. She pulled a steel knife from her belt and sliced it back and forth in the air in front of Marcy. Marcy moved back again and again, working to avoid the blade.

"Marcy!" Michael yelled. "Catch!" He had ripped off his shirt, balled it up and threw it to her.

She caught it and wrapped it around her left arm. "Nobody touches her but me! You're mine, bitch!" Marcy yelled. "This is way past due!"

Lizbeth lunged at her, knife held forward. Marcy moved her left arm in front of her. The knife blade bit into the material, but didn't slice through. She grabbed Lizbeth's wrist with her right hand and twisted it hard. Lizbeth brought her other hand up, curled into a fist, and slammed it against the side of Marcy's head. Marcy went reeling, landing on the ground. She shook her head, moved to get back up. Lizbeth kicked at her, aiming for her head. Marcy rolled, evading the hit, quickly got up.

Lizbeth came at her with the knife again, and again Marcy grabbed her wrist and started twisting it. Lizbeth resisted, tried hard to pull her arm away, but Marcy held fast. She grunted loudly, twisted harder, and the knife dropped to the ground. She punched Lizbeth in the chest.

Lizbeth reeled backwards, arms pin wheeling as she tried to keep her balance. She landed on her ass, picked up a handful of dirt and flung it at Marcy's face as she approached. Marcy shook her head, wiped her eyes and opened them just in time to see Lizbeth charging into her, knocking her to the ground.

They scuffled, swinging wildly at each other, sometimes connecting, sometimes punching air. Lizbeth shoved her down, gained the high ground, her knees pinning Marcy's arms down. She picked up a rock and held it over her head.

"Now! You! Die!" Lizbeth spat out in staccato venom.

Marcy kneed her in the back, broke one arm free and jammed her fist into Lizbeth's neck, crushing her windpipe. Lizbeth dropped the rock to the side and got up, clutching her throat, doing a deathly dance back and forth, gurgling and gasping for breath but coming up empty. A few moments later she collapsed on the ground, dead.

They all looked at her, lying on the ground, a grimace locked onto her face, then looked up at Marcy.

Ted grabbed the end of the rifle pointed at him and pulled it toward the ground next to him. Robert fell forward as this happened, Ted's fist smashing into the side of his head. Ted was up in a second, the rifle pointed at Michael.

"I'm gonna die, but so are you!" he snarled.

Robert's open hand connected with the rifle, forcing the barrel down and away just as Ted pulled the trigger. The bullet exploded into the ground. Michael moved forward immediately and kicked the rifle from Ted's hands. Ted squared off in front of him, fists up, one oozing blood from the earlier gunshot wound.

Marcy had picked up her pistol and pointed it at Ted. "On your knees or I'll shoot!" she yelled.

"No, Marcy!" Michael yelled. "He's mine! Let's see what you got, *Big Foot!*" Michael looked directly into his eyes, searching for the hint that would signal the first swing. He saw it a split second before Ted stepped forward, putting his full weight into the punch. Michael stepped back a half step just out of reach, then spun around, making a fist as he did, and connecting with the side of Ted's face. Other than a slight tick of his head, Ted didn't flinch. Instead, he swung his left fist at Michael, who turned just enough to take the blow in his shoulder.

"Let me take him!" Robert yelled, the rifle in his hand.

"No!" Michael yelled back, getting a few steps further away from Ted. "Stand down, Robert!"

Ted charged at him, full speed. At the last second, Michael

sidestepped and grabbed Ted's outstretched arm, pulling in the direction the big man was headed. Ted went flying, going down a half dozen steps from a group of his men. He put his hand out to one man, who tossed a pistol in his direction. A gunshot rang out from across the field. A bullet hit the pistol, knocking it off its trajectory and away from Ted.

"Smiling Bobby Ray!" Robert whooped.

Ted looked around, grabbed a rock the size of a small bowling ball, then started toward Michael. He grunted as he swung the rock. Michael danced back and forth on his toes, avoiding contact. As Ted started pulling his arm back to throw the rock, Michael charged him full bore. He drove his head hard into Ted's gut, knocking the wind out of him and forcing him to the ground.

Ted rolled, got up and faced Michael again. He drew his arm back, swung at Michael, who sidestepped. As Ted regained his footing, he charged again and grabbed Michael in a bear hug, lifting him off the ground and trying to squeeze the life out of him. Michael struggled to escape but quickly realized it was no use. He forced his head far enough forward to clamp his teeth onto Ted's left ear, biting down hard and ripping a piece off. He spit it out.

Ted yelled out in pain, put one hand over his ear, giving Michael the chance to wrestle one hand free. Holding it briefly a foot from the man's face, Michael smashed his open palm into Ted's nose, pushing up as he connected, driving the cartilage into his brain. A second later, Ted let go, dropping Michael to the ground. He staggered back, a surprised look on his face, then collapsed.

Michael got up, walked towards Ted's men, most of whom were still holding their weapons. "Any questions?" he growled.

Almost as one, they dropped their guns. Jake motioned a few of his men to move into the group to collect the weapons. Marcy came running over.

Michael grabbed Marcy and pulled her to him, kissed her hard on the lips. She laughed. Tears rolled down her face. "You always did like being in control," he said. "I'm glad you came."

"You know I hate missing a good party," she said, hugging him back.

They heard the distinctive backup beeping of two APCs off in the distance.

"Davis!" Robert yelled, turning in that direction. "I've got to...."

"Guy named Bucky's got the other one. You'll never catch them," Michael said. "They'll be out of here like bats out of hell. But get back to the building and call Betsy, let her know to set up defenses, just in case they show up there."

"God help 'em if they do!" Jake said.

The two-way handheld Marcy had dropped, clicked to life.

"Get over here fast," Bobby Ray yelled. "Jimmy's hit...hit bad. He needs help now!"

Marcy picked up the unit. "We're on our way."

Michael took off even before Marcy answered. The first to reach them, he saw only Jimmy's back. Bobby Ray had a hand around the teen's mid-section. Michael gently rolled the boy onto his back. Bobby Ray held a bloody shirt against Jimmy's stomach. Michael peeled it back. The wound was massive. The skin and muscle had been ripped in half. Bloody intestines, in clear sight, jiggled just inside the wound.

"He's unconscious," Bobby Ray said.

"He's passed out from the pain! Keep light pressure on it," Michael said.

Marcy and Bob arrived, told them Bill was getting a vehicle.

<hr />

Michael and Dr. Watts worked on Jimmy for over six hours, trying to stabilize him as best they could, but they both knew they were in way over their heads. They were not experienced surgeons, and knew that even if they had one there, that doctor would likely not be able to help the boy either. He was bleeding internally from multiple sites and there was nothing they could do to stop it. He was losing blood faster than the IV could bring the universal into his system.

"Jimmy? Can you hear me?" Michael said. "Jimmy?"

The boy opened his eyes ever so slightly, shut them again, then opened them a bit wider. "Michael?" he said, his voice weak, a slight gurgle to it.

"I'm here, Jimmy."

"How…ba…ba…bad?"

"You're going to be fine," Michael lied.

"If…you…say so…but don't…feel like…that."

"You need to rest now, Jimmy. I'm going to get Bert."

"Okay…Bert…," he said, his voice trailing off as he closed his eyes.

Michael instructed Ronnie, one of the people trained as a nurse, to monitor the boy, use the two-way if things started changing.

"Check the output from the drainage every five minutes. If it increases by more than five ccs call me right away," Dr. Watts explained.

Bert was standing outside the door, waiting for word. He saw the look in the doctors' eyes and knew the news wasn't going to be good. They took the man to Michael's office, asked him to sit down.

"Shit," Bert said, shaking his head. "I know it's bad, but how bad?"

In medical school, doctors-in-training were taught how to break bad news, using a set of words that was supposed to gently present the severity of a situation. *But they never prepared me for this!* Michael thought. Yes, Jimmy was his patient, and yes, Bert was the closest person to the boy, but both had also been friends of his for quite some time.

"He has a lot of internal bleeding and he's losing blood faster than we can push it into him," Michael said.

"We don't have the equipment…." Dr. Watts said.

"Or the knowledge and skills," Michael cut in, "to stop it. He's dying, Bert, it's just a matter of time."

A look of horror set into Bert's face. He was unsure what to say or do. His feelings jumbled up in his head creating a logjam of helplessness and anger and sadness. He wanted to scream at them to fix the boy, but he knew that was neither fair nor helpful. His eyes welled up. He took in a long breath.

"How long?"

"Until we stop pumping blood into him, or until we run out," Dr. Watts said.

"Then we need to get him to the hospital. I'll call 911," Bert said, realizing as quickly as he said it, that it was no longer an option. "What am I saying? Okay, so how much of that stuff do you have?"

"Our supply is already running low. Theo, John and Russ are also using a lot on their patients."

"Well, can't I give him some of my blood?" Bert asked, hoping beyond hope.

"I'm sorry, but the damage is just too great," Michael said. "We'd just be postponing the inevitable. And his level of pain is going to increase with each hour that passes, so we'd have to keep him almost unconscious to stand it."

"This can't be happening!"

They saw the look of horror on Bert's face and watched his eyes moving rapidly back and forth, searching for something he could grab onto, something that would tell him this wasn't real. They watched as he mentally left the room, came back only to leave again. This was his boy.

"Bert," Michael said gently.

The man turned in Michael's direction, but it was clear he wasn't seeing him.

"Bert!" Michael said, sharpening his voice.

He saw the man's eyes focus. "Bert, we have to make a decision now."

The two-way crackled. "Dr. Watts, his output has increased over six ccs in the last five. Over."

Michael pressed the button. "We'll be there shortly." He turned back to Bert. "We have to decide now."

Bert looked at Michael, looked away, pounded his fist onto the table, then looked back. "Let me talk to him first, let him know what's happening. Just after his parents died, some of the people he dealt with didn't tell him the truth, you know, trying to protect him, and it meant he didn't have a chance to say goodbye to them. When he came to live with me he made me promise to always tell him the truth, and I have never reneged on that promise. I'm not going to start now."

About fifteen minutes later, Ronnie, at Bert's request, called them to the surgery room. Bert stood next to the table, his hand resting on Jimmy's shoulder. They had both been crying.

"We talked it over. Can you give him a shot or something to move this along? He's in a lot of pain and he doesn't want to use more of the blood supply that could help someone else out," Bert said. "That's my boy: always thinking of how to help out. Always the team player. Shit!" Bert started to cry again.

Michael felt a tear run down his cheek. "I can do that. Tell me when, Jimmy."

"He's having trouble putting his words together, so he asked me to ask you if you can take him outside to do it. He'd rather be out there than in here, and he'd prefer the front of the building. He was so blown away the first time he came out here. And he wants to see Mica one last time, said he really enjoyed babysitting for him, spending time with him."

Michael got on the two-way, called Marcy and spoke with her for a moment. She informed him that Heather and the others had arrived back an hour before, bringing all the kids with them.

They unlocked the gurney wheels and started moving Jimmy through the hall toward the stairs. Bill met them there, and the four of them carried the gurney up the stairs into the living room, then out the front door. They wheeled him across the parking area and faced him toward the building, tilting the head end of the gurney up enough so that Jimmy had a straight-on view.

A steady stream of people walked around the right side corner of the building. Another bunch approached from the left. Within ten minutes there were seventy to eighty Berk Shire residents forming a semicircle around the gurney. Some reached out to Jimmy, touched him on the leg or shoulder or head; others simply stood nearby.

Marcy brought Mica over, held him close to Jimmy, who extended his hand to the toddler. Mica reached out and grabbed one of his fingers.

"I love you, Mica," Jimmy whispered between his tears.

"Jeemy," Mica said, then waved his little hand.

"Bye, Mica. Bye, bye."

Marcy leaned down and kissed Jimmy's forehead and ran her hand gently over his cheek.

The boy turned to Michael and gave a subtle nod of his head. Tears flowed down his face. "Thank you," he said quietly to Michael. "Bye, Bert. You were…a good…dad."

Bert took his hand. "Son." Tears streamed down his face.

There was complete silence as Michael inserted the syringe into the IV line, hesitated for a moment, then gently pushed the plunger.

<hr />

Bill and a crew jury-rigged two large, spare refrigeration compressors into two big outbuildings to keep the bodies from the battle cold so as to slow decomposition. Floor to ceiling shelves were hastily constructed to maximize the space.

It was decided that the Berk Shire residents' funerals would be spread out over the first three days. Three rows of fourteen funeral pyres were erected on the baseball field. A single additional pyre was set in front of the others. A rotating crew of twenty people was used to watch over the prisoners during the funeral ceremonies.

Jimmy's service was first. His body was placed on the single pyre, to honor his sacrifice. He was the youngest member of Berk Shire to die. A number of people, Michael and Marcy included, got up to speak about their experiences with the boy. Bert delivered the eulogy. He stood on the makeshift podium, a lit torch burning off to one side at the base of the stairs. He looked out through red, bloodshot eyes at those in attendance, cleared his throat.

"I've known Jimmy all his life, him being my sister's kid, and she and Ray, her husband, living right there in Warren. They only had one child on account of something happening to her during the birth, something the doctors couldn't fix up. For whatever reason, the Lord saw fit to take them home early, leaving Jimmy with me when he was eight. Hell, I knew it was the right thing to do, but I wasn't sure what I was getting into. I didn't have any experience as a parent."

Bert looked up at the sky for a moment, sniffed. "Good kid...real good kid. Never complained, 'cept when he was real young and got lied to by some people trying to spare his feelings.

"He had a bit of a hard time in school that first year, but we got him back on track and he always did well after that. Came to work in the store when he was nine, helping out by sweeping up, moving boxes, stuff like that. Real hard worker. And when he got onto the football squad...well, let's just say that he was great at helping others make the big plays. Never said boo about not getting the headlines, but I'll tell you, he did get mentioned for helping others make those plays...a lot. Almost every article had a line about him assisting. He just loved being part of the team."

He rubbed a kerchief across his forehead and eyes, sucked in a big breath. "I don't know if he ever knew what he brought to my life. It wasn't all one-sided, me taking care of him. He taught me so much, brought me so much. He somehow got me to see things a little differently than I was used to…and that was real good. He taught me…he…." He brought out the kerchief again to wipe away his tears, then, realizing it was a lost cause, stuffed it back into his pocket and sniffed hard. "He taught me what love truly was. Go with God, Jimmy." Tears ran down his face.

Amidst absolute silence, he walked slowly down from the podium, took the torch from its stand and went to the first pyre, stood there for a few moments before touching the flames to the tinder. The wood quickly caught fire. Bert seemed to mentally drift away, because he just stood there. Bill had to gently pull him back to keep him from being burned by the rising flames.

Michael officiated at the funerals for the other forty-two Berk Shire residents. The ashes were scattered into an unplowed field, to be tilled under as Berk Shire got back to putting in crops. The deceased would, in that way, continue on within their community.

He spoke with members of Lizbeth's group, let one of them take on the job of facilitating at their funerals. Of the two hundred and eighty-five dead, those without any family connections were burned in a single large pyre. It took six days to eulogize and cremate the ninety-seven that did.

Quite a number of Berk Shire residents, including Michael and Marcy, stood off to one side of the ceremonies, to show their respect for the dead. Guards were posted around the edges of the field, but were told to leave their weapons on the ground. There were no incidents of violence. There were not even any harsh words spoken between the two factions.

The first war of the new order had ended. It left no victor.

Michael, sitting in the conference room, exhausted and frustrated, shook his head and thought: *A battle that didn't have to happen, a battle that caused the unnecessary deaths of over three hundred and twenty-five human beings. What a waste! And now ninety-one prisoners of that war to complicate matters even further.*

The group shuffled into the room to discuss the disposition of the prisoners. Execution was not even raised. It was out of the question. In battle they had been forced to kill, but they were not killers. To execute the prisoners...it was not what was in the soul of Berk Shire.

Michael listened to the ideas put on the table. *Take them all back to Boston and let them loose. Separate them into groups of four or five and drop them off in different places hundreds of miles from Berk Shire. Send them back to the food distribution warehouse and leave them without weapons, let them finish whatever food was there and then screw them.*

Michael tapped his hand lightly on the table to get the others' attention. "I would like to remind you all that these are regular folks in desperate times, manipulated through misinformation supplied by Lizbeth and Ted. They're not criminals, and only a few are even actual soldiers. So, here's what I propose."

He told them what his idea was, why he thought it best, and, as usual, the others saw the wisdom in it. He had always been one to look forward and see possibilities no one else did.

"But," he said, "we need to put this to a vote with the entire village. To not do so could result in a lot of unrest, and that we do not need, especially at this time."

Robert and the soldiers, who had been polled privately, watched over the prisoners while the villagers met and discussed and voted on Michael's proposal. Only a handful balked at the idea.

The prisoners were assembled outside the main building, a single line snaking from front to back. They were brought down in small groups to a waiting area in the basement. One by one, each prisoner was guided into Michael's office where he asked the same set of questions. *What did you do before all of this happened to the country? Do you have any family members in the group outside? Do you still feel like we're the enemy?* If he sensed contrition about what they had done, if there was no belligerence, no attitude, he asked them one final question: *If we can find you a place to live, either here or at one of the neighboring colonies, would you promise to work hard to fit in and become part of the team?* If they answered yes he drew a single line on their right hands and sent them back out with instructions to talk to no one. If there was attitude or the answer to the last question was no, they received an *X* on their left hands.

Outside, those leaving the building were checked for one line or an X and were sent to one of two holding areas. Each of those carrying the single line were told that if they so much as spoke with another person in the line to go in, they would immediately be removed to the group that would be dealt with harshly. No one tested the rule.

Michael had conferred with Robert on the wisdom of offering amnesty to the six soldiers in the group. Robert's feeling was that because they had been part of a highly elite unit under the command of Davis, and because Davis had escaped, should ever he return, their loyalty would almost certainly go back to him. They would therefore present a potentially grave danger to Berk Shire. He said it was not worth taking the risk.

"Why wasn't Davis put in charge of the group?" Michael asked.

Robert thought for a few moments. "Most likely Davis thought that Lizbeth and Ted could pull it off. He'd let them do the dirty work, take the casualties, which would knock down the amount of people to oppose him when he overthrew them later."

"You're saying he would have thought this all through."

"Special Ops training - consider all intel, all options, all variables, then act in the best interest of the mission and the men. It is always about accomplishing the mission, and his was to secure and run Berk Shire for his benefit. Lizbeth's ego wouldn't have allowed for Davis to be in charge."

In the end, after eighty-five interviews, only seven were marked with an X. Michael lined them up, took multiple pictures of each, then addressed them and the six soldiers, letting them know that they were to avoid, under penalty of death, any other colonies. They would be dropped off at various sites and were encouraged to find a place to call their own and set up camp.

The following morning, they were divided into three groups and transported - blindfolded - to three different spots, all at least one hundred miles away from Berk Shire, fifty to sixty miles apart from each other and remote enough to limit the possibility that they would make their way to other colonies. They were given minimal weaponry, one rifle and pistol for each group, fifty rounds for each weapon, and a compound bow with a dozen arrows. In addition, each group got one plasteel bow saw and axe, two knives, enough food and water for a week, some cookware and utensils, a few plastiseal tarps for tenting, and two good lengths of rope.

Pictures were distributed to all colonies they passed with which the groups might possibly come into contact. The Berk Shire people doing the transporting explained the situation to the leaders of the colonies, along with their recommendation that any of the group members should be considered armed and extremely dangerous, and should be dealt with swiftly in whatever way they saw fit. It was made clear to the colony leaders that if any of these prisoners came back to Berk Shire, they would be executed on the spot.

After accounting for how many cabins were opened by the deaths that had occurred, Chrissy announced they could take in about thirty-five of the newcomers. A lottery was held to choose that number. Joe and Jean Walker and their two children were among those who won places at Berk Shire. The remaining people were relocated to other colonies. Families were kept intact, wherever they ended up.

Bob and Heather welcomed a healthy baby girl in mid-April. They named her Mikella. Heather explained that they wanted a new name for the new times into which the child had been born. It was obvious they were also paying respect to Michael. Mica Martin had been the first true child of Berk Shire; Mikella had now joined him with the honor of being the first female child born there.

Wayne's old Border Collie produced six pups. He chose the pick of the litter and presented that dog, a female, to Michael and Marcy. They named her Neila. She and Mica Martin quickly became quite attached to each other and were, for the most part, inseparable.

The opportunity to have their sperm tested was extended to all the males in Berk Shire and Morgansville. Four men in addition to Michael tested out fertile in Berk Shire; none did in Morgansville.

"Looks like the five of you are going to be quite busy," Marcy said.

"We'll have to mix it up," Michael said. "Chrissy has already started a registry of births and lineage to avoid...uh...."

"I believe it used to be called intermingling," Marcy said, "but I have no idea if that word would even apply now. Still, it's better to keep things as separate as possible."

"And then there's this thing of writing down the rules of Berk Shire. All I thought about when I started setting all this up was surviving as comfortably as possible, and here we are starting a colony with rules - laws, I guess - and a government. And that's another thing: we need to start holding elections, so rules need to be set up for that, and...."

Marcy gave him a look. "Michael," she said.

"But there's so much to do."

"There's always so much to do, and that's why we're going to work on you learning to delegate better."

⸻ «◉» ⸻

Elections were held in early June when a lull between planting seasons occurred. Michael and the core group decided that utilizing a seven-member Board of Selectpersons would limit any one individual's potential power. Terms would initially be staggered, with some lasting one or two years, others lasting three years, and thereafter lasting three years, with reelection limited to three consecutive terms total. After a break equal to one term, a person could run again. A Head Selectperson would then be voted on by the board. After discussing the matter with Marcy, Michael made it clear that, if elected to the board by the general population, he would not accept a nomination for the Head Selectperson. He did say that he would remain in an advisory position to the head person. Anyone sixteen or older would be given a vote. Those being nominated had to be twenty-one or older.

John was elected the first Head Selectperson. The other six members of the Board included Dr. June Watts, Robert, Will, Bert, Barbara Murray and Michael. The Selectpersons met frequently in the beginning to come up with a list of rules to be voted on, and to develop plans for the continued, but controlled growth of Berk Shire. At the first meeting, everyone looked to Michael to start. He simply smiled and looked at John, who laughed quietly before tapping a small block of wood on the table to get the Board's attention.

At first Michael found himself having to remain very conscious about holding back in the meetings. Marcy continued teaching him the practice of mindfulness. As the summer moved on, he found it easier and easier to simply be one more voice and vote at the meetings.

By his second birthday that August, Mica Martin was speaking in complete sentences using what Bert deemed *five dollar words for a kid that young*. It was clear he was very intelligent. With a little help from Marcy and Michael, Mica taught and practiced commands and tricks with Neila.

As a gift to Marcy, Michael and friends built a three bedroom cabin in a new neighborhood which would, at least for the time being, be the furthest away from the main building. Although she knew about the newest area and construction projects, she did not know the cabin was for them until it was done and Michael brought her and Mica Martin there. He told her it was to keep him a good ways away from the eighty-hour work weeks.

"I just love this farmer's porch," Marcy said. "Don't suppose you and Bill could put together some rockers for it."

Michael laughed, told her it was a great idea. "And one of these days I'm going to step back, let go altogether, and let this happen on its own. Then we can spend more time rocking away," he said. "That will be a very good day!"

"I'll tell you my favorite day…well, one of them, anyway," Marcy said. "It was the day you taught me how to plow a straight line. I think that's the day I really started to fall in love with you."

"Mine, too," Michael said. "That and the day Mica Martin was born." He looked into her eyes and smiled, told her he loved her, then leaned in to kiss her.

"We're going to be all right, aren't we?" she asked, slipping her arm around his back.

"There'll be other storms, but this colony is strong enough to weather them," he said. "So, yes, we're going to be okay."

—«◊»—

Thank you for reading my novel. My current plan is to release

Book 2 in the series early in December 2016. I will give updates on the SEER Facebook page. You can also access my website by going to Outskirtspress.com, clicking on the Bookstore tab and entering Seer in the search box.